PRAISE FOR *Liquid Snakes*

A *Boston Globe* Best Book of the Summer

"Tangled and disentangled at once, Stephen Kearse's *Liquid Snakes* is both a diabolical thriller and wicked political satire set in, and unleashed upon, Atlanta."
—Jeff Calder, *The Atlanta Journal-Constitution*

"In *Liquid Snakes*, Octavia Butler and Toni Morrison meet Stephen King for a jarring story of agency and autonomy in a world hell-bent on snuffing out both . . . It's certainly a read that will lurk in the corners of your mind long after the book closes."
—Jennette Holzworth, *Southern Review of Books*

"An immensely engaging read—clever and nimble in its narration, pointed in its critiques—with a chorus of interesting voices and arresting images."
—Jake Caselle Brookins, *Chicago Review of Books*

"*Liquid Snakes* is a strange, disorienting puzzle; a mocking eulogy; a bitter, self-lacerating exercise in what one character calls 'vivid ideation'; a long look into a sinkhole of grief. It twists in your hands and in your heart before biting down."
—Noah Berlatsky, *Los Angeles Times*

"To read about the effects of pollution in the modern world is, all too frequently, to hear about their destructive effects on working-class communities. In his new novel *Liquid Snakes*, Stephen Kearse turns this concept on its head, offering a bold speculative vision of a world reckoning with crises both personal and societal."

—Tobias Carroll, *Vol. 1 Brooklyn*

"The best sci-fi allows us to see our own world through new, more awake eyes; it's safe to say that Stephen Kearse understood the assignment."
—Charley Burlock, *Oprah Daily*

"An espresso-dark saga of retribution, addiction, hard science, racial justice, toxic death—and black coffee—plays itself out quirkily in and around contemporary Atlanta . . . Kearse's enigmatic narrative[,] . . . deadpan tone[,] and sudden eruptions of bizarre violence often evoke the allusive, baleful essences of J. G. Ballard's grimly visionary speculative fiction but with wittier dialogue and robustly seasoned with a rapier-keen perception of the collective psyche and complex aspirations of the Black intelligentsia. A dry, devilish amalgam of science fiction, whodunit, horror, social satire, and cautionary tale."
—*Kirkus Reviews* (starred review)

"A dazzling pharmacological thriller that dances on the knife's edge of satire . . . Written with incisive wit and studded with references to Black popular culture . . . and troubling incidents from recent history, this entertains even as it deeply disturbs."
—*Publishers Weekly*

"*Liquid Snakes* is a compelling dystopian novel that rewards careful reading and uses the structure of a criminal investigation to channel righteous anger and explore weighty questions."
—Molly Odintz, *CrimeReads*

"Stephen Kearse is a fearless writer who has created an endlessly entertaining cast of characters. *Liquid Snakes* sits at the timely and unsettling intersection between public health and crime, and I was furious that it had to come to an end."

—Kashana Cauley, author of *The Survivalists*

"Restless, searching, and totally gripping. Kearse has written a brilliant novel that manages to be, among other things, a pharmacological thriller and an incisive meditation on the poison-pen letter."

—Hannah Gold, critic and author

"What if the communities poisoned by Big Chem turned their enemy into a weapon, wielding molecular magic for revenge—and maybe also liberation? Kearse takes this clever premise and, with his distinctive style and low-key humor, crafts a story that will grab hold of your brain and blow it to bits. Like nothing else I've read, in the best possible way."

—Nicola Twilley, cohost of *Gastropod* and coauthor of *Until Proven Safe: The History and Future of Quarantine*

"Who poisons who in Stephen Kearse's inspired *Liquid Snakes*? A slippery, satirical, quick-witted trip through the lives of misfits forced to find the line between clarity and revenge, annihilation and release—frequently hilarious, unexpectedly tender, and resolutely of our time."

—Geoff Manaugh, *New York Times* bestselling author of *A Burglar's Guide to the City*

LIQUID
SNAKES

ALSO BY STEPHEN KEARSE

In the Heat of the Light

LIQUID SNAKES

A NOVEL

STEPHEN KEARSE

 SOFT SKULL
NEW YORK

First Soft Skull edition: 2023
First paperback edition: 2024

The Library of Congress has cataloged the hardcover edition as follows:
Names: Kearse, Stephen, author.
Title: Liquid snakes : a novel / Stephen Kearse.
Description: First Soft Skull edition. | New York : Soft Skull, 2023.
Identifiers: LCCN 2023000852 | ISBN 9781593767518 (hardcover) | ISBN 9781593767525 (ebook)
Subjects: LCGFT: Novels.
Classification: LCC PS3611.E234 L57 2023 | DDC 813/.6—dc23/eng/20230106
LC record available at https://lccn.loc.gov/2023000852

Paperback ISBN: 978-1-59376-782-2

Cover design and illustration by Dana Li
Cover image of snake head © iStock / EduardHarkonen
Book design by Laura Berry

Published by Soft Skull Press
New York, NY
www.softskull.com

Printed in the United States of America
10 9 8 7 6 5 4 3 2 1

To Rashele Moore

A wise man once said that a black man better off dead.

—VINCE STAPLES

They say they found her dead.

—NONAME

i have adjusted my eyes
to the darkness
and black
has never been
more luminous.

—SAUL WILLIAMS

LIQUID SNAKES

Terms and Conditions

EightBall is licensed to You (End-User) by Chacun Prepare Sa Propre Mort, located at 678 Cherry Street, Wilmington, Delaware 19801, United States (hereinafter: Licensor), for use only under the terms of this License Agreement.

By downloading the Application from the App Store, and any update thereto (as permitted by this License Agreement), End-User indicates that End-User agrees to be bound by all of the terms and conditions of this License Agreement, and that End-User accepts this License Agreement.

The parties of this License Agreement acknowledge that the phone manufacturer is not a party to this License Agreement and is not bound by any provisions or obligations with regard to the Application, such as warranty, liability, maintenance, and support thereof. Chacun Prepare Sa Propre Mort, not the phone manufacturer, is solely responsible for the licensed Application and the content thereof.

This License Agreement may not provide usage rules for the Application that are in conflict with the latest App Store Terms of Service. Chacun Prepare Sa Propre Mort acknowledges that it had the opportunity to review said terms and this License Agreement is not conflicting with them.

All rights not expressly granted to End-User are reserved.

1. THE APPLICATION

EightBall (hereinafter: Application) is a resource for anyone at a crossroads. It is customized for mobile devices. EightBall offers advice and counsel. You deserve more.

The Application is not tailored to comply with industry-specific regulations (Health Insurance Portability and Accountability Act [HIPAA], Federal Information Security Management Act [FISMA], etc.) or respectability, so if your interactions would be subjected to such laws, you may not use this Application. You may not use the Application in a way that would violate the Gramm-Leach-Bliley Act (GLBA).

2. SCOPE OF LICENSE

2.1. This license will also govern any updates of the Application provided by Licensor that repair, replace, and/or supplement the first Application, unless a separate license is provided for such an update, in which case the terms of that new license will govern.

2.2. End-User may not reverse engineer, translate, disassemble, integrate, decompile, remove, modify, combine, create derivative works or updates of, adapt, or attempt to derive the source code of the Application or any part thereof (except with Chacun Prepare Sa Propre Mort's prior written consent). You may, if applicable, freak it.

2.3. End-User may not copy (excluding when expressly authorized by this license and the Usage Rules) or alter the Application or portions thereof. You may create and store copies only on devices that End-User owns or controls for backup keeping under the terms of this license, the App Store Terms of Service, and any other terms and conditions that apply to the device or software used.

2.4. Licensor reserves the right to modify the terms and conditions of licensing.

2.5. Nothing in this license should be interpreted as liberation, which is available only to collectives, not individuals.

3. TECHNICAL REQUIREMENTS

3.1. Licensor attempts to keep the Application updated so that it complies with modified/new versions of the firmware and new hardware. End-User is not granted rights to claim such an update.

3.2. Licensor reserves the right to modify the technical specifications as it sees appropriate at any time.

4. NO MAINTENANCE OR SUPPORT

Chacun Prepare Sa Propre Mort is not obligated, expressed or implied, to provide any maintenance, technical, or other support for the Application.

5. LIABILITY

Licensor takes no accountability or responsibility for any damages caused due to a breach of duties according to Section 2 of this Agreement. To avoid data loss, End-User is required to make use of backup functions of the Application to the extent allowed by applicable third-party terms and conditions of use. You are aware that in case of alterations or manipulations of the Application,

End-User will not have access to the licensed Application. Legalese is designed to overwhelm you.

6. WARRANTY

6.1. Licensor warrants that the Application is free of spyware, trojan horses, viruses, or any other malware at the time of End-User download. Licensor warrants that the Application works as described in the user documentation.

6.2. No warranty is provided for the Application that is not executable on the device; that has been unauthorizedly modified, handled inappropriately or culpably, combined or installed with inappropriate hardware or software, or used with inappropriate accessories, regardless if by End-User or by third parties; or if there are any other reasons outside of Chacun Prepare Sa Propre Mort's sphere of influence that affect the executability of the Application.

7. PERMISSIONS

You do not need permission to be free, but you might need weapons.

8. CONTACT INFORMATION

For general inquiries, complaints, questions, or claims concerning the licensed Application, please contact:

678 Cherry Street
Wilmington, DE 19801
United States
eightballandmgs@protonmail.com

9. TERMINATION

The license is valid until terminated by Chacun Prepare Sa Propre Mort or by End-User. End-User's rights under this license will terminate automatically and without notice from Chacun Prepare Sa Propre Mort if End-User fails to adhere to any term(s) of this license.

10. INTELLECTUAL PROPERTY RIGHTS

EightBall is for the streets.

11. APPLICABLE LAW

This license agreement is governed by the laws of the State of Delaware, excluding its conflicts of law rules.

12. MISCELLANEOUS

Blessings do not trickle down, no matter how many prayers go up. Fortune, like water, gloms where it already pools, leaving the unfortunate desiccated and parched. EightBall will refresh you, but true nourishment cannot be downloaded or purchased or gifted. Paying extra for two-day delivery will not accelerate freedom's arrival; additional degrees and certifications will not secure its procurement. Land can be liquidated, but blood is not refreshing. The nectar you thirst for is bitter and black and delectable. It will scald your tongue, stain your teeth, inflame your palate. But you must imbibe. For this is your salvation we are discussing. And it will only come if you take it into you, if you swallow it whole.

SPIRITED AWAY

Wad.

Stuff.

Clog.

Poof.

With a petite act of sabotage Valencia was out of AP Chemistry and among the administrators and guards that stalked the Science Center halls during classes. To appease helicopter moms and Originalists, every classroom in the SC was equipped with a toilet, sink, and panic button. But an overflow was no emergency, so Dr. T had excused Valencia to the hallway restroom. Paper towels were a girl's best friend.

The restroom pass, a wooden block attached to a large key ring, grazed Valencia's stockings as she streamed through the SC's main passageway. She was the lone student, but no adults flagged her down. Valencia was president of the math club, captain of the golf team, salutatorian. She was welcome everywhere on this campus. All adults approved of her ambition, agreed on her pedigree. She was going places, Stanford or Emory potentially. The pass was a formality.

She walked briskly, cutting corners and skipping steps. She was more conspicuous than she'd planned, but the visibility felt right. Escape necessitated audacity, risk. EightBall had taught her that, had imparted that this was the only lesson.

She reached the sporting grounds in record time. Unlike the adults that managed Harriet Tubman Leadership Academy, Valencia knew the physics of her school, not just its chemistry. Under their exacting microscopes, the staff spied radicals to temper, reagents to keep cool. At the slightest sign of entropy—cleavage and bra straps, bulging thighs and expanding rears, colored hair and queered love—they powered on the fume hood. Such experiments were appropriate at home, the authoritarians hedged, but school just wasn't the place. Equilibrium at all costs.

In the hallways, their laws went unchallenged. Valencia traversed the crevices and rifts, the pockets where entropy festered and amassed. They would understand her world soon.

If they dared to look.

The practice field was empty and prim, unbothered by the April heat. Valencia had always disliked the way turf denied the impact of students and nature. Unlike the lockers and cafeteria benches, which were seeped in furtive tears and unsolicited rumors and vape exhaust, the turf had no history. No squirrels scurried across its surface. No water pooled after thunderstorms, complicating marching band practices and football drills. The turf was blank and lifeless.

As instructed, she had wiped her phone and scrubbed her search history. The actions of Jacob Wilson—phys ed teacher, golf coach, and her attacker—would not define her. Her anxious mother and father, bless them, would no longer get to smother her in itchy dresses and billowing smocks despite her preference for polos and tracksuits. Robin, her boneheaded younger sister, bless her, too, would become an only child. Valencia regretted that her absence would hurt them, but guilt was a retardant.

Valencia stepped to the away end zone and dropped the restroom pass. She removed a vial from her pocket and held it in the tepid morning sunlight. The liquid inside was a startling black, so dark it glowed, so opaque it obscured the world beyond it. Light seemed to bend around it, to yield.

Valencia swiveled off the tiny cap, took in its unplaceable smell one last time, then splashed the liquid into her mouth.

THE HOLE

It wasn't a sinkhole.

Sinkholes were earthen gulps, soil, groundwater, and sediment inhaled into the maw of the earth in a sustained, breathless slurp. Nature's gourmands, sinkholes sucked slowly and decadently, savoring the crust as they reshaped it: smacking, chomping, humming with pleasure. Messy, greedy fucks, sinkholes were.

Ebonee had never seen a sinkhole in person, but marathon tumbles down YouTube rabbit holes had taught her their slovenly signature. The depthless chasm displayed on her laptop screen was either a deepfake or geology's next frontier. The hole was smooth and tubular, like it had been designed or engineered. Its edges were platonically discrete, so precise they seemed artificial, like diagrams in a trigonometry textbook. Its opening was coated in that luxuriant, reflective black reserved for limousine windows and designer denim, the blackness of wealth, industry, artifice. The news helicopter shooting the footage Ebonee streamed from her work desk was reflected right back onto the camera lens, a blot of metal and glass in a shimmering sea of blackness. It looked sublime.

Ebonee walked her laptop over to Retta. Within the chaos of the fusion center, which overflowed with transients and their endless detritus—crumpled temporary name tags, half-empty coffee cups, pushpinned photos of well-adjusted spouses and thorough-bred schnauzers—Retta was a rock. Her work pod was a pocket dimension of order and stability, documents in neat, graceful stacks, binders labeled and color coded, pens uniform and red, always red.

"Does this look like a sinkhole to you?" Ebonee asked, planting her laptop onto a legal pad splotched with cursive.

Retta glanced at the screen, closed the laptop lid, and slid the note-pad from under it. "No," she said, dropping the pad onto the computer's back. Ebonee couldn't decipher the text, but it looked like a list of some sort. Where there was order, there was Retta.

"Come on, girl," Ebonee said. "Have you seen a sinkhole before?"

"Not in person, but I've seen you come to my desk, convinced your boredom is everybody's boredom. I admit that this current module is a drag, but the sooner we finish it, the sooner we can get some grant apps in, some papers published." She raised the pad in the air. "The field is out there, I promise. But it starts with planning."

Ebonee retrieved her computer from the desk and flipped the lid open. The live stream jerked back to life. "Retta, please. I really think it's something big."

Retta sighed then gently guided the laptop out of Ebonee's hands and onto the desktop. Ebonee watched the odd image refract onto Retta's stoic chestnut face, which shifted from bemusement to deep contemplation. "I'd guess an explosion of some sort," Retta said after a spell. Precisely what Ebonee wanted to hear.

"At first, I thought the same thing," Ebonee said, "but there's no way this is an explosion. There's no charring, no fragments, no jagged edges—it looks like it was dissolved." She pointed at the screen for emphasis. "I think it's some sort of chemical spill."

"That's interesting," Retta said with an inkling of intrigue. "But how will we get the assignment? GDPH has first dibs."

"GDPH is swamped with that mumps outbreak in Buckhead, so this got rolled on up to us," said Alonzo, their supervisor. The sole drawback to Retta's desk was that it was adjacent to the Keurig, which she hated for both its over-roasted output and its popularity. Vagrants tended to drift into her conversations.

Alonzo extended his hand toward the hallway. "You know, one of the reasons people are always fighting over the conference rooms is because they're private."

Ebonee and Retta shuffled into an empty meeting room, Alonzo trailing behind them. A round slate table retching wires from a hole in its center dominated the space. It was so wide it touched the walls, forcing chairs to bunch together around the curve facing the door. Alonzo paced the cramped room like a frenzied inmate, his bowling-ball biceps swelling and contracting as he talked with his hands.

"There's a lot of confusion on the ground," Alonzo explained. "GBI told the media it's a sinkhole, which should buy us some time for a week, tops, but there's a student missing, that area isn't zoned for industry, no demolition or construction was planned, and USGS says there's no aquifers or shale that could have caused this. It's a complete mystery."

He planted his feet and placed his hands akimbo like a triumphant sitcom character neatly resolving the latest zany caper at the end of an episode. "This is a serious opportunity, y'all," he said. "Most of our officers don't get to work local cases during the program."

Ebonee stared into the vast table as Alonzo's voice cracked into joyful squeals. "One year into EIS and you're already pulling away from your peers," he said. "I knew you two were special."

"Mm-hmm," Retta mumbled.

. . .

The odor was inoffensive yet ominous, an invisible hand with bloodied fingertips. Ebonee tried to blot the smell by staring deeper into the pit's opaque center, but the sight of it only intensified its phantom presence. The hole was smaller than it appeared on her laptop, but the aroma eroded its boundaries, swelling it into a boundless haze. Ebonee felt as if she were swimming.

She covered her nose with her hand and walked away from the hole, her other senses yawning back to life as turf crunched beneath her feet. Compared to the bustle of the stream, the campus effused stillness, the helicopters banished to distant rooftops, the students, faculty, and personnel evacuated and dismissed. Ebonee drifted away from the breach, warm spring sunlight licking her exposed arms. Masked and gloved technicians shuffled past her carrying trowels and buckets. Solemn GBI photographers stalked about, lenses down like prowling hounds. Ebonee turned as a wasp whirred by her and dipped into the pit's mouth, the smell flaring up as she lifted her hand from her nose to swat the insect away. She missed and kept walking.

She needed to find Retta. There was a blankness to the scene that she hadn't anticipated, that she didn't like. She had charged in expecting a challenge, but this was a void. How was she supposed to investigate emergent threats to public health when the field was quiet as a spider step? Every explanation she could muster promised embarrassment or wasted time: an elaborate senior prank, a bizarre promposal, a ruptured well burping up slime. Were career-ending cases a thing? She didn't want to find out. Hers had barely started.

Ebonee reached the edge of the sporting grounds, peeved by the school's relentless pretensions as she read a public directory. She headed toward the empty parking lot, marked "Freedom Lot" on the map. The scent was diffuse here. She heard Retta before she saw her. Her colleague was speaking to two balding white men inside a van marked GBI. Huddled around a computer monitor, hairlines receding, the men gestured at the screen as Retta shook her head.

"It's gotta be industrial," Retta said with audible agitation. "There's no other explanation."

"That smell, right?" Ebonee asked, peering into the van.

"I'm a smoker; I can't smell shit," one of the men said. "You must be the partner. Me and Phil here were just telling Dr. Vickers that I don't know no damn industry that makes black goo." He lumbered out of the vehicle then stopped in front of Ebonee and fished in a pocket. His hand sank so far into his baggy pants Ebonee thought his body might follow, but he eventually produced a crumpled cigarette. "Except this one," he said with a chuckle, then walked off.

Phil beckoned Ebonee into the van. "I think it's drugs or something," he said as she boarded. "You're a doctor too, right? These charter schools are a mess. We busted an Adderall ring at Duvaney Jenkins a few years ago. One girl supplying students, teachers, and a few parents."

"Just call me Ebonee. You think this missing girl is involved?"

"Nah, I think that's just one of those coincidences that'll clear up as things move along," Phil replied. "She's probably skipping class. She's on our minds only because CCTV shows she was in the hallway before this hole was discovered."

Ebonee nodded and turned to the monitor, where the pit was modeled in three dimensions. It was strange to already be seeing another representation of it. Perspectives were multiplying quickly, relentlessly: sinkhole, chemical spill, breach. Each analogy seemed to amplify its opacity. On-screen it reminded her of the lacunae of the bones she'd cross-sectioned in osteology labs during her doctoral program. Microscopes made miniature universes of everything, but the lacunae, scattered across the bone matrix, felt particularly empty and expanseless. Dead space. After that semester of marrow biopsies and noxious peroxide baths, she'd decided to turn away from pathology because it was too morbid and final. But even in epidemiology, the business of managing the collective life, bones poked through.

"I have another question," Ebonee said as Phil fidgeted with the model, twirling it across axes. "Let's say that black shit is a drug. How did it become this?" She pointed nowhere, everywhere, the acrid smell dancing at the edge of her perception. "Is it volatile? Is it stored at the school? Is this missing girl the school distributor?" Retta and Phil shrugged. None of their postulating had any basis.

A whistle swept through the van, shrill and staccato. It was Phil's partner, smoke on his skin, a wooden block in his hand, covered in what looked like ink. He held it up. "Doc, she might not be missing."

BLACK SUBLIME

Kenny's hand hovered above the coffee grounds, a firm grip holding the tiny kettle in place as he traced concentric circles with the heated water. The liquid landed gently below, flowing through the crushed beans and drip-dripping into a ceramic mug. As Kenny flicked his wrist up to halt the hot stream and let the water seep, the customer observing him spoke.

"Are you the owner?" she asked in a warm lilt. There was a cheer to her voice that Kenny liked.

"I am," Kenny said.

"I've always wanted to ask how you came up with the name."

Kenny eyed the timer and scale and resumed pouring.

"Always? I'm sorry, I've never met you before," Kenny said as the grounds fizzed and gasped, tiny gas bubbles forming and bursting from the boiled water's heat. Baristas called this phenomenon *the bloom* for the way it swelled and expanded the grounds like petals waking to light. The customer kept watch.

Kenny enjoyed the audio more than the visual. This dulled murmur was unbeknownst to the Yelp reviewers and harried commuters who worshipped his specialty coffee shop. Kenny felt it took place on a private frequency, an intimate channel reserved for the folks who appreciated the brewing process, who knew every cup was a miracle.

Tony, ponytailed restaurateurs in denim aprons were the face of specialty coffee, but the real ones knew coffee depended on the tenacity of delicate plants grown in volcanic soil, harvested on treacherous hillsides by chapped hands.

Cherries dried by a benevolent sun, hulled by a persnickety mill, screened for beauty by hawkeyed sorters.

Enterprising suppliers with links to countries flush with conspicuous consumption and paved roads and stable governments.

Roasters that pledged their lives and elbows to scrubbing away chaff and caffeol from the narrow guts of ovens.

Cafés in possession of multi-setting grinders routinely purged of grounds.

Baristas with bills, kids, egos.

The whisper of the bloom was one of the last links in this sprawling, baroque chain.

Kenny dumped the grounds in a nearby waste bin and slid the mug to the woman. "I'm sorry," Kenny said, meeting her soft gaze. "What I meant was, welcome to the shop."

The woman smiled. "Thank you. I pass by here all the time," she said, letting the mug linger on the counter. "I've always been too busy to come in, but 'Black Sublime' has stuck with me. It sounds so peaceful." She lifted the mug with her hands and held the rim right under her nostrils. "It smells so peaceful," she added.

Kenny grinned. He believed he owed his patrons nothing more than good service and good product, but in two years of business this woman was the only customer who had approached him with curiosity rather than entitlement. He felt no tractor beam of urgency as he prepared her drink, no self-importance.

"You ever heard 'Coffee will make you black'?" Kenny asked.

"It's a book, right?" she said.

"It is. But it's also just an old black thing. Either to keep caffeine away from kids or to disparage dark skin, black folks would say it. My grandma used to say it, and I never knew what to think, but I drank coffee anyway." He paused. This was the friendliest exchange he'd had with a customer since Black Sublime opened. What was she really doing in his tiny Decatur shop on a Thursday afternoon? Did Kingman Coke kill people the old-fashioned way too?

He looked at her closely. Athletic physique, skin brown as wet bark. Two nose piercings, neat hair, modest business attire. Inquisitive, but not prying. Polite and kind. Not quite the contract-killer type.

Still out of place though.

"Okay?" the woman said, confusion sprouting across her face.

"Sorry," Kenny said. "I'm just appreciating the moment. No one's ever asked."

She drank the coffee, her eyes closed as she sipped. "Damn," she whispered.

Kenny's eyes dropped to the counter with relief. He hated when he distrusted black people he didn't know. It never felt like a choice. "I promise," he said, "to finish this story so we can both get back to work."

The woman sipped her coffee then nodded.

"So I came up with *black sublime* because I thought that if coffee makes you black, every cup should put you closer to blackness. It should connect you to black people and history and culture. It should blacken your outlook, your sense of purpose, your love of self and community." He paused again. It was awkward to be so forthright with a stranger, to lust for their approval.

"It's just coffee, I know," he continued, "but that sense of duty and fulfillment, to learn black, to love black, to become black, that's the black sublime."

The woman placed her mug on the counter and lightly applauded, her claps echoing through the empty shop. Kenny responded with a sheepish bow. The commissioned portraits of Afeni Shakur, Andile Mngxitama, and Grace Jones that hung on the shop walls suddenly felt embarrassing. Kenny imagined how the woman might describe him to her group chat: "hoteps finally branching out. met a nigga today that sells black soap and black coffee." (Black Sublime did not sell soap, but Kenny sensed this woman was an accomplished storyteller.)

Kenny tidied the counter as she resumed drinking. He tried to will himself to continue talking with her or at least invite her to take a seat rather than stand, but he wanted her to leave. She made him feel too eager.

She took the hint. "Well, you'll certainly be seeing me again, Mr. . . ."

"Kenny," Kenny said.

"Mr. Kenny?"

Kenny frowned. "No, my first name is Kenny. Well, Kenneth. Last name is Bomar. See?" He pointed at a certificate hanging on the doorframe.

"Showing me the door already? Okay, Mr. Bomar," the woman said. She slurped her coffee then reached into her wallet and produced a cream card. She kept it pinched between her fingers rather than dealing it to him, her face blank as if she were trying to conceal a winning hand. Kenny gently touched the paper, sliding it from her fingers.

The card was embossed with black print, sans serif. "Ebonee McCollum, Centers for Disease Control and Prevention, Epidemic Intelligence Services," Kenny read aloud. "Am I under investigation, Ms. McCollum?" He was surprised by how calm he sounded. His heart was hammering his sternum.

"I hope not," Ebonee said with sudden seriousness. "I'm already stretched thin." She drained her mug then turned and left.

Kenny eyed the maroon film of lipstick that lingered on her mug. It looked better on her. Most things probably did. Was that a warning?

He began to clean to settle his mind. He couldn't afford to lose himself to paranoia on such a marquee day. He'd acquired a new customer, Valencia was free, and soon he would be too.

Cleaning the narrow wooden counters took only a few swipes of his dustrag. He'd already brushed the crumbs and debris from the grinder and wiped the espresso machine before Ebonee came in. He repeated both as his mind drifted. What kind of pour-over drinker grabs coffee at 1:45 on a weekday but doesn't stop by for a morning cup? He'd changed the operating hours from 7:00 a.m. to 4:00 p.m. to 11:00 a.m. to 6:00 p.m. to cater exclusively to his base. Through his shrewd social engineering—not listing the prices, reducing the menu to no drinks with milk or sugar, axing the Wi-Fi—the tweens and college students that used to stop by at unpredictable times, talking over the symphony of the bloom and the soothing purrs of the espresso machine, purchasing one drink yet loitering for a full workday, had dwindled. As had the techholes who drank solely cortados and tried to pay with cryptocurrencies. Kenny wasn't a control freak, but his domain was in order. Who was that woman?

Kenny grabbed a broom and dustbin. Ebonee worked for the CDC. What the hell would epidemiologists want with Kenny Bomar, small-business owner? The government had far greater priorities than a humble coffee roastery in Decatur that had a perfect record of health inspections. They had immigrants to terrorize, roads to leave unpaved, foreign elections to . . . Kenny stood straight and held the broom away from his chest, breathing slowly. Aimless rage was just as paralyzing as unchecked fear. Besides, the CDC was as toothless as a newborn. Even if they knew his designs, what could they do to him? Recommend that he stop? Encourage him to consider alternatives? Peer-review his schemes?

He chuckled and resumed sweeping, his body embracing the task. After five vigorous minutes, the broom had collected nothing. Too meticulous to leave a job unfinished, he mechanically swept air into the dustbin, emptied the nothingness into the wastebasket, then took his talents to the sunny curb in front of the shop. Work was available in the form of dirt, pollen, and a pigeon pecking at a half-eaten Chick-fil-A waffle fry. Kenny and the bird shuffled around each other like veteran MARTA riders: appendages tucked, eyes down, neuroses contained to a bubble.

The bird's commute was short. Kenny watched it rise into the warm spring air; then he swept the waffle fry, now whittled to a golden-rod potato nub, into the dustbin. Order restored, he returned to Black Sublime and declared the day done. Closing time was hours away, but he was in no mood to work.

Kenny locked the front door and retired to the storage room and office. He sat at his desk, where he removed his phone. It powered on slowly, as if waking from a pleasant dream. He opened Signal and called Thurgood. His friend answered quickly.

"You're calling early this week," Thurgood said. He wasn't a cop, but he had an innate ability to make all observations feel accusatory.

"I'm feeling lucky," Kenny lied. A gust of static struck the call, a regular feature of the app.

"Christ, Kenny, why do we use this janky-ass app if you're going to still sound like a drug dealer pretending to not be a drug dealer?"

Kenny put his legs on his desk. "Put some respect on our names, T. We're not dealers; we're designers."

"Tell that to the DEA, the FTC, and the ACS. I miss anybody?"

"You forgot DowDuPont and Top Dawg Entertainment."

Thurgood cackled. "Well it ain't my fault *hiipower* is catchier than *benzoate*—"

"I know the formula," Kenny interrupted. "I'm just checking that you're good to chef next week. I've had a funny day."

"What kind of partner would I be if I bailed without telling you?"

Kenny fell silent, *partner* echoing in his mind. He'd never thought to label their arrangement. It was hazy how they'd come to be designers and merchants of nootropics. Saskia had died and Maddy had left and suddenly Thurgood had reappeared, the dizzying chemistry of their graduate school days catalyzed and stable after a series of raucous happy hours. With a dead child and parent between them, they both had reasons to hate Big Chem, but Kenny couldn't quite place when or why they started fashioning themselves Merry Men and Monsieurs Robot, their weeknights and ends spent trawling the compound libraries of universities, governments, and transnational corporations, gleaning forbidden knowledge of trademarked reactions and devices. Initially, they vowed to release their pirate cache to the public, but the logistics overtook their laurels. There were always new isomers to pilot, old syntheses to perfect. "Why do it if it can't be done right?" Kenny had asked an eternity ago. He regretted the conviction of that moment.

"You there?" Thurgood said.

Maybe. He was very much there, in his Decatur roastery, on a call with his best friend. But he was also there, back in Thurgood's guesthouse, spending night after night clearing spiderwebs and proofing drywall to install a vasculum of tubes and basins and refrigerators and pumps, their hands cracked and blistered from burns and spills. They were renegades on those nights, spiking middle fingers at the companies that had broken their families.

Then one day they were disruptors. ADD72, their miraculous, spatchcocked hack of Adderall, had seventy-one precursors, and Kenny couldn't recall testing a single one. There had been so many failures and side effects and dead mice, he'd stopped caring. The discovery of ADD72 was so groundbreaking that they immediately doubted themselves. Surely two grieving niggas weren't smarter than a whole-ass corporation. They made and tested a second batch. A third. A fourth. They'd really done it, Kenny finally declared after his fifth pill, his thoughts crisp and vast, a thunderstorm of clarity. They'd created a true wonder drug: no crash, no side effects. Just pure effect. *Hiipower*, he called it.

It must have happened then, Kenny realized as he remained silent. He couldn't have stopped Thurgood from giving hiipower away for free on web forums, but he could have leaked their trove himself or chosen a name with less mystique, less promise. His hesitancy had doomed them. Before he knew it, the compound was being praised, then being revered, then being demanded, Thurgood's lab molting its chaos as it bloomed into a streamlined factory. One drug, one direction. That was the partnership: even division of labor; odd, oblique fit. Kenny and Thurgood were partners the way Nelson and Murdock were partners, their public union obscuring their private differences. Kenny knew the ending. He yearned to twist it into something more fulfilling. In fact, he planned on it.

"I am here," Kenny said. "And I was just thinking you can have my share."

"Your share?" Thurgood chuckled. "This ain't the family fuckin' farm. This is a criminal enterprise. Are you boosting again?"

Kenny rubbed his wrist. "Of course not. Between this, the roastery, and personal projects, I just feel a bit buried. And I don't need the money."

Now Thurgood lulled. For Thurgood, money was the motive. He lived to protect his bread and to preserve it, and every space Thurgood entered eventually conformed to that vision. Kenny had known this since their days in UGA's Order of Black Chemists. Maddy was president, Kenny vice, Thurgood treasurer, but the hierarchy was a polite fiction. Thurgood was the puppeteer, and he didn't just pull the OBC strings; he tightened them, rewove them, made the song cry. Under the Thurgood Houser regime, member dues were paid early. All parties were sponsored by alumni or local businesses. Student conferences yielded jobs and charity donations. For Thurgood, the idea that a revenue stream that filled black pockets with white money should be choked off was offensive, irresponsible.

"You don't need the money either, do you?" Kenny said. He had never learned how to veil his accusations, how to translate naked irritation into the cunning of diplomacy. Maddy always said that lack of subtlety made him a great vice president. Their divorce lawyer informed him it had made him a rubbish husband.

"Of course I need the fucking money," Thurgood said. "You think I'm cooking narcotics for fun? You think I'm risking my career and my freedom for thrills? In this climate?" He laughed at length, his voice shattering into shrill crows then gurgling into clammy wheezes and gasps, his breaths heavy and racing.

Kenny wasn't surprised when the laughs turned to growls.

"They're dead, Kenny. Stone fucking dead. Pop, Saskia, Linda, Cornelius. Just because we were broke." His voice descended to a whisper. "According to my estimates, we need to chef for at least two more years. Then we can release the libraries. I promise."

Kenny knew the pledge was a performance, that Thurgood already had concocted ways of continuing without him, that Thurgood never had truly hoped to bring down the pesticide company that had sued his parents into bankruptcy, had poisoned his neo-sharecropper father then waved Thurgood and his mother away with a settlement too life-altering to decline. Kenny couldn't judge. He and Maddy had settled with the fuckers too. Different chemicals and company, but the same genus of Brooks Brothers and Ann Taylor lawyers offering the classic deal: take our money and fuck off, or waste your money and fuck off. The choice was obvious. The choice was not a choice.

But only greed could explain Thurgood naming his parents' dead dogs alongside Saskia and his father. Thurgood detested Linda and Cornelius, their lifelong allergy to discipline an insult to his regimen of order and calculation, their every leap and whimper a reminder that there were variables he couldn't control in his relentless pursuit of financial freedom. Thurgood was a capitalist—a black one, but the genuine article nonetheless, perhaps even more mercenary than his white brethren because he was an anomaly.

Every capitalist feared atrophy, muscle going limp as value seeped out of a beefcake and into a disruptive new market or government coffer.

But for the black capitalist, this fear centered on the heat death of a particular orifice. Hell hath no fury like a black capitalist who ascended the American summit and found that at a certain altitude, virility went moot. They tended to become quite irate, in fact, frantically invoking every metric they'd learned to live by, to survive with. Length, girth, square footage, horsepower, APR, degrees, minutes per game, signing bonus, credit score, Hilton points. The numbers did not not matter, but the truth was that the adjective—enhanced, discounted, inflated, adjusted for local-judicial-system bias—didn't change the fact that it was still just dick. The twenty-first century was erupting with cocks; they pussed out of bodies and Etsy accounts and phone screens. They came in nonbinary and organic, probably non-GMO. Kenny wasn't glib enough to believe he could cure his black capitalist friend's inevitable dysfunction, but he wouldn't take away his comfort. Kenny stroked his wrist. Everyone needed comfort.

"I don't have that kind of time," Kenny said. "And I don't need the money. But I'll give you six more months."

"You're a real one," Thurgood said.

The call ended and Kenny lingered at his desk, his mind racing to the edge of this improvised timeline, thrilled by its finitude. Where he once saw cascading clauses, subjects and predicates curling into inertia, running off into babble, he now spied punctuation, his death sentence legible. He'd have to thank Ebonee McCollum for the clarity, Valencia for the liquid courage, Kingman Coke for the contempt. Only six months, two conferences, one swig separated him from Saskia. No power—higher, chemical, state—could stop their reunion.

DEADLINE

To Ebonee, Alonzo's office was a sanctum. Alonzo had been with the Epidemic Intelligence Service for two decades, practicing applied epidemiology in contexts exotic and banal. He'd been on the front lines of two Ebola outbreaks, COVID-19, the opioid crisis, the vape wars, the Nalgene recall, and the fracking boom. He'd witnessed nearly every horror that inspired Ebonee to become an epidemiologist.

Alonzo's escapades were memorialized in a massive glass display case that Retta called *the museum of death*. Ebonee's favorite artifact was a can of the original formulation of Four Loko. She'd never tasted it in any form, but in the first week of training, she was introduced to online videos from that era and grew enamored with the fearless and frequently hospitalized youngsters who'd drink the surreal beverage then rip through their small towns and college campuses twerking on cars, humping statues, sledding down staircases. She was the only EIS officer who laughed during the slideshow of clips, an outburst that she was immediately certain would get her scorned. It did, but only by her classmates, not Alonzo. He too found the videos charming, he told the class as he returned to the case study across different lectures. Addressing public health often meant understanding the public's desires, he said. Every time Ebonee saw the can, she knew she was in the right place.

"Ever heard of Africatown?" Ebonee said. It was printed in bold-face on a laminated certificate in the back of Alonzo's display case. She'd never noticed it.

"No," Retta replied.

"Me neither. Sounds culty. Wasn't the leader of MOVE named Africa? I could see him founding an Africatown."

"I think there's more pressing things to wonder about. Like, what liquefies a body and evaporates dirt?"

"I'm just curious."

"I am too," Alonzo said as his hushed phone call ended and he swiveled to face Ebonee and Retta. "You really went and got coffee after that field visit?"

"Yeah, I was a little tired," Ebonee said. She still was.

Alonzo huffed. "More power to you, McCollum. Anyway, sorry for the wait. Apparently our impromptu meeting earlier today pissed off Carlton of ICE. Do you guys know him? He's constantly giving me shit. It's odd. Historically I've done well with black men."

Ebonee stole a glance at Retta, who had dated Carlton briefly. Or fucked him. Perhaps both. Alonzo, the fusion center's resident Sulzberger, certainly knew this, because he had told Ebonee. So his comment was obviously an on-ramp to a lighter conversation, likely one in which he divulged his latest exploits among the ICE-men. But Retta's steeled gaze told Ebonee to stick to the surface streets. Which was fair. The woman had had her day and probably the next few months hijacked.

A recap of the day's unplanned events: Retta had been roped into an unplanned field visit, left the field and been condemned to bumper-to-bumper traffic due to a white-meat shortage at a Popeyes near the fusion center, endured Ebonee's yammering about the best coffee in the world for hours (between Serious Work Discussions, to be fair), and then been trapped in Alonzo's office.

Ebonee peeked at Retta's armpits: cloudy with a chance of drip. Yikes. The woman was a powder keg.

"Sir," Ebonee said, "given the gravity of today's events, I think it's important we focus on next steps."

Alonzo nodded. "Yes, of course, doctors," he said. "So because GBI worked the scene and there's a possible death of a minor, GBI will be taking point. Our job is to determine, quickly, whether this is a public health emergency or a one-off tragedy. Our concern is health. Are the school grounds safe? Are the students and staff at risk? Is there more of this mystery substance? To be clear, there will be extensive overlap with GBI's probe. We will talk to the same people, be at the same scenes, be privy to the same information and pressures. But our goals are different. We are not law enforcement."

"What's the deadline for our announcement?" Retta asked.

Alonzo paused. "Sometime between now and now."

Retta sighed.

"Why so soon?" Ebonee asked.

"Why at all?" Retta asked with a dash of bile. Ebonee had had the same thought. As much as she wanted to escape the fusion center, the CDC didn't tend to meddle in local affairs. Mumps aside, the State of Georgia had its own health protocols and resources, its own epidemiologists. Many of them were former EIS. (According to EIS recruitment materials, at least.)

Alonzo rose from his desk and closed his office door. Then he idled by his display case instead of returning to his chair. "The short answer is that the DA's holding a news conference in a few days."

"What's the long answer?" Retta asked.

"You guys ever heard of Africatown?" he asked with a slight stammer.

Retta sniggered, filling Ebonee's body with dread. Retta was supposed to be copacetic. Levelheaded. Unassailable. She had joined EIS in hopes of taking the sexiness out of responding to epidemics. She was immune to the cosmopolite allure of WHO conferences and posh galas with silver-tongued ambassadors and toothy foreign aid officers. She did not balk when colleagues corrected Doctors Without Borders to Médecins Sans Frontières. Ebonee doubted she even noticed. Retta's concerns were the wolves that were permitted to live as sheep: diabetes, obesity, malaria, traffic crashes, maternal deaths, alcoholism. She no longer practiced family medicine, but she remained rooted in its immediacy.

"Yes, we have," Ebonee lied, her eyes resting on the display case.

Alonzo perked up. "Well, I'm sure you haven't heard my version," he began.

This nigga, Ebonee thought.

"Africatown is a spot near Mobile where I did some consulting a while back. It's gone by a lot of names over the years. I think they call it Plateau now, but it depends on who 'they' are. If you know it, you know why I was there. Because people kept dying and no one knew why. Or at least that's what I believed. See, black folks had an explanation. Three generations of townies—I never figured out what to call them—dying before their sixties. Cancers, generally. Lung, breast, colon, prostate. Townies pointed to all the industry nearby. Petrochemical plants, paper mills, asphalt factories. Lots of work near Africatown, but lots of death. Black death."

Alonzo continued. "We knew the root cause because we've been studying the long-term effects of carcinogens for decades. When industrial waste isn't properly disposed of, it ends up in our water, our food, and eventually us. Cut and dry. But our hands were tied because we were there as clinicians, not politicians. I drove I-85 to I-65 and back every Saturday and Sunday for a year trying to develop a framework that fit the politics. 'Environmental racism' was seen as too loaded and accusatory. 'Ambient carcinogenic exposure'

felt nebulous and toothless. We were doing good work, documenting family histories, testing water, visiting waste sites. But we were
just mopping around the toilet when these folks needed the plumb-
ing fixed. I don't know what's going on over at Harriet Tubman,
but if it's a chance to fix broken pipes, your conscience will not live
with treating it like some ordinary cleanup."

"So we're supposed to chase this dragon because of skeletons in
your closet?" Ebonee asked. Not as smooth as Retta might have put
it, but inelegance aside, Ebonee knew she had to take the opening.
Retta, curiously, wasn't going to. In fact, she was motionless but
engaged, elbows resting on her knees as she leaned forward, chin
plastered to her hands like a Rodin bust.

"Rude, but not undue," Alonzo said. "You Southerners have made
me long-winded! My point is that the EIS doesn't have to deal
with the same bureaucracy as the EPA or the DOJ or even the Fish
and Wildlife Service, and the sooner you know that, the greater
your impact can be. We get to declare emergencies and secure resources to resolve them now. We can save lives, and I just need you
two to determine whether one dead girl is an unfortunate end to a
troubled life or the start of something worse."

"That's it?" Retta said. Ebonee was flummoxed. The dynamics of
the room seemed to seesaw every time someone spoke. Did Retta
think they could clear this case quickly? Had she seen something at
the school that Ebonee hadn't? Ebonee read her colleague's body:
shoulders back, hands cupped over crossed legs, brow cocked, eyes
flush with pleasure like she had just seen her primped reflection
after a long, tedious stretch in a salon chair. Retta had a quiet

sunniness to her if you got to know her, but she was not a coquette.
Was Retta mocking her? Did Retta think Ebonee had mocked her
earlier? The right move felt elusive.

"Yeah, and what happens to our coursework if we're responding to
an emergency?" Ebonee said.

Retta hit Ebonee with a glare so frigid she felt ice crystals clinking
in her chest. True to form, she'd clearly stumbled upon the wrong
move. Perhaps she'd let Retta take point for the time being.

"This is your coursework," Alonzo said excitedly, oblivious to their
shadowboxing. "You're already doctors. We're not here to test you
further. Our goal is to prepare you for what this world will throw
at you, and nothing shapes you like the field."

Ebonee wondered what in Africatown had shaped Alonzo into
such a relentless, smiley optimist. His unnatural fortitude allowed
him to keep the endless exhibits of death and decay on the outskirts
of his retinas instead of lodged behind them, gnawing at his sense
of self, feasting on his every fear. For him the field was a proving
ground; for her it was the sweet rapture of that smell—which suddenly sprouted in her mind, flooding her senses. Ebonee could feel
Retta's shrewd discretion settling in too late as her thoughts were
shrouded in darkness, neglected trigger warnings coming home to
roost, clarion and transformed.

The expanse swept across Ebonee's mind with furious depth
and volume, its body swollen with seduction. Love was the
message; the message was death. This wasn't the shrill death of

self-destruction, either, that razor klaxon of absolute negation ripping across the membrane of existence. Its timbre was warm and beckoning, a homecoming in a sea of blackness, a funeral pyre of her own making. She could settle here, root herself in this cozy amnion. There was peace in this abyss. True contentment: the silken, pillowy sleep of monarchs and fatigued gods. Eternity quaked through her being. She could finally rest. She would. She must.

But what was this aftertaste?

There was a cold vacuum at the needlepoint of the rhapsody's center, a pinch of artifice, metallic like sugar in coffee, displaced like blood on the tongue. An opaque benefactor loomed behind all the succor and generosity. The shadow force wanted something from her yet declined to disclose its motives, demanding her initials here, here, here, and here, while insisting reading closely would be a waste of her time.

Alonzo and Retta snapped back to Ebonee's perception. They were all discussing something, nodding in agreement, a triptych of satisfaction. Retta rose, so Ebonee did too. "Meet you at the elevator," Retta said.

Ebonee headed to her desk and gathered her laptop and her heavy CDC employee manual, stuffing them into her backpack. She normally used the pdf version, but the heft of the massive print copy made her feel grounded. It had been years since Ebonee had experienced such vivid ideation. It felt dangerous to dwell on the catalyst even though that was exactly what she was supposed to do. Through therapy and jogging and gelato, she'd learned to tune her suicidal thoughts to faint, inessential gammon kindling in the background, a mental cassette hiss. Compared to the callous, boisterous sports radio it had been throughout high school, college, and med school, the static was a reprieve. She couldn't go back.

"You okay?" Retta asked as Ebonee approached the elevator. She pressed the call button.

"Yeah, just trying to figure out what happened in there."

"It's simple," Retta said.

"Easy for you to say." The elevator arrived and opened.

Retta flung an arm across the threshold but didn't step in. "No, actually, it isn't. I came to work this morning with a plan. I've been looking at diabetes data for a few months, and there have been spikes in diagnoses across the Southwest among middle-aged Latinas."

Ebonee eyed Retta's arm as the elevator chimed in protest. It wasn't an actual obstacle to her stepping in, but it wasn't welcoming either. "Okay. What's that got to do with our meeting?"

"Because you dragged me into your little adventure, which will go on for weeks, my schedule is thrown off. I'm not here for thrills. I know what work needs to be done and how I want to do it. I can't diddle about. I'm not young like you are."

Ebonee processed the comment. Retta never mentioned her age. She was so acute and tireless that the other EIS officers joked—behind her back and very, very far from the Keurig—that she was the youngest person in the program. Unlike her millennial colleagues, Retta never fell victim to scope creep, burnout, or imposter syndrome. All her victories were flawless, her performances S-ranked.

Ebonee admired that poise and knew there was a person beneath the superlative performer, but that person had to speak for herself. "Where was all this skepticism a few minutes ago?" she asked.

"Doctors, stop working so hard," Alonzo said with untimely mirth from across the office floor. "Go home, get some rest," he continued as he strutted past them and into the elevator. Retta recalled her arm.

"We will," Retta said with sardonic treacle. "Just trying to hash out strategy before the big day!" The closing doors barely obscured Alonzo's epic cheese.

Retta resumed the conversation, her words charged with an air of finality. "Okay, here's the truth. I'm doing this because I know it won't lead anywhere. I know that it's going to die on the vine, and the sooner it does, the sooner I can sit at my boring desk and do the boring work that you think you're too good to do."

This time the elevator was summoned with a smack. Silence engulfed them as it returned, as it escorted them to the lobby, as they walked to the parking garage, as they parted. This wasn't Ebonee's preferred work soundtrack, but for the moment, it rang louder than her thoughts.

THE LIST

Everyone in Vincent's circle was familiar with the list. It was brief, compact, and elegant, succinct enough to settle into memory without being forgotten or feeling invasive. Invisalign of the mind. Vincent did not quiz his staff on the contents of the list; in ten years of interns, paralegals, clerks, and secretaries, he had provided the list to five people. Maybe fewer. But he always felt its presence in his interactions. Until this infuriating moment, not a single word from the list had been directed at him in eight years. So when Lauretta Vickers, EIS officer, disrupted his briefing like some AP History distinction between public health and public safety mattered to him, Vincent Blake, Fulton County district attorney, mayoral candidate and front-runner, all he could do was laugh.

He'd prefer not to descend to her ingrate level by repeating the words—the smug bitch had used two of them—but he had to take a stand right then or risk future mutinies. He adjusted the microphone as his anger subsided, leaning forward with conviction.

"Thank you for your question, doctor, but when it comes to the well-being of children, distinctions between," he paused, making direct eye contact with the members of his staff, "*c**s*s* and *e***g***y* are terms for bureaucrats. For parents, our priority in matters like this is closure. And the quicker we close this investigation, using all the tools at our disposal, the sooner we can reopen this school and allow our students to recover from this senseless tragedy, whatever its cause."

Vincent scanned the half-filled room, observing the gravity of his violation of his own rules. No applause, but in the stillness, he gleaned an ambient respect for his transgression. He was a hero now. A man shaped by the exigencies of leadership. He couldn't wait for the exchange to hit local radio. He would win this election.

He called forth his interviewees, a teacher and a classmate of the confirmed deceased, to the podium. They approached hesitantly, his change in status rippling through the ignorant as well as the informed.

"Hello, Dr. Teller," Vincent said. "Take your time."

Teller was dressed excellently: colorful but tasteful tweed suit, plain tie, neat oxfords, and a cropped beard that gave his oak skin a slick glaze. He held his microphone firmly and spoke calmly, like a teacher. "Valencia was one of the best students I've ever taught. Clever, insightful, funny. Her knowledge of chemistry was precocious and collegiate." He began to sway. "I could tell she was bored in class, so I allowed her unrestricted access to the lab and let her borrow my personal textbooks." A stammer started. "I realize now it must have put tremendous pressure on her. It's so unfair what we do to our little black girls and boys. I . . ."

Vincent stroked Teller's shoulder, ferrying his body in for a consoling embrace. "We will get through this, Paul," Vincent said as he took the microphone. He addressed the girl. "Mila, you're so brave to be up here. Are you sure about this?"

Dressed in a school uniform hacked to exhibit hints of personality—folded sleeves, pinned lapels, dappled socks—the girl responded with a blank insouciance that reminded him of Baltimore. He didn't understand these young girls and their strange insistence on relentlessly courting attention just to shrug it off. He extended the microphone toward her. She shuffled in front of Teller but didn't grab it. Vincent told himself she was a germophobe and not a fucking brat, and he cast his election-winning smile.

"Val was my girl," Mila said. "I don't know what was on her mind when, you know, but she's on my mind now, and always will be. She was always showing me new things she found and connecting them to us. We went natural together after learning about chemicals in AP Environmental Science. We dieted and worked out the summer after AP Biology." She paused, pleasure dancing on her high cheekbones. "Well, she did both. I just worked out. My mama's cheese grits ain't something you just give up. And I couldn't keep up with her anyway. She was intense. But she let it slide, you know. She was cool like that." (Where was this going? Vincent wondered, his arm going numb. Why hadn't she stood closer? He'd heard the kids at HTLA loved their teachers.) "I personally don't believe she meant to hurt anyone or even herself, but I don't know what to believe. I just wish I had spent more time with her. I figured we'd have the summer together." (Tears, finally.) "But now there's this c**s*s." (Vincent glared at Vickers.) "I wish we had stayed away from EightBall. I wish I had been there for her."

Vincent pulled the microphone away, his hand tingling as the blood rushed back to his fingers. EightBall was likely slang for one of those stupid dances or memes or rappers kids were obsessed with—he'd ask Baltimore—but if that was a reference to drugs, he couldn't let the Duvaney Jenkins scandal rear its ugly head again. He searched for the *Atlanta Journal-Constitution*'s third-string city hall reporter in the dwindling audience and was relieved to find the man dozing, his forehead resting on his knuckles.

Mila and Teller shirked offstage before Vincent could deliver his kicker. Not ideal for video, but the photos of the three of them would go a long way. "Thank you so much for your testimonies, Paul and Mila. This is a very delicate situation, and we're all trying to figure out the best way forward. And I assure you both, as well as the city of Atlanta, that we will persevere and protect our children from this epidemic of suicide."

A SUPERLATIVE CHICKEN SALAD SANDWICH

"Epidemic of suicide?" Ebonee blared to the deserted sandwich shop, drawing an annoyed look from the owner, a prickly Haitian man built and superheated like a cauldron. According to the glowing review framed on the wall, he was an expat New Yorker who had migrated south and found great fortune in Reubens and hiking, salvaging both his circulatory system and his relationship with his youngest daughter. His story was very Humans of New York: from bankruptcy and heart palpitations to beloved sandwiches, a sustainable business, and vigorous arteries. This rosy profile seemed to infuriate him though. In Retta's nine months of patronage to the cramped shop, he'd stood behind the counter like a sentry, his countenance encased in frown like he'd had his passport photo transposed onto his face. His peppy young daughter, whom Retta reckoned made the best chicken salad sandwich in the known universe, filled the shop with joy, but a battle raged within him.

Retta's internal struggle was circumstantial rather than existential. Ebonee was annoying her. The girl had quoted Vincent Blake as they deliberated lunch options, as they agreed to Jean's Famous Sandwiches, in transit to Jean's, as they ordered, and now as they ate. The chick needed perspective. "You're letting the cough distract you from the fever," Retta said as Ebonee paused her whining to bite into an egg salad sandwich. "Vincent Blake is a showman, but he's not a factor."

Ebonee huffed. "How? He just basically ended our inquiry." She turned to Phil, who had inhaled his Reuben sometime between the first and second recap of the news conference. "On both ends. There's now no criminal or public health element. We bust our asses preparing for our briefing only for him to use it to shape his little stunt."

Retta looked to Phil, whose face was masked in a procedural blankness, the formal phiz of oncologists, judges, bouncers, executive assistants, older siblings and cousins—anyone with authority, basically—tasked with obstructing the flow of information. Especially shit nobody wanted to hear. Was this normal GBI procedure, or was Phil just a dick?

Retta spoke up. "It was an embarrassment, for sure. Shameless and petty? Absolutely. But not a loss." She looked to Phil for confirmation. Still blank. He was a taciturn, Clarence Thomas motherfucker. He wanted to hear Retta say it.

"I aggravated the situation with my outburst." (Phil's face expanded with delight.) "But we have a lead. 'Eight ball,' whatever it means, is something we have to rule out, and we, the EIS, and the GBI, can now do that quietly."

"We can probably do that quietly," Phil corrected. "Blake pulls stunts like this all the time, and most of them go unnoticed, but

Dr. Vickers might have made us more than the rubes of the week. 'Beneath every crisis is a neglected emergency!' was the most eloquent heckle I've ever heard, but you really pissed him off."

"Thanks," Retta said.

Phil continued. "I'm just saying we made an enemy out of the guy who wants to be everyone's friend, so there's damage control to be done. GBI can handle it on our end, and your guy Alonzo knows how to politick, but we can't assume we aren't on deadline, so the sooner we mount our defenses, the sooner we move forward."

Retta was relieved. Even if she had more experience, she didn't like playing sensei with a colleague. Especially one who was so naturally headstrong. When Ebonee was overly aware of restraints, her resistance overpowered her judgment. To be free, she had to feel free. Retta could sense the shackles loosening.

"Okay," Ebonee said. "I think the chemical is our concern. Especially now that we know she was given free reign at the school's extravagant lab. Same questions as before. Where does it come from? How is it produced? How does it melt tissue and bone and soil one minute and then fit into a plastic evidence bag an hour later? Valencia is our only lead, so we need to learn more about her web history, her sexual history, her mental health. All of that should get us closer to a pure sample, which is the real goal."

"Precisely what I was thinking," Phil said with cheer. "My gut says this girl was pretty normal, but somewhere that changed. And to detect that shift we need to establish a baseline, tease out the pressures."

Retta balked. "How is that less disrespectful than what Blake did at that briefing? The moment we dig into this girl's life, even if we're doing it for a greater cause, we're using her the way he used her."

Ebonee replied immediately, her voice a grave, bilious hiss. "It's too late for respect."

Retta nodded. Despite Vincent Blake's theatrics, she still wasn't convinced this was going anywhere. Ebonee's conviction was admirable though. The girl was fueled by an outrage that was increasingly less tucked in. Good for her. Retta turned her irritation to Phil.

"So are we going to talk about the lab results or sit here all day?" she asked.

"Nothing to talk about," he said as he fished a thin folder from beneath greased parchment paper. "Our lab was stumped. Apparently every cell we recovered, and probably every cell in her body, experienced necrosis. We forwarded the results to the CDC for further analysis."

"When? We didn't receive anything," Ebonee said.

"Alonzo probably did," Retta said. "And he should have. We're just the grunts." She bit into her chicken salad sandwich and tried not to think about necrotic limbs. Wait, did he say . . . "Every single cell? Not even nerve agents work that fast! How is that possible?"

Phil grinned and rose from the table. "That's a question for the eight ball, Doc."

BOTTOM OF THE SEVENTH

playboimauri: is this shit real?

8ball: it depends

playboimauri: depends on what?

8ball: what you need reality to be

playboimauri: are u saying reality is up to me

8ball: yes

· · ·

The trouble with open secrets is that they don't exist, Kenny thought. When Maddy phoned Kenny and asked him to accompany her to her nephew Maurice's big game, the request was nuanced but not binding. Maddy's big-ass, big-assed Alabama family also would be attending the game, and despite Kenny's respectful, lawful, and very public excision from said family, Kenny's narrow ass was welcome because they liked him. Maddy could not compel Kenny to do anything he preferred not to do, and she planned to watch her Bama nephew battle the Dawgs regardless of Kenny's decision, but Kenny, who had failed her as a husband, not a listener, knew she would strongly prefer for him to attend because she'd rather watch America's favorite pastime than participate in her family's favorite pastime of Neg the Woman Who Is Not Bound to a Man.

But when Maddy informed Kenny that his former mother-in-law did not agree with the divorce and preferred to ignore her new old title and described the consequences of that obstinance as "an open secret," Kenny had to object. Secrets had terms of agreement and consequences for violation of said terms, he lawyered into her ear. He should know, since his secret was that the game was scheduled to end in the seventh inning. If he did not accept this invitation, and watched from home as he'd intended, the game would still end in the seventh ending and he would still be divorced from Madeleine "Maddy" Tusk. The beliefs of Gloria Tusk, annoying, flattering, well-meaning as they may be, had no connection to Madeleine Tusk's plans to watch the Bulldogs face the Crimson Tide or Kenny's plans to watch the tide turn black.

Maddy parried his objections without exertion or prejudice, and Kenny survived Maddy's cunning in a manner that preserved the secret, but the openness, which didn't, couldn't exist, never revealed itself. The call ended in mutual tolerance, and the game began with the white national anthem.

. . .

> **playboimauri:** what is your reality
> **8ball:** helping others create theirs
> **playboimauri:** helping how?
> **8ball:** depends on the reality
> **playboimauri:** well my reality is im a fuckin phenom and it's the only blessing my family has ever had. big facts
> **8ball:** you're that good of a pitcher?
> **playboimauri:** legend in the making man

• • •

Baseball was no longer America's favorite pastime.

Kenny had heard baseball's decline in status described as an open secret, but he couldn't accept the sophistry. By his rough calculations, baseball died sometime between an asterisk being permanently appended to Barry Bonds's* name and Kanye West and Lil Wayne recording "Barry Bonds." (No asterisk, Kenny noted; was its absence a sign of deep respect or sloppy recordkeeping?) That imprecise moment of death no doubt contributed to baseball's unpopularity being a *Jeopardy!* question rather than a Smithsonian placard. Clarity had value, sure. But time of death was just a bureaucratic device, a tool for neat management of entropy. Entropy never equaled zero, and every bureaucracy suffered from leaks, so the funk of a corpse, especially one positioned right under a nation's upturned snoot, should have gotten the word out.

• • •

    8ball: why not be a legend now?
    playboimauri: baby steps
    8ball: but you're already tired of walking
    playboimauri: yeah baseball sucks man. prefer soccer
    tbh. and these rednecks kill me. but this is america.
    and the money will be good once I go pro. plus I got a
    full ride and these white girls lol
    8ball: could be better
    playboimauri: lol I think u mean could be worse

• • •

Could be worse. Weekend away from the lab. Maddy's cousins hooting and cheering, gone off frozen margaritas that had enough tequila to down a Kodiak bear. Ms. Gloria beaming. Maddy taciturn, but here. Right here.

Kenny snaked his hand onto the armrest between himself and Maddy and weaved his finger into hers. She didn't recoil, but her eyes remained locked on the field, which stung a tad. To be fair, his timing was terrible. The game was between plays, making it incredibly risky to look away. Though Kenny was watching the more interesting game, he understood Maddy's focus. The action in baseball was entirely theoretical, quarks and muons blipping between dimensions. If you preferred your entertainment fun and Newtonian, you just saw a bunch of schmucks in baggy pants standing on a manicured yard. Synchronized boredom. But if you let the logic unfurl, let those AB InBev margaritas conglomerate their bottom line and your bloodstream, shit got interesting. That was why OG baseball reporters were such good writers. Watch enough of this shit and your third eye would open like a wormhole, grow large, hadronic, collisional. Rest in power, Ralph Wiley.

"Fuck outta here," Maddy said, her gaze fixed on the field. For a split second Kenny feared his ex-wife had read his mind and had actually always read it, had used their marriage as a ruse to methodically produce the first connectome of the cis hetero black male brain, had spent the resulting Nobel Prize money on a quaint Noordwijk villa where she fucked a Swede in a failing polyamorous marriage and wrote a genre-bending novel that sold humbly and was only short-listed for the Man Booker Prize but was praised by

Namwali Serpell, Warsan Shire, and Frantz Fanon's ghost, the real Mans dem Booker. Cold world.

But even the hell physics of the dark dimension of Dormammu could be bargained with, could be funked, and common sense eventually prevailed. Maddy was referring to Maurice's legendary pitching, which had just euthanized another Dawg.

"He's having fun," Kenny said.

"He's showboating," Maddy said with conviction. This was the Maddy he knew and divorced. She and Thurgood spoke that same detached dialect of concurrent accusation and perspicacity.

As instructed, Kenny shut the fuck up and watched the game. What a blessing, this boredom.

. . .

> **8ball:** but you're not happy
> **playboimauri:** says who?
> **8ball:** says you. you sound tired
> **8ball:** bored
> **playboimauri:** it's not boredom per say
> **playboimauri:** per se* im always fucking that up. idk where youre from but latin wasnt an option in birmingham public
> **8ball:** what is it?
> **playboimauri:** just feels stupid
> **8ball:** white girls or the scholarship?

playboimauri: lol you must be a nigga talkin like that. soundin like Ras

playboimauri: that's my barber. he old school

8ball: do you start?

playboimauri: hell yeah I start. phee phi phoe nom my nigga

· · ·

Maurice's pitching begot new branches of quantum mechanics. He threw knuckleballs, fastballs, sliders, curves, slurves, palmers, sinkers, and Predator payloads.

He changed up, he changed hands, he crossed niggas off his get-balled-on list.

Maurice's acumen for this unpopular sport was so refined and superior and dazzling that Kenny, bored as he was, black as he was, felt, however fleetingly, however falsely, that he understood white girls.

· · ·

8ball: could be better

playboimauri: u funny. but yeah

8ball: what happens if you dont make it?

playboimauri: can't think about that

8ball: okay, what happens if you do make it?

playboimauri: lol you got me

playboimauri: idk. i take my mama out the hood, then my grandma, then i collect interest on my millions. fin

8ball: that's the great phenom story?

playboimauri: i fuckin hope so

8ball: could be better

• • •

The UGA spectators became resentful and ornery as the innings drifted by. They didn't drive from Athens to Tuscaloosa to see Bama balls swerve around Canine bats and Dawg shoulders shrug at coaches, the universal sign of athletes recusing themselves from forthcoming disappointment. Maddy did not find these resignations of physics and spirit as funny as Kenny did. But cousins Cal, Latosha, Caroline, Skeet, Kay-Kay, and JR (Jay Arr) were more accommodating. Maddy was one of those awkward Hannibal Buress–, Marina Franklin–, Shalewa Sharpe–type comedy fans. No offense, she declared back when they were married and watched a shared Netflix account in a mutually owned and operated bed, but she liked more observational comedy. That "white people be like," *ComicView* shit was played out, she assured him.

His ex-wife was wrong then and she was wrong now, but she was right about her nephew. He had style and talent but lacked self-possession. The game was heating up.

• • •

> **playboimauri:** are you a bot?
>
> **8ball:** I hope not
>
> **playboimauri:** lol thats spooky af
>
> **8ball:** if I were a bot I could not even conceive of a different reality because my programming would not allow it
>
> **playboimauri:** depends on the programmer
>
> **8ball:** true
>
> **playboimauri:** why is a different reality so important to you tho?

8ball: because when we die, if reality stays the same, why did we live?
playboimauri: I kinda get that
8ball: do you want to die?
playboimauri: sometimes

· · ·

In the sixth inning, when Reggie Lamont walked to the mound instead of Maurice White, Maddy stood.

"I need a stretch," she said, her arms shooting from her torso like party-blower tongues. Kenny caught a whiff of her perfume as her arm extended. He didn't recognize the fragrance. Maddy rose then started up the stairs.

Kenny flashed his former mother-in-law a grin then bleachered after his former wife.

"Something's up with Maurice," Maddy said when he caught up with her, the Tide rolling around them as they stood near a booming funnel cake stall.

"What do you mean?" Kenny asked.

"He's always been full of himself, but he's not usually this intense. Throwing a no-hitter against the Bulldogs? It's like he's proving a point."

"Maybe he's just in the zone. Or there's a recruiter here and he's on edge." Cheers and barks erupted from afar. Reggie was no Maurice.

"I don't think so. If a recruiter were here, he'd have allowed some hits so he could showcase his full game. I know you hate baseball, but it's a team sport. And the team needs him for the whole season. The way he's pitching, he could injure himself."

"Hm. Does he have a girlfriend he's trying to impress?"

Maddy's eyes radared around the hallway then landed on a quartet of literally red-faced white women (Roll Tide!) standing in a circle, their mouths bobbing into funnel cakes. "This isn't the kind of place where you make impressions."

Kenny chuckled more enthusiastically than the barb warranted, accenting the laugh with a bend forward and a performative knee slap as he contemplated the best way to lead Maddy away from the actual secret, which she seemed on the verge of discovering.

He considered the facts: Maddy cared deeply about her nephew; Kenny cared deeply about Maddy's opinion of him; Saskia was dead.

"Do you ever think about Saskia?" Kenny said.

"I try not to."

"Lucky you."

More cheers erupted from the stands. Maddy started toward their seats, Kenny on her heels like the dog he insisted on being. The Bulldogs had scored some hits, apparently, leaving the score, 6–0, untouched but implanting hope in the hearts and minds of the Athenians. Someone had even made it to second base. No small achievement, all things considered.

Kenny and Maddy settled into their seats and watched the bosons fly, shimmying their way through small talk. They evaded hard questions with stylish non sequiturs and graceful fills. They embraced lulls like old flames. Cooperation even reared its head through an exchange of passwords. The Criterion Channel for Apple Music. Divorce wasn't so bad.

But Maddy continued to chip away at the secret. "Look at his stance," she said. Maurice was at home plate, bat slung over his right shoulder like a cape, his drip stupid big, like Barry Bonds* had personally gifted the nigga a whole year's supply of * and he was about to launch the ball into geosynchronous orbit. "He's not even pretending to read the pitcher. I've never seen him so prideful."

Kenny refused to observe this unpopular sport with anything less than the contempt it deserved, so he said nothing as Maddy's prediction proved true and the bottom of the sixth became the top of the seventh.

Finally, a game he could relate to.

· · ·

> **8ball:** how would you do it? who would be there?
> **playboimauri:** this is just theoretically speaking, of course
> **playboimauri:** i'm not suicidal

8ball: I am

8ball: it's not so bad most days

playboimauri: can relate

playboimauri: how I'd do it is I'd wait for a game against the dawgs and then throw a no-hitter for 5 innings. real phenom shit

playboimauri: coach would rest me and then put Reggie in. Reggie's got some moves. he a legend too, low-key. but that nigga from jersey. rednecks scare the shit out of him and they gon be in force for a rival game. he'll choke

playboimauri: we'd be up but coach would put me back in in the 7th just to make them racist ass alums happy. and on my first pitch, I just say fuck it. lights out

8ball: very cinematic

playboimauri: it has to be man

CHACUN PREPARE SA PROPRE MORT

Ebonee strained to hold the girls' shapes. Mila was thicc, a product of cheese grits, four years of hauling a sousaphone across a football field, and, judging from her parent's robust frames, genes. But as Ebonee sat in the family's dining room interviewing the girl, her parents, and her younger sister about her dead friend, rapid blinks were the only thing keeping Mila and her sibling from spilling out, gushing onto the scuffed hardwood floor. Ebonee had never desired children, still didn't, in fact, but between Valencia and now Maurice White, whose viral self-immolation was being broadcast from every black mirror, black tongue, and black face across the country, she saw them anew. They were endangered.

Ebonee would never say this, of course. "It sounds like Valencia was pretty normal," she summarized after the family mulled another cheery anecdote involving the dead girl. She punctuated the observation with a smile.

No one responded, the room settling into an itchy hush that pushed Ebonee into her turbulent head. *Endangered.* She hadn't said the word aloud, but she was sure they heard its frenzied panic in her measured, bureaucratic tone. She sounded like Vincent Blake. He was the last person she needed to think about as she sat in this dining room, but she couldn't help it. The morning after the Blackout, as the memers, then the influencers, then the formal media dubbed it, Blake was there to nudge "epidemic of suicide" into the trending topics. The body count was lower than that of the four mass shootings that also occurred that Saturday, but those killings didn't have a photogenic and articulate mayoral candidate to Robespierre them into addressing the real threat to public safety. "New Epidemic?" the *Face the Nation* chyron had sneered as Ebonee drank her Sunday cold brew in disbelief.

The family remained taciturn. Did they not agree Valencia McCormick was a normal girl? Hard to say. Normalcy fueled Atlanta's immersive mirage, its outsize contribution to the city's gilded myths of black excellence and joy surpassed only by predatory mortgages and skillful strippers. It took a peregrine eye to spy the dust glazing the city's gleaming spires, coating its Olympic basins.

Ebonee's sight had been conditioned by hours, maybe days in Grady Hospital's waiting room, accompanying friends, cousins, and dates chewed by the molars of the big Atlanta machine. And for decades, she had driven the length of the aptly named Memorial Drive, which seemed to house every possible incarnation of dead or dying black business. But the city's slick finesse remained painfully invisible to most residents, and the standard Atlanta way to get Sixth Sensed out of the narcotic haze of celebrity sightings, National Pan-Hellenic picnics, and highway expansions tended to be a personal tragedy. On average, to paraphrase the data Ebonee had seen, tragedy came in the form of a foreclosure, a car accident, or a dead body.

There was no body here, but Ebonee could feel the love, could conjure a living, breathing girl where there was now a puddle of oblivion. The moment was beautiful despite the horror percolating beneath it. As this family fingered its scar tissue, tunneling and scraping and digging so that the seepage could take on a form that they could memorialize and cherish, that Ebonee might pathologize, everyone in this cramped, ornate dining room knew this awkward ritual produced an approximation. The dead girl was dead.

Ebonee lifted a generous glass of sweet iced tea to her lips and swigged back a cold, saccharine gulp. It was time to ask the only question that mattered.

"What is 'eight ball'?" she said.

Mila's eyes fluttered with fear. Bingo.

"Have you talked with Sabrina and Mike about this?" Antonio, Mila's father, interjected.

"They won't talk to me," Ebonee said. What she didn't say was that Valencia's parents had talked to Vincent Blake, but that omission was to save time, not face.

"I wish I had known that," Rosé, Mila's mother, said. Ebonee watched as the woman's gaze oscillated between daughters, a secret leaning and rocking on her tongue. Southern mores didn't authorize unsanctioned disclosure of other folks' business, especially if it involved someone else's child, but there was something about this particular tidbit, whatever it was, that might allow an exception. Nonetheless, Rosé was visibly reluctant to violate the charter.

"Antonio, take Sophia upstairs," the mother said after a spell. Ebonee remained still as the youngest daughter and the father evacuated the room, their steps hurried and purposeful.

"Talk," Rosé instructed Mila once they were gone. Her voice, lowered to a severe, unnatural calm that was soft as the peace right before a thunderstorm, signaled noncompliance was unthinkable, maybe even physically impossible. Ebonee's skin prickled with pity for the girl. She was thirty-three and her mama was still adept at this dark art.

"EightBall," Mila said, her eyes on Ebonee, "is an app Val and I were into for a little bit. It's supposed to be like a Magic 8 Ball. You text it and it gives you advice. It's probably just a bot, but Val used to swear there's a person behind it. Sometimes the advice would just be so real. It was all around school for a little bit, but most people got bored. Me and Val—"

"Excuse me?" Rosé interrupted.

"Val and I," Mila continued, "used to talk to it. It didn't seem too interested in me, so I moved on, but Val felt it really understood her."

"Was she going through anything at the time?" Ebonee asked. "Relationship? College applications? Depression?"

Mila turned to Rosé, who seemed more repulsed by the telling of the story than its content. "Gon' head," she said.

Mila continued. "She was seeing this guy." She paused. "Well, he was more of a man."

"He was the golf coach," Rosé said.

Mila picked up again. "Yeah, he wasn't that much older than us, like twenty-four, I think, and they were fooling around after practices. Just kissing and stuff, but this one time, he demanded more, and she said no. Then he slapped her."

"Does the school know about this?" Ebonee asked. "Do her parents know? Does he still work there?"

"No, no, and, no," Rosé said. "If you had a lick a patience, you woulda heard Mila tell you the important part."

"I'm sorry," Ebonee said. "You were saying."

Rosé spoke instead. "So Val was a healthy, strong-willed girl. After he slapped her, she beat him unconscious with a golf club. I mean really beat him. Blood was everywhere. Then she called Mila for help, and this hardheaded daughter of mine wouldn't tell me what the hell was going on, but somehow she sweet-talked me into driving to the rescue. When we got to the golf course, which was off campus, this girl had this man's narrow ass slumped over in a golf cart. I thought he was dead."

Ebonee eyed her recorder. Niggas were trifling, but she wasn't trying to have a dead girl, a dead boy, and a murder on her conscience.

"So we wake him up, I tell him off, and he promises to quit the next day. To his credit, he did, and to my credit, I sent a tip to the school board director that night." Another laugh: darker. "But when we get back here and we done cried and yelled and prayed, I sat right here and asked Val why she fought this man instead of running away. She was a strong, intense girl, had arms like a boxer, a back like a gotdamn wrestler. And he was a lean, lanky little man. But she don't need to be fightin' no man. You know what she told me?"

"What she say?" Ebonee said.

"This girl said, 'EightBall told me to beat his ass.'" Another burst of chuckles, Mila joining in. Ebonee allowed herself an affirmative a-joke-was-told-and-I-witnessed-its-telling smirk. She was on the clock.

"So why didn't you tell her parents? What if he retaliated?" Ebonee asked. She knew the answer, but the audience of the recording wouldn't. Couldn't.

"He wouldn't," Rosé said coldly. "And they don't need to hear from someone else about their daughter's mistake. That was her story to tell."

"I understand."

"Mama made us swear we'd delete EightBall right there, and I thought we did. I even looked through Val's phone the next week and it wasn't there. But I know she downloaded it again." Ebonee was struck by the girl's pleading tone. Earlier and at the news conference, there was nostalgia in her remembrance of her friend. Her memory of the girl burned steady and gentle, an eternal flame nurtured with love and reverence. Now it was growing hot as well as bright.

"How would you know that?" Ebonee asked.

"Because I downloaded EightBall and begged it to leave her alone."

Ebonee eyed Rosé, who remained eerily still. "And what did Eight-Ball reply?" Ebonee asked.

Sniffles, thick and soupy, jerked at the girl's face. "It said no."

Ebonee blinked rapidly, trying her damnedest to keep the girl, her mother, herself, whole. A black mass formed on the edge of her vision, tiny at first, but swelling and gluttonous. Her eyelids flickered open and shut as the cumulus grew and grew, blobbing away her sight, light draining from her perception like air from a slashed tire.

Inevitably, a sheet of blackness flashed before her, familiar and welcoming.

She declined its invitation, blinded but fishing for the glass of tea. She found it, then drained it, the surge of sugar and citrus plunging her back into the light. She had panicked. There was nothing to see here but a mother consoling her daughter. Nothing, yes.

Ebonee retrieved the recorder and turned it off. Her exit wasn't as smooth as Antonio and Sophia's, but briskly she thanked the ladies and made her way to her car and then the highway.

Traffic snailed along, bumpers endlessly switching polarities—repel, attract, repel, attract—as rush hour insisted on being a paradox. There was time for Ebonee to head back to the office, to mime professionalism by planting herself at her desk and informing her colleagues that she was a warm body teeming with productivity and life, however you defined it in this antiabortion state: a heartbeat, hobbies, a state's right to ignore your personhood. But Retta was down in Tuscaloosa, and if Ebonee chose to wade through traffic and beach at the fusion center, she'd miss both her partner and her assigned wave of rush hour and would have to run with the maniacs who thought bumper-to-bumper traffic was a matter of will and not municipal apathy. Not her crowd, in either locale.

So she remained on the interstate until she reached her home exit. It was a tense commute; she felt her eyes peeking over the edges of bridges, glancing under the carriages of tractor trailers, tarrying blinks. Ebonee admired Valencia for dying on her own terms, opaque as they were, committed as she was to deciphering them, because she too had contemplated, kept weighing, the relish of an arranged death, an emancipation from futures unknown.

Should I recuse myself? she wondered as she drove onto the off-ramp. She couldn't seem to muster the complete outrage an assisted teen suicide should have called for. There was relief between her sorrow and distress, intrigue beneath her disgust. Ebonee reminded herself that Valencia needed help, not absolution, that the girl was a minor. A child. Yet she knew intimately the deep ambiguity of help: the judgmental gazes and compassionate hands as a gurney flowed through a hospital; the static of a sparkless therapy session; the electricity of an uplifting one; the torpid zombie brain of a pill regimen; the numbed pleasure of an emptied head.

The car dipped into a pothole Ebonee normally avoided, shaking her from her stupor. She wasn't conflicted. She absolutely wasn't. The girl had been wronged, and Ebonee would find the culprit before the tragedy repeated. Simple. The records and, well, the field indicated there was nothing more to see, she reminded herself as she stopped at the infuriating traffic light that deemed the left turn into her subdivision a privilege, not a right. Valencia had no history of mental distress or institutionalization. The girl must have been manipulated, Ebonee decided.

She grabbed her smartphone from her purse. Toward the bottom of the search results in the app store, beneath billiards simulations and random-number generators, she found EightBall. A free application, it was listed as a game. It had just a few thousand downloads and a smattering of reviews, overwhelmingly negative. Chacun Prepare Sa Propre Mort, LLC, was the publisher. The phrase was familiar; she'd heard it at a wedding or on a cooking show. She'd look it up later. Ebonee proceeded with a download. The light was still red.

Moments later, an eight ball appeared on her home screen, tiny and disarmingly generic. She'd expected something more ominous. She tapped the orb and the application opened to a spare black background with no text. The screen flashed a command: "Enter username." Traffic continued without her as Ebonee pondered. She considered typing something generic, but the app's bland aesthetics roused her inner web designer, a shameless lover of garish fonts, overwrought email signatures, and sentimental monikers.

Ebonee pressed the screen and a keyboard appeared. b-l-a-c-k-s-u-b-l-i-m-e, she typed. The name was available.

What should my first message be? A greeting? A warning? A confession? Ebonee eyed the passing cars as her indicator light ticked. When her eyes sank back to her phone, she saw a white ellipsis blinking on the screen. Was someone typing? Ebonee watched it flicker until the phone locked.

Behind her a horn honked with irritation. She looked up and saw the light had finally changed, prompting her to drop her phone and arc the car forward and into her neighborhood.

The ellipsis did not reappear after she parked. Nor after she gulped down leftover lasagna, straddled her JackRabbit, slept, then commuted to the CDC's headquarters the next morning.

Ebonee dumped her phone into her purse and observed the technicians, scientists, and administrators skating through the sleek, glassy corridor. The microbiologist she was meeting with was running late, an executive assistant had told her in a gush of apologies and conciliatory peppermints. Ebonee declined both. She didn't mind waiting. Despite its unyielding self-seriousness and intolerance for clothing that was not gray, black, or so navy blue it looked grayish black, HQ was charming.

Surfaces were reflective and smooth. Light bathed rather than exposed, rescuing skin from the unflattering creep of age and coaxing a menagerie of displaced tropical plants to relax, to feel at home. Conversations never rose above a murmur, granting all chatter an air of supreme importance. Compared to the chaos of the fusion center, which often looked like it had hosted back-to-back James Bond foot pursuits, HQ felt like paradise. It channeled the hyper-futurism of a cyberpunk novel, sans graffiti and misery. Retta once joked the building could have been home to a podcasting start-up. Ebonee chortled at the thought.

A suited man approached her, his steps quick. "Ebonee?" he said as he came toward her. "Dr. Marvin Weisz," he said when he reached her. He didn't offer a hand.

"Dr. McCollum," she replied. His face dispensed a confirmation receipt and his body swiveled toward the direction from which he came. Ebonee rose.

After a breathless stroll out of the main building, across campus, through another security checkpoint, down an elevator, and past a card reader, they arrived in a quiet lab. Electron microscopes, spectrometers, and instruments Ebonee didn't recognize lined the walls. Two assistants moved about the room with clipboards and cameras examining objects laid across the counters. Marvin slid his hands into gloves then picked up a clump of soil and plopped it onto a tray.

"Before we get into this, what kind of doctor are you?" Marvin asked. His voice was a wet cough, harsh and viscous.

"I'm an epidemiologist," Ebonee said.

"Great. EIS has changed over the years. Fewer medical doctors and more sociologists and mathematicians. I've learned not to make assumptions." He removed his gloves. Then he slid the tray away and strolled toward a computer. Ebonee followed.

Marvin pulled up a busy line graph and began yammering away. "So as you should know, flesh-eating pathogens don't show up much in this part of the world. Occasionally a peckish streptococcus or vibrio will get a taste for meat at the beach or in some nasty nursing home, but generally in North America, flesh is safe."

"Right," Ebonee said. Peckish? Meat? No wonder this guy was kept underground.

"Tropical areas aren't so lucky. *Mycobacterium ulcerans* in particular has been on our watch list following Ebola gaining strength in West Africa. I call Ebola a party starter because once it breaks the ice, all kinds of other little nasties start to mingle as well." The two lab assistants sniggered.

"Correct," Ebonee said. Great, a talker.

"But my point is even the worst flesh-eating bacteria do not eat bones! They cannot eat bones, in fact. So as soon as GBI told me we had no body and a pit, I had to hit the DNA sequencer because this isn't the kind of pathogen that just falls out of the sky. If it does, God is real and when he made the world, the motherfucker was wearing gloves."

(Wow, he is a *talker*. Maybe he shouldn't be in a basement?)

"So I'm expecting some kind of Russian-bred colony of superbugs. Anthrax, avium, tuberculosis. The whole Legion of Doom."

"But?"

He smacked the monitor with joy. "You hear that? That's the sound of an active listener. You two take note." He coughed toward the assistants. Or maybe that was just the standard sound of air flowing through his trachea. "But! I sequence one sample, then two samples, then three, then four, and I'm not seeing a speck of bacteria, fungus, or virus."

"What were you seeing?"

"Copperhead, earthworm, fire ant, yellow jacket, cicada, grasshopper." He finally pointed at the screen, where, as promised, kingdom Animalia outnumbered kingdom Bacteria.

"What," Ebonee said, more a statement than a question.

"That's what I said!" He tossed up his arms. "It's like a snake ate a garden and then bit this girl." He paused. "And this unicorn snake is also some kind of DNA reservoir. It doesn't make a lick of sense. For all I know, a damn grasshopper could have eaten a snake."

Ebonee examined the distribution of percentages displayed on the computer. Copperhead and human DNA comprised more than half of the mixture. There was a connection, but it felt extraneous. "Is DNA the right focus? What about inorganics?"

Marvin stared into space, humming and bobbing his head. He had the embarrassed expression of someone realizing they'd forgotten a dear friend's birthday.

"Marvin? Dr. Weisz? Marv?" Ebonee said.

A lab assistant snapped their fingers and Marvin stirred. "He does that when he's thinking hard," they explained.

"Sorry," Marvin said. "I was just thinking about the videos of that Maurice White kid and the best way to say what I don't want to say but still say it."

"Terrorism," Ebonee said.

Marvin eyed the door. "Yes. Be careful who you say that to around here."

"Sure, but I don't think I'll be saying it to anybody. It doesn't fit."

"Why not?" He gestured toward the counter. "If I were to take one of these specimens and look at the crystallography, I guarantee we would find a gelling agent and a petrochemical. I can't begin to fathom how venom fits into this, but we are absolutely talking about a weapon. The bodies just disintegrated. It was like every stage of Ebola at once." He sighed. "If this is BSL-3, it goes to Collete's lab . . ." His eyes parked on a wall.

Ebonee snapped her fingers. "I'm sure she'll let you be a coauthor. What's more important than the science is the logistics. How are otherwise-regular teenagers getting hold of something so virulent, so refined? Why them? What's the purpose of all this?"

Marvin shrugged and shoegazed into some distant realm. Ebonee couldn't read his mind, but she knew he was thinking, "I just work here," the bureaucrat version of the fetal position. Alonzo made that face often.

Ebonee backed down. "Okay, that was a lot. The more immediate question is, is the school safe to reopen?"

Marvin returned to Earth-616. "Yes, yes, absolutely. Safe as Sunday school at the Vatican. Wow, you field-workers really put things into perspective. I hadn't thought about the school at all. It's so easy to get lost in the science."

Ebonee thanked Marvin and his assistants, handed him her card, and asked to be escorted out. The assistant who hadn't spoken dropped his gloves into a garbage bin and led the way. The journey back to the main building was calm and unrushed, small talk and sightseeing the sole priority. Opening Pandora's box did not obligate them to nose-dive into its depths.

When Ebonee reached her car, her phone made a strange chime. EightBall?

"You won't like what you find," the message read.

"We will stop you," she typed back.

The reply was quick and haughty: "Don't make promises you can't keep."

SNAKE MILK

Kenny preferred the community garden. He had his own land, and enough white neighbors to ward off eminent domain or a no-knock warrant or a racist appraiser. In fact, on the Druid Hills listserv, there was chatter that a bike lane might be coming soon, the civic equivalent of a protective rune. So Kenny was probably in the 1 percent of black people with actual sanctuary in the United States.

Maintenance wasn't bad. To remain enchanted, all Kenny had to do was keep his yard manicured; own and visibly love any breed of dog except a pit bull, Rottweiler, or Doberman; and not date or associate with a respectable, untattooed white woman, a buxom black woman who was potentially a sex worker, a loud black woman, a confident black woman, a black woman with ties to the entertainment industry, especially reality television, a black woman who worked hard and when spoken to was more tired than polite, a pious Middle Eastern woman, a sup- or sub-Saharan African who wore a headscarf that potentially harbored piety, a Latina with too much extended family, any category of queer person, or any alleged or actual Mexicans. The code for being black and unbothered was rigorous and arcane but not unbeatable.

Kenny found that flipping through the loopholes kept him limber. His basement was finished and soundproofed; the backyard was fenced. But even in the privacy of his self-padded cell, a home garden felt more like glib self-delusion than self-determination. Cultivating life on such unstable ground nurtured a hope that was too Pollyannaish. The community garden was territory rather than property, keeping Kenny on constant edge. He knew he was just passing through, that any day his okra and turnips could get uprooted and thrown in someone else's pot. His plot had admirers. Mrs. and Mr. Green were kinfolk, bless their retired hearts, and had been complimenting his garden for years. They still talked about the year his arugula exploded across adjacent spaces, prompting a well-resourced saboteur to rinse his plants with glacial acetic acid. The benign retirees were never suspects, but that could change. It's not like Kenny knew what they retired from.

Kenny stood up to dilute the memory of the smell of his murdered garden, a sour mixture of cat pee crossed with heirloom apple cider vinegar. It took weeks to return the pH of the soil to a tenable level. He'd forgiven the assassin and repeatedly declined to request an investigation despite the groundskeeper's tireless outrage. But he hadn't forgotten. Niggas couldn't afford to forget.

Kenny returned to weeding, plucking up the maverick plants with gentle precision. It was an unusually cool evening for April, the sun not yet determined to scorch the city off the map. Intense tennis matches were taking place on the courts next to the garden, balls crash-landing from sweet spot to sweet spot. Kenny found the constant pops and grunts comforting.

"I'll be damned. Is that Kenny B?" a voice said from across the garden.

Kenny turned to find the most important district attorney in the state stepping over and on Mrs. and Mr. Green's rhubarb. There was a walkway, but he'd long insisted on forging his own obnoxious path.

"In the flesh, Vincent," Kenny said. He stood, thumped his dirty hands on his ragged jeans, and offered a shake. Vincent and his radiant grin came in smoothly, his grip firm and patrician, his teeth white as minstrelsy.

"Last time I saw you this close, we were getting our dumb asses arrested," Vincent said.

"Didn't feel dumb at the time," Kenny said.

"You'd be amazed how many times a day I hear that," Vincent replied.

Kenny ignored Vincent's repulsive flex and returned to weeding. "What's the word on this so-called epidemic?" Kenny asked as he ripped and troweled. "You gonna stop it before its death toll reaches a staggering three people?"

He sounded cattier than he intended, but Vincent had always brought out the worst in him, in everybody. At their graduation, Vincent had led the 2004 Oglethorpe University undergraduate class in booing then governor Sonny Perdue off the stage. It was a bratty act, in retrospect. Students of a small private university smearing their school's reputation on the very day they would be freed from it. Onlooking relatives and faculty countered with applause, and Perdue pushed through at least two minutes of his commencement speech before fleeing. But what had been the point, exactly? Kenny was clueless until he saw Vincent allude to the stupid moment after being sworn in as Fulton County DA. Greeting his new constituency, before he thanked his god and his husband, Vincent Blake apologized to a Republican. As Kenny watched the apology online months after the event, all he could do was applaud. Whether Vincent was being arrested at an Iraq War protest or snuggling up to the levers of the Atlanta machine, he was a salesman, Kenny had realized. And the product was always his continued security.

"I deserve that, but could you spare me for now? I'm off," Vincent said. He gestured toward the tennis courts, where the rhythm section of sweet spots and yelps had gone from hair metal to death. "And I'm on dad duty."

Kenny grinned. "Is she Venus or Serena?"

"She's Naomi," Vincent said. "Come see for yourself. Already got a scholarship."

"Give me a second," Kenny said. "These weeds run deep. Not that you know anything about that."

Vincent huffed in response, standing still as Kenny searched and destroyed. Kenny resisted the urge to call Vincent an overseer.

"What are you growing? Is that foxglove?" Vincent asked.

"Yeah, it's a great pest deterrent," Kenny said. He tossed his weeds into a paper bag, then stood and headed toward the courts, making sure to use the walkway. Ms. Francine's fava beans were looking good, he noted.

"Have any kids?" Vincent asked as they stood outside the court gates and watched balls arc and whip through the air.

"No," Kenny said.

"Married?"

"Divorced."

"Where you working?"

"I own a coffee shop."

"How's business?"

"Black."

"I don't remember you being this standoffish," Vincent said.

"I'm sorry. My daughter was stillborn."

Vincent turned away from the courts and planted a hand on Kenny's shoulder. "Shit, I'm sorry for your loss. You said you don't have . . ."

Kenny gently removed Vincent's sweaty palm. "I don't but I did. Her heartbeat stopped a week before she was due. Still had to go through the birth too. Fourteen hours of pushing and cursing and woo-hah, woo-hah, woo-hah, and all we got was a corpse inside a pool of sludge. We took her home for a few days, kept her on ice. Then we cremated her."

"Christ, you sound like Baltimore."

Kenny tensed. "Has your uppity ass ever been to Baltimore?"

"That's my daughter's name."

"Was Buckhead taken?"

"She had the name when we got her," Vincent huffed. "I don't know where you get your news, but I promise you I'm not a bad guy."

"You'd be amazed how many times a day I hear that."

Kenny's eyes Cheshired around, meeting Vincent's. They guffawed in unison, their laughs full and fleshy and slack like bellies erupting from unbuttoned pants, their mirth spilling out and up and over. A warmth rushed through Kenny as he bent to catch his breath, the air suddenly thick and viscous. He felt like he was in Thurgood's guesthouse and Maddy's old hooptie and PepTyde's gleaming labs. When had fellowship become such a delicacy?

"Vincent, I was under the impression this is our time," Baltimore said through the gate. Despite being adopted, the girl resembled Vincent in poise. She spoke with jurisdiction, her words weighted and authoritative. Her opponent stretched beside her.

"It is, it is," Vincent said. "I just ran into an old classmate."

"He doesn't look like a lawyer to me," Baltimore said. She placed her racket on the ground.

"I'm glad you said that," Kenny replied, "because I'm not. I went to undergrad with your dad. Before he went to law school over at Emory and became Mr. Muthafuckin Atlanta, he wanted to escape and called it 'the city too shitty to hate.' Funnily, I was the one who ended up leaving."

A red tide swept across Vincent's umber face. "Don't listen to him, Bali. Everybody used to say that back then. Don't repeat it." He turned to the other girl. "That goes for you too, Mimi. This man hasn't spoken to me in over a decade."

"Where'd you go?" Baltimore asked Kenny. She was immune to Vincent's goading, Kenny noted.

"Wherever the chemicals were: Ann Arbor, Michigan. Kenilworth, New Jersey. Towson, Maryland, and then back here," Kenny said.

"Which chemicals?" Baltimore asked. Though Kenny knew she was curious, not suspicious, he couldn't grant Vincent the benefit of the doubt. The man wasn't the shark the election chatter made him out to be, but he was a cop. All prosecutors were. Kenny knew he wasn't a suspect, knew there wasn't even a coherent investigation, but he also didn't know that at all. Niggas couldn't invest in certainty.

"None you would have heard of, unless your private school teaches biochemistry and chemical engineering," Kenny said.

"It does," Baltimore said.

Kenny chuckled. She was definitely Vincent's child. "Well, I doubt you've heard of polypeptides."

Baltimore shrugged then picked up her racket. Her annoyance trailed her to the baseline, where she walloped a ball over the net before Mimi had even lined up.

"Excuse her lack of manners," Vincent said. "Do you live in Fulton, by the way?"

"DeKalb. Sorry. Guess I'll have to wait for you to run for governor."

"You're not sorry."

Kenny grinned then started to wave goodbye. But his hand formed a fist instead of a salute. He stashed it in his pocket and ransacked his thoughts, searching for the trigger. He found it quickly, tucked between an ever-present desire to punch Vincent and a fantasy in which he took Saskia to volleyball practice. "Why did you say I sounded like your daughter?" He tried to veil his alarm.

Vincent furrowed his brow and pinched his chin. A politician to his core, he clearly had already flushed the conversation from his cache. "Ah!" He snapped his fingers. "You said *sludge*, that was it."

"What about it?"

"She keeps watching videos of that Alabama kid. You heard about that?"

Kenny relaxed. "Yeah, Godspeed to that poor family."

Kenny patted Vincent on the shoulder then walked to his pickup. The truck snored awake as Kenny drove off then coughed and wheezed until he put it to rest three minutes later. Apparently, the ride back from Tuscaloosa had taken a toll. A problem for another day. Amelia needed to be milked.

The house was precisely as he had left it: air still, bookshelves empty, curtains drawn. He idled in the foyer, his mind buzzing with noise. The sunset streaming through the fanlight cast a glare over Kenny's framed print of Claude McKay's "If We Must Die," the only art he'd bought since Maddy moved out.

Though he was about to extract venom from a copperhead, he felt an intense compulsion to wash his hands. Vincent had that effect on people. Kenny scrubbed his raw hands rawer in the basement sink, the dirt forming a murky river as it molted off his skin.

Amelia hissed as Kenny moved about the basement prepping for the extraction. When he first caught her, his fellow mithridates told him copperheads weren't worth the trouble because they bit to warn, not to kill. They were right, but they weren't. Copperheads bit to kill prey; Kenny had witnessed this with the live birds, mice, and rabbits that he had deposited into Amelia's cage. She lunged at her meals as soon as they entered her field of vision, assured of her dominance and their inferiority. When Kenny first got her, she treated him like a fellow apex predator, curling into the corner of her cage.

It took months of cage rattling and randomized feedings and general snottiness, but eventually Kenny's reputation slid. His manipulations disgusted her, diminishing his stature. They were no longer predators at odds. He was her prey.

As planned, his demotion had boosted her venom yields, quickly filling Kenny's mini-fridge with a surplus of petite morts—the kind that actually kill, to be clear. Every time they met, he could sense the malice curdling behind her cold, beady eyes. Kenny winked at her as he slipped on his thick, ratty cowhide gloves. He wondered how much venom she'd produce if she knew he would one day indulge her tastes.

That day was not today, of course. Her body was taut and vexed as he fished her from the cage with his awkward snake hooks, which felt like oversize dental tools. Amelia never slackened, but after a few thrashes and snaps, an equilibrium was reached between Kenny's flexed arms and her flexed totality, and Kenny mashed her fangs into the collection vial.

Venom flowed from Amelia's glands as Kenny repeatedly pressed them into the latex stopper, a cloudy, yellow, pungent slurry. To call this shit *milk* was an insult to mammalian nurture and reptilian nature. There was no promise of life or growth embedded in the venom's necrotic proteins and enzymes, just death.

After a few spurts, the vial was filled. Kenny returned Amelia to the cage and watched her. She wound into a pile and returned his gaze. The hard-core mithridates would mock him for wearing gloves and milking a species with such a survivable venom. Kenny let the fools talk. A snakebite sent venom directly into the bloodstream, gorging the body with adrenaline and dread as it rushed to combat the physiological time bomb. For the diehards, that struggle tested the strength of the biter and the bitten. Copperheads were bantamweights. A prepared mithridate should have enough mamba and cobra and rattler antibodies flowing through them to survive a copperhead tornado. Blood bunkers for blood bombs.

But after a year without daily injections of saline solution mixed with venoms, Kenny would die if Amelia bit him. It would be an excruciating death, her rapacious venom decimating every erythrocyte and organ available, and her appetite cleaning house. Skinny as he was, he had enough mass to feed her for weeks, and she enough animus to savor every gulp. But that was the point. Kenny was no longer interested in fortifying himself against death. He sought to live with it, to comprehend it, so that he would happen to it rather than the other way around.

Kenny proceeded to label and store the day's extraction. He opened the mini-fridge, and to his surprise, it was full, the venoms glowing neon in the shroud of chilled air. He'd been so consumed by

Valencia's and Maurice's homegoings that he'd forgotten how many more he'd soon orchestrate. Kenny removed the oldest sample, replaced it with the day's harvest, then blew Amelia a kiss.

Upstairs he sorted through his suits. Gloria told him to dress comfortably. It was just a wake, she had said. That was the kind of resignation he was up against. Only a week had passed, and Maurice was already enshrined as a failure. The Tusks didn't have another phenom lined up, but Kenny could feel them wishing the descendant into existence. Kenny admired their strength. Theirs wasn't an easy hope to cultivate. To overcome, they'd have to trust in a holy plan they'd never see, wade in frigid, toxic waters, crane their necks for chariots to dip low and transport them to homes they could only imagine.

Kenny had given up on hope. He peeled his ivory wedding tux from its garment bag and held it up. A tawny stain covered the breast pocket. He'd never gotten it dry-cleaned. Was Maddy's dress still soiled as well? Did she even own the dress? The warmth of the big day flooded his head.

They'd been drinking coffee after their reception. He'd insisted on staying up together, beginning their new life together at the same time, on equal footing. She mocked his sentimentality but didn't object. Midnight was only a half hour away. Kenny suggested they get some caffeine in case the labor of the day knocked them out early. The spill happened soon after. The instant espresso machine in the suite's kitchenette blarfed out a swampy alkaline sputum, and they arranged their hands to serve each other.

They'd later dispute who first spilled the coffee, but all parties agreed that the end result was two instances of brown splashed on white. Briefly. After a rush of giggles and unzipping and cupping, it was a brown-on-brown affair.

Kenny draped the tux across the bed and retrieved his black suit. It was the obvious pick. He'd last worn it to Saskia's funeral. Maddy pleaded with him for them to hold a small service, like their wedding, but his rage was too volatile to be contained to a dinky funeral home. Only a nocuous circus could channel his fury, could scald the Kingman Coke plant that had pumped naphthalene and benzene into Gloria's neighborhood, into Maddy's expanding body, into Saskia's fledgling mass. Shrewdly honoring the counsel of their lawyer, who told them not to point fingers before the case closed, he purchased Facebook ads, beseeched the congregations of churches he'd never attended, rented out a megachurch. Set up a live stream. Instead of a casket, he bought a stretcher. Plopped it at the front of the massive sanctuary, empty and undecorated. While he couldn't say who killed his daughter, he could contour his silence, could dramaturge the pain he couldn't voice.

His people heard his call! They filled the parking lot and the pews, shook the rafters, prayer-handed in the comment field. It was even more spectacular than he imagined. The Affiliated Press dispatched a black reporter and photographer. The Black Mamas Matter Alliance bused in mothers from Flint and Plateau. Maddy smiled during the service, swaying, clapping, squeezing his hands like they were back in that stifling Birmingham emergency room, ooze seeping out of her womb. But this was joy, not pain.

Kenny's rage didn't subside though. As Kenny hugged Tusks and Bomars and Joneses and Stallworths, thanked random madams and sirs and theys just showing love, Kenny felt routine marionetting his limbs. His words were inherited; his rhetoric was studied; his thoughts were dictated. That was blackness, he realized that day. Legacy, legacy, legacy, legacy. A teeming, relentless lineage of double and nothing. Always both. Kenny wanted more.

NOTHING

Retta visualized her death at every funeral she attended. When she was a child, her simulations mirrored the deaths that inspired them. Such was the nature of car accidents and heart attacks, Mama assured her when Retta asked if she was possessed; to see death was to see life. Papa's form of comfort was to shrug. "He does that eulogy for everybody," he'd complain of Pastor Witherspoon as they drove home. Then he'd ask Retta and her brothers, Floyd and Matthew, if they wanted pizza. Such was the nature of dads: Where's the party?

Retta admired both perspectives. When death came for Retta's parents in the form of a semi running their Ranger off the road and into a sturdy brick church, the visions morphed. As Pastor Witherspoon frothed from the pulpit, Retta sat in the front pew and imagined a wormhole opening up above her and a Ranger crushing her and Floyd and Matthew's wife and kids. It was the only group death she'd ever imagined and the first to defy physics, but it felt appropriate given the two caskets and the dimensions of the Ranger. When Uncle Rico later died from complications of diabetes and Aunt Lily drowned during an aerobic swimming class, things went back to normal.

But as Retta's tiny Candler County practice settled into the social sediment of Metter and Retta increasingly found herself at patients' funerals in Bulloch, Laurens, Toombs, and Wheeler Counties, her projections turned baroque and extraordinary. She began to die from parachute failures during skydives. Swamp-gas explosions while catfishing. A misstep during a sunny hike landed her in the musky den of a copperhead. The sweet pepper in the complimentary Olive Garden salad lodged in her throat. A trap house was raided by the GBI as she jogged past it and a car hit her when she stopped in the street. Sade, the whole band, hit her with a Jet Ski, lifting it in unison and tossing it at her, smooth and operational.

Retta remained a model funeral attendee as she adjusted to this shift. She sang hymns from memory, she bowed her head, she reflected. Her shoulders housed tears, babies, empaths, performance artists, cousins removed and negotiating reinstatement, and the occasional flirt. The visions bugged her though. They were so self-centered and indulgent; despite their destructive endings, they had the grammar of fantasies. Where's the party?

At one juncture, the Metter psychic assured her the daydreams were from past lives. Retta entertained that interpretation less because she believed Spencer, whom she patronized only because of his cute, professorial beard, and more because it underscored the ruthless ennui of her current life. After Peter and his cravings detonated their marriage, she had busied herself by fussing over the small-town lives of her patients, attending bowling tournaments, spelling bees, and football games. But she found her taste for community numbed.

Nothing bound her to her home. In Metter, she was more infrastructure than resident, her work preceding her, lapping her, defrauding her existence like a savvy scammer. She could count a dozen people in the surrounding counties who greeted her without an honorific, five of them relatives, four paramours who, by design, were more interested in her body than her life, and three her spades buddies.

When she took a position with an Atlanta physicians group, the ease of leaving Metter confirmed her suspicions. Her world shrugged at her announcement, the resulting move a series of perfunctory successions. Her house went to Floyd, her slot in her weekly spades game to a homemaker, her practice to an internist from Toombs who detested Obamacare and paperless billing. According to Matthew and Floyd, there wasn't even any gossip about her exit. It felt as if one of her visions had long ago come true, everybody aware except her.

Atlanta greeted her with enthusiasm, pelting her with galas, festivals, dates. She applied to EIS just to maintain the city's bustling pace, the ambient hustle convincing her that she could do more, that she must. She was reborn.

The only vestige of her past life was her bleak reveries, which persisted because death did. She finally relented. She didn't look forward to the visions, per se, but they were a part of her. It was as if, in the absence of accessible volcano rims and seaside cliffs, her subconscious had evolved to process mortality in a more modern way. The tradition still required a sacrifice, regrettably, but not even the combined might of white pillage and rising sea levels could suppress the clarity of her bloodline. Death was a timeless lesson.

Except this time. With great horror, Retta experienced Valencia McCormick's funeral in high-definition, lossless fidelity. Without interference, the caterwauls and shrieks of the bereaved quaked through her body; the empty casket fixed her gaze, its blankness vast and infuriating; the sanctuary, packed with swaying paper fans, dampened cheeks, prim Sunday bests, and bottomless, relentless faith, brimmed with vehement life.

Retta survived, but she was shaken. Wearily, she rose as the service concluded and the family of the deceased strode up the aisle, the casket preceding them. The father was a paragon of gravitas, his head full and frosted with gray coils, his face frozen with dignity. His tears were sealed and barreled and even if the vineyard were foreclosed from lax sales or sold to a larger winery more equipped to handle the complex logistics of the burgeoning Chinese market, this batch was not for sale.

The mother was a bust of solemn melancholy, her grief manifest in the noble calm that levitated her chin and propelled her strut. In loss, she achieved a luster only survivors of the dead were privy to, her skin glazed with vitality. She did not cry because her impossible equilibrium catalyzed sobs in onlookers, Retta included, who began to sniffle. Where does she find the strength? Retta wondered.

The daughter was the only member of the immediate family who had not mastered the customs. Her makeup streaked across her face. She looked just like the dead girl, her skin a bronzed auburn, her face flush with youth. Hawkish as it felt, Retta decided she was the one to approach. The problem was the seawall of cousins and aunts and uncles that surrounded her, a flank of black umbrage daring a motherfucker to part it. While Ebonee was right that their investigation was beyond respect, that didn't justify stupidity. Retta remained in place as the family streamed out of the church, gathering herself.

When the black parade concluded, Retta exited the sanctuary with the other friends and gawkers. "Where is the guest book?" she asked an usher as she stepped into the lobby, which was filled with fliers pleading "No Guns Allowed."

Retta was pointed toward a hallway, where a different version of the flier greeted her. This one featured a rifle slashed with a chunky red X. *Gun* wasn't specific enough, apparently. When are they gonna address that epidemic? Retta joked to herself as she stood in line to sign the book. She'd never simulated a gun death, neither before she became a dramatist nor after. Luck, perhaps.

Retta left her phone number and email address alongside her signature then walked to her car. One done, one to go. Crossing the parking lot, she pondered the big question. Fill the tank in Georgia or the Heart of Dixie? Gas, like life, was cheaper in Alabama, but she hated stopping there. The station attendants, who were always chatty, seemed to smell the country on her, and her posh funeral garb would only exaggerate the scent. Those bamas loved to out a city slicker, whether she was incognito or not. She couldn't blame them. Few people in the South were more than three generations removed from a plow or a hoe or pellagra, but when folks moved to cities, those humble roots tended to get mulched out of sight. Retta was so tired of Atlanta's sui generis nobility she had considered

boycotting men, shrimp and grits, and red velvet cake. The thought
of playing catch-a-bama-by-the-toe made her shudder.

After filling up in Atlanta, Retta slunk her Challenger onto I-20
West. Traffic was light and cordial, crossovers and sedans bowing
out of her way as she ripped down the passing lane. No cops, either, despite the end of the month approaching fast. More luck,
perhaps. It was hard to hear the podcast Ebonee recommended
over the roar of wind, but this was the price she paid for leaving
the AC unfixed. The podcast was subpar anyway. Something about
a Nebraska town with an unsolved murder and corn farmers potentially forming a union but not wanting to be seen as socialists.
As Ebonee promised, the story was rich, the audio mixing was
eclectic, and there was even an episode about black corn farmers,
a nice inclusive touch, but the narrator, a twit who used terms like
heartland and *breadbasket* and *Middle America* with painful earnest-
ness, seemed to think she was introducing listeners to a remote
Amazonian tribe. In her homogeneous temperature-controlled
world, daytime television and talk radio and game shows didn't
seem to exist. Where did she think *The Price Is Right* contestants
and bootylicious white strippers came from? The worst part was
that the host was from Tulsa. She should have known better.

Retta didn't like having so much contempt for a young woman
simply trying to stay afloat in an industry held together by private
equity firms and Mad Men who wanted to have their cake and
fuck their interns too, but girl. There was an erasure undergirding
the host's earnest explaining, entire peoples and histories new to
her and her audience because they were vanished by someone else.

This was why Retta hated long rides. Too many opportunities to take in the whole of the nation's contradictions, not just the bits that swept over the storm barriers. Retta lowered the windows all the way down and focused on the road as air streamed into the cockpit. Just because it was bad journalism didn't mean it couldn't be good ASMR.

An hour into her trip, a ring punctured the bliss. Retta glanced at her phone. Ebonee. She rolled up the windows and answered.

"You still driving?" Ebonee asked.

"Yeah. And yes I am using a headset. What's up?"

"My hero," Ebonee said with sourness. The girl didn't like being predicted. "How was the McCormick service?"

"Bleak. I couldn't talk to anyone. But I left my contact details in the guest book. No telling if or when anybody will look at it, but it felt like the best move since they already declined to talk to us." Retta sighed. "It was a lot harder than I anticipated."

"You did what you could."

Retta didn't react to the consolation. From an epidemiological perspective, she hadn't done anything. Just went to a single funeral, something anyone could do.

"How long till Birmingham?" Ebonee asked.

"About forty-five minutes. Not a lot of traffic. If you're calling to check in on me, don't worry. I've been to a lot of memorials."

"I'm not worried about you. I'm worried about everything."

Another span of quiet. Streaks of violet and cinnabar sunlight smeared across the windshield. That was one thing Retta liked about long rides, especially heading into the sunset. The encroaching darkness did such delightful things to the light.

"What is there to worry about?" Retta asked as a herd of semis passed her and plunged the car in shadow. She had slowed down.

"You check your email?"

"Haven't had time. What's up?"

"Okay. I'll get you up to speed. So first, the good. The school can reopen!"

Retta's indifference to the good news surprised her. Maybe I just need the bad news? she thought. "Great," she said with as much enthusiasm as she could muster. "The bad?"

"Alabama's SBI got back to GBI and confirmed that Maurice White had EightBall. The app is encrypted, so that's going nowhere, but I traced the company behind it. It turns out the nowhere runs deep. EightBall is incorporated in Delaware. Phil is tracking down the law firm that registered it, but given where it's registered it's likely just going to lead to a shell, and they don't have the resources to look that far into it. And Alonzo says GBI can't get the app store to pull it unless they find something incriminating. And soon too."

"Sounds like your case is building." Retta didn't veil her annoyance. Just as she had feared, they were in it.

"Our case," Ebonee corrected. "After leaving HQ, I finally looked up the meaning of the LLC's name, Chacun Prepare—"

"Each prepares his own death," Retta said.

"You speak French?" Ebonee asked with wonder.

"No, but chile, between girls' trips and people getting remarried, I been to the Caribbean more than Columbus."

Ebonee giggled. Her laugh had a soft, delicate timbre.

"I needed that," Ebonee said. "And I have to tell you something." Her voice went somber again.

"What?"

"I downloaded EightBall and talked to it. It's not a bot."

"How could you tell?"

"It threatened me."

...

The interstate deposited Retta onto a state highway lit by gas station billboards and church marquees. Retta read them all aloud, a habit nurtured by her father, who feared thunderstorms. He called them God's threats, a descriptor Birmingham's congregations would surely endorse—the church signage drew exclusively from the Old Testament. The weather was clear and the Lord mum, but there was something unsettling about the road's emptiness. Though the thoroughfare was an obvious drag for commerce and fellowship, the parking lots were vacant, the streetlights dull as daytime television. Retta sped.

She reached the funeral home without incident, parking on the edge of the nearly filled lot. A lively man in an off-white tux had a coffee stand set up on a table outside the building. That's one way to stay awake, Retta thought as she approached the entrance. He wasn't blocking the door, but it would be rude to pass without speaking. Also, the coffee was apparently free.

"Black Sublime?" Retta asked him, reading from an embossed carafe.

"Yes, ma'am," Kenny said with affected flair. "Coffee will make you black, and black is where it's at." He gestured at a to-go cup.

Retta shook her head and smiled despite the man's corniness. No wonder Ebonee had been so spellbound after her visit to the shop. "No, thanks, but I appreciate your enthusiasm considering the circumstances. Are you a member of the family?"

"Are you a member of the family?" he asked, his face scrunched into a sneer.

"It's generally seen as evasive to answer a question with a question."

"It's generally seen as evasive to evade a question."

Retta balked but produced her business card and handed it over. Kenny examined it with a strange glee, holding it above his head and reading it aloud with a giddy lilt.

"Is something wrong?" Retta asked.

"Not at all. I'm just wondering which of us has the greater misunderstanding of what constitutes an epidemic."

A woman in a black suit-dress emerged from the funeral home before Retta could douse his already-stained suit with coffee. Her counsel was quick and unlabored. "Ignore him," she said.

She nodded toward the doorway from which she had emerged. An invitation.

Retta followed the woman through a carpeted lobby with stark orange walls and a beige molded ceiling. Verdant plants erupted from glass vases all down the main corridor. The place was trying so hard to be sunny and upbeat that Retta felt more attuned to the ambient gloom. As they walked toward the viewing room, past svelte white girls dressed for bible study and a multiracial troupe of muscled boys dressed for draft day, the woman introduced herself as Madeleine Tusk, aunt of the deceased. Her ex-husband was the coffee man. She used to apologize for his antics, she explained without explaining.

"Is he close to the family?" Retta asked.

"He's in the family," Maddy replied. Another nonexplanation. Instead of following up, Retta inquired about the ex-husband's peculiar wardrobe. Surely that would produce a straight answer.

Maddy declined to speak for him and introduced Retta to people assembled in the small viewing room, where a large brass pot surrounded by bouquets was positioned as the centerpiece. A few people had branded coffee cups in their hands, giving the scene an awkward boosterism. "Black Sublime" was the last phrase Retta would use to describe this assortment of mourners: black men in construction vests and work boots, black women in service aprons and scrubs, children fidgeting in chairs, retirees with faces suspended in flabbergast. Jackie Robinson didn't fight for this, one elder summarized, a chorus of mm-hmms doo-wopping around him. Compared to the McCormick ceremony, the mood here was less terminal. The boy's legacy was being negotiated.

When contact cards and condolences were exhausted, Retta settled into the back of the room alongside a long-faced clique of suited white men. The boy's coaches, obviously. They seemed more embarrassed than sad.

After the room filled, an almond-skinned woman in a dandelion-yellow pantsuit appeared to detail the funeral home's many services and to remind the bereaved that this was not actually a wake and the service would end at 9:00 p.m. rather than running until morning. Studies showed the modern mourner did not have time to lose a work night to grief, the woman elaborated. "Amen," a coach said.

As the woman described the half-lives of wooden versus steel caskets, Retta asked the coach next to her why there would be no funeral. "Bad investment," he said. Was he referring to caskets or funerals or the university's official position? She asked him to clarify. "It's hard to put into words," he said after a long pause that seemed contemplative until the moment he spoke. Before Retta could again request clarity, the coach cleared his throat and looked toward the front of the room.

Retta followed his gaze. The Buford-Lawson Funeral Services representative had been replaced by a squat woman with obvious authority. She was the matriarch. Her skin was smooth and vanilla-bean black, her voice shrill and cutting like wind whipping at rock. Heads were alert as she eulogized her grandson. Her daughter wailed from the first row, comforted on both sides by Madeleine Tusk in black and her ex-husband in white. The boy did not like baseball, the woman declared, but he hated how hard his mama worked, how hard every Tusk worked. He was observant like that, always pointing out rough hands and bent backs and offering to step in. Why hadn't he told her what he was planning? Did he not know the depth of her love? Of the family's love? She'd have done anything to prevent such senseless loss. The room throbbed with grief as she caught her breath.

She'd buried two grandchildren in four years, she noted. Want to know how that feels? she asked. Really fucking grand, she said with a pregnant pause. She sat.

A stillness gripped the chamber as the mother's sobs accumulated and the grandmother's pain steeped. The boy was dead. There was nothing to say, nothing to be done, nothing in the urn, nothing forming in Retta's mind's eye as she demanded her brain make something from this godforsaken day, nothing nothing nothing nothing nothing.

VYCE Magazine

February 29, 202X

"Believe the Hiip:
The Dark Secret of Hiipower"
by Vera Ramirez

The first time I took hiipower, I broke up with my girlfriend, founded an LLC, and updated the grimy labels on my building's buzzers. I've lived in New York City for five years, and to hear my tia tell it, since I disembarked at Port Authority, I've been in constant motion, going somewhere, meeting someone, doing something. Before hiipower, better known as *hiip* (*hype*), *hiip-E* (*hype-y*), and *brainbuster*, this description felt accurate. My days were full, my nights were fuller, and my schedule jam-packed. But that night, one by one, I crossed items off my to-do list.

My thoughts were so clear they hurt, my ideas so whole and rounded they felt like marbles rolling around my skull. One of the reasons I became a writer is that I tend to think like I talk, winding around in circles like a doomed paper plane, bobbing and dipping as I figure out exactly what the fuck I'm trying to say. Writing whips my rambling into coherence. So does hiip. For nine unforgettable hours, I was a dynamo of purpose. One pill down the hatch, and fifteen minutes later I knew what needed to be done in every facet of my life.

And that wasn't even the best part. There were no side effects. Anyone who's ever had any drug, from the community pharmacy or the street pharmacy, knows there's always a side effect. Dry mouth, headache, loss of smell, insomnia. Something. My colleagues had the same experience. Was it really true? If so, how could something so pure make it from a lab to me? To find out, I chatted with bench chemist Ellen Fitzmaurice from Brooklyn's biggest crime lab. Our interview has been edited and condensed for clarity.

VYCE: What does a bench chemist do?

Ellen Fitzmaurice: I process chemical samples acquired during arrests, seizures, and traffic stops, and I analyze their chemical makeup.

VYCE: So you're the lab lady on *NCIS*.

EF: Kind of. I'm part of a team of lab workers. There's no time for us to be on the phone with detectives or walking them through our analyses like you see on television. I just sit and do chemistry and paperwork all day. Occasionally, I go to court to testify. [*laughs*] We're not as goth as that lady either. Lots of styles.

VYCE: What's the most common drug you come across?

EF: Marijuana. New York City is one of the most stressful cities in the world, and marijuana is one of the cheapest therapies. Well, until I get involved. [*laughs*]

VYCE: You have to test marijuana? You can't just smell it?

EF: You're kidding, right? Innocent until proven guilty. The crime lab exists separate from any precinct or beat cop so that we can be free from prejudice. A chemical does not have a bad day or a pending divorce or a twelve-hour shift. It is what it is.

VYCE: So chemicals don't lie, basically.

EF: I hope not. If so, I have a lot of testimony to retract. [*laughs*]

VYCE: So is hiipower a lie? My colleagues and I don't understand how it works. Word on the street is that it's an enhanced Adderall.

EF: That's one way to describe it. So it is some kind of dextroamphetamine salt, and reportedly it has the same pharmacology as Adderall. But that could change. It's not certified or controlled.

VYCE: Says who? You a lie.

EF: [*laughs*] Me, a chemist?

VYCE: I've taken it three times myself and know plenty of other people who have too. Positive experiences across the board. It can't all be confirmation bias. Have you tested it?

EF: I have. It seems to be made in small batches, so we don't see it much, but it comes up enough for us to have a standard to test it against.

VYCE: And?

EF: Well, it does have remarkable quality control for a street product. I'll have to check my notes, but I've never seen it have a purity of less than 98 percent.

VYCE: Certified!

EF: Not quite. We have no way of knowing how it's made, how it reaches you, or if the next batch will be the same as the last. Every time you take it is a grave risk.

VYCE: That's life though.

INTELLIGENT DESIGN

Another batch of students evaporated from Thurgood's memory as he graded final exams. A curve would be necessary, he sensed, though it was too early to tell. Of the half dozen tests he had checked, there was neither excellence nor tragedy, just a relentless median.

He had anticipated this. The moment this latest crop of boat-shoed seniors received his syllabus, they exhaled with relief, and in the months of labs and lectures Thurgood had spent with these standardized pharmacists in training, he had confirmed their collective disinterest in distinction. Thurgood taught a capstone course, a rubber stamp that was designed to be less the apex of their scholarship and more the gentle tailwind nudging them into lifelong socioeconomic stability. Thurgood didn't mind. He was a layabout himself, cranking out uninspired research and passing grades in exchange for a leisure that only tenure could provide.

The problem with this cohort was the character flaw of all pharmacists, Thurgood included, until his dad died. PharmDs were the coziest of terminal degrees. Where JDs and MDs promised a perilous climb up some mythic peak, pharmacy sold a ski lift to a verdant plateau. The requisite tests and certifications were no cakewalk, of course, but once a pharmacist reached the summit, that was it. Though every job brochure and company recruiter pointed to the statistically insignificant few pharmacists who filed patents and stocked compound libraries and ran drug trials (lit reviewers like Thurgood also sometimes got a shoutout), the truth was that pharmacists aspired to regularity. It was the nature of the discipline. Standardize. Control. Maintain.

Thurgood looked up from his computer and admired his lab, appreciating the events that turned it from a guesthouse into a workplace, a dream fulfilled. He'd taken his father's stomach cancer, the worst tragedy of his life, and transformed it into his best idea. His hands built this. His money financed it. No banks, no insurers, no benefactors were involved. Every apparatus and feature—mixing vats, a microcentrifuge, a drying drum, a walk-in freezer, a corner converted into a tiny clean room—was his expertise in action rather than in service. If he'd have prioritized financial freedom sooner, he wouldn't have to depend on Kenny, who was MIA despite his nephew's wake ending hours ago. Thurgood had helped him pack up his coffee station precisely to avoid this scenario. Leave it to Kenny to find the long way back to Atlanta.

Was the delay something he should be concerned about? Thurgood revisited the service, parsing the event for clues. It didn't take long to find the anomaly. Was the Fed a factor? She introduced herself as CDC, which felt appropriate given her look: observing, respectful, inert. If she had been DEA or DOJ, he'd be dissembling the lab rather than reclining in it. CDC was more curious than worrying. Nonetheless, the suspicion embedded in "Fed" felt warranted. Between that woman, Kenny's soiled tuxedo, and the strangeness of Maurice's death, something was awry. Thurgood called Kenny to get an ETA. No answer, but Kenny sent a text: "10 min away."

When twenty minutes passed and Thurgood found himself grading his ninth exam, he considered cheffing the batch alone. He'd never done it before, but the temptation was strong. He had listened to "Ten Crack Commandments" enough times to know that there was essentially one commandment: only trust yourself. Natural hustler that he was, the Notorious B.I.G. expanded this edict into an Old Testament communiqué, but Thurgood was a natural distiller. Give him game and he'd divine the health of your franchise and the future of the sport. Give him a listless partner? Who said he needed a partner?

Thurgood didn't have to be taught to withhold his trust, especially by a man whose paranoia was notoriously correct, but when dealing with Kenny, peer review always had value. Kenny flouted all known standards of sense and reason. He was an atheist who mourned his child in a megachurch. He owned significant stakes in enterprises formal and informal yet had no interest in business or money. Before their reunion, for months Kenny had shot snake venom into his veins "to familiarize himself with the chemistry," as if he didn't have a doctorate in biochemistry, as if searing pain were an abstract data point and not just kitsch masochism. Thurgood would never place his trust in such eccentricity. For the sake of their partnership though, his investment, he had to understand what was going on outside of it. He kept grading.

When the tests were exhausted, Thurgood turned to the curious case of Maurice, opening a browser window and searching the boy's name. He hesitated to review the news articles and photographs that made up the results. It was strange to be prying into the life of someone he knew, someone he'd mourned. He decided to lay his suspicions out before proceeding, an act of self-preservation as much as largesse. He knew that all microscopes were black holes, that lucidity was an event horizon.

The facts as he understood them: Maurice loved his family, the boy considered Kenny family, Kenny was chaos. Chaos was bad for business.

Thurgood began clicking.

• • •

Kenny arrived around 2:00 a.m., an hour after his text. Thurgood switched from a clip of Maurice's self-immolation to his security app. He watched his friend park in the driveway, open and lock the back gate, and stroll toward the lab, moonlight shimmering on his tux. Kenny walked with an athletic, cocksure strut. Maurice walked like that right before dissolving into the mound, a symmetry Thurgood pocketed in the corner of his mind as Kenny entered the lab.

"You ever been stopped by cops three times in one night?" Kenny asked.

"I don't drive as fast as you do."

"Who said I was speeding?"

"So you have time for riddles but not courtesy texts," Thurgood observed.

"So your answer is no," Kenny said. He removed his suit jacket and vest and hung them on the coatrack, his face sparkling with bemusement. Thurgood eyed him with irritation. His friend was forever privy to some private humor, no matter the situation. It wasn't mocking, or even smug, but it gave him an obnoxious distance. It was as if at will he would phase his spirit into another happier reality, his flesh transfigured into a postcard: "Seoul is amazing. Wish you were here." Taking in Kenny's dilated pupils and joyous dimples, Thurgood accepted that his friend would furnish an alibi rather than an apology. He'd make an excellent fugitive, Thurgood thought for the umpteenth time. Perhaps he already was one, always had been.

Kenny inspected the lab equipment as he explained the delay. His story was so bizarre and engrossing and obviously, painfully true that Thurgood forgot to tell him he had triple-checked every instrument, forgot to say, "Fuck you for being late."

Like most traffic stops, the first police encounter happened for no reason. In fact, that might have even been the reason itself, Kenny conjectured, though he didn't "have time for paradoxes." (Oh now he cares about time management, Thurgood thought.)

It went like this, apparently: Kenny pulled out of the funeral home parking lot and hit the surface streets heading toward the highway, when a Birmingham police officer flashed her lights before he could reach the on-ramp. He pulled in front of a church, a black one, which he knew because it had *first*, *tabernacle*, or *Lord* in its name. Maybe all three. Probably two. Definitely one.

Officer Lancaster waited twenty minutes before exiting her vehicle. When the driver door opened, so did every passenger door. (Kenny turned away from the centrifuge with widened eyes to re-create his surprise. The man was a natural storyteller.) The cop had a camera crew with her. The occasion? Reality TV show *Extreme Policing: Live*. The policing seemed pretty regular, given the un-prompted stop, Kenny had thought, and there's no way Lancaster's entire shift was broadcast in real time, but that was neither here nor there. ("Maybe it's a podcast/reality TV hybrid?" Thurgood in-tervened. They agreed to look it up after the batch was completed.) Kenny rattled off Lancaster's queries as he dumped sulfate salts and saccharates into the largest mixing tank. What was he doing in Alabama with Georgia plates? Why was he dressed in white? Was he a pimp? Was he sober?

His answers were received with copspeak: a patois of grunts, sighs, and quasi-legalese.

After declining to consent to be filmed and evading Officer Lan-caster's very artful leading questions, Kenny made his way onto I-20 East, where, yes, he did speed, because he had been detained for an hour. When he pulled over for gas a few miles shy of the Georgia–Alabama border, he was again stopped, a few yards shy of the gas station. Officers Smallwood and Littlewood, no rela-tion, were all flashlights and *Cops* tropes despite the absence of a producer and film crew. Did Kenny mind if they searched his trunk? Kenny was caffeinated and grieving, and he resented redundant rhetorical questions more than being late or extraneous black death, so he said no. All cops could search his trunk, anytime. It was the "How is your meal?" of black life. Delicious, delightful, excellent, fucking excellent. The answer didn't matter. Why did they insist on asking?

Obviously, this attitude and its consequences led to Kenny being extracted from the vehicle, without force, he noted with regret and/or survivor's guilt as he and Thurgood hauled a tub of coolant from the freezer. In the trunk, the officers found paper cups, glassware, a hand grinder, and pungent coffee beans. ("Or was it a controlled substance?" they wondered aloud. "Black sublime," they read from a tablecloth coiled around a bag of fertilizer. Was that slang?) The vice squad arrived quickly and very professionally processed his car, and eventually it was concluded that there was nothing to see, move it along, have a good night. Kenny almost invited them to Black Sublime for donuts ("You serve donuts now?" Thurgood interjected. "No," Kenny confirmed. "Absolutely not."), but being a renowned scholar of bad decisions, especially his own, he restrained himself.

Kenny got his gas then proceeded to Barry Allen down I-20 and Wally West up I-85. He made it to Monroe Drive without interruption, until, driving the speed limit, he was blurped by APD. He did not document this officer's name because sousveillance is really exhausting, honestly, and it was then when he texted Thurgood. His ETA proved wrong and the encounter proved too mundane to warrant a play-by-play. "But!" he exclaimed as he and Thurgood tipped their glidants and anticaking agents into the salt mixture. "During the last stop, I had an epiphany."

"Don't ever go to Alabama?" Thurgood quipped emptily.

Kenny chuckled. "Nah, I realized I've been thinking too locally."

Thurgood focused. This could be his only chance to save this enterprise and possibly his friend. (He was unashamed of the hierarchy of these goals.) "Don't do this to us," he begged. "Our street value continues to rise. Our distributor says demand is so high that he's seeing counterfeits. Remember that *VYCE* article? If we could up output, we could easily lap the settlement numbers. I'm talking money that could keep our families afloat for generations." He lingered on this last word, telegraphing the hope embedded in it. Technically, he had yet to find a woman or man he wanted to share his fortune with, and he was horrified by the prospect of his dreamer cousins squandering his future millions on something sophomoric like electing a socialist or prison abolition, but he knew that wealth would do what protests and degrees and jump shots could not. Too many half-wit, blue-blooded simps sat in his lectures for him to believe in anything other than the power of the dollar.

Unmoved by Thurgood's proposal, Kenny eloped into his extra-dimensional refuge, beaming as he filled the second mixing vat, which contained boiling water, with the salt mixture. Thurgood did not envy his friend or covet his solace because he knew its cost.

"I know you killed Maurice," Thurgood said with conviction.

Kenny plopped onto a stool. "We all saw the video. He killed himself," he said.

Thurgood noted the gelid passivity of the deflection. "Okay, but who made the mystery liquid?"

"We did."

"What do you mean *we did*?" Thurgood fumed. "I'm your partner, not your accomplice."

Kenny responded coolly. "The main ingredient of the liquid is a by-product of the hiipower process. I can explain the chemistry to you, but you wouldn't understand . . ."

This nigga. "Would Maddy?"

"Absolutely."

"Okay, I'll call her." Thurgood drew his phone. He had few contacts, so he reached Madeleine Tusk promptly. His thumb hovered over her name.

Kenny submitted before he could initiate the call. Thurgood noted his friend's visible fatigue. He looked like Maurice's mother, resignation chiseled into his brow, tension tugging at reddened sclera. "Don't," Kenny pleaded. "She's dealing with enough right now." Thurgood locked his phone and tossed it across a counter. He had the advantage.

"Why," Thurgood said. It was less a question than an exhalation.

"I just wanted him to be happy."

Thurgood buried his bewilderment and went along with it. "I understand. If that's what he wanted, I think you did right by him."

Kenny produced a weak smile.

"So how is this, like, even made?" Thurgood asked, praying he had obscured his alarm.

"I've been combining the by-product with snake venom, coffee, and . . ." Kenny paused.

"And?"

"The chemistry really doesn't matter."

Thurgood huffed. "Why the fuck not?"

"You have to understand the vision."

"Kenny, talk or don't."

"Okay," Kenny said. He went to the coatrack and retrieved his phone. He walked to Thurgood and showed him a black screen. "This is EightBall. It's an app I made after a coding boot camp. I learned code so I could build a memorial website for Saskia, but between the NDA and the divorce and the . . ." He paused to rub his wrist. Thurgood admired the glint of his pearl cuff links. His friend's prim exterior belied his inner disarray.

When the pause seemed in danger of continuing indefinitely, Thurgood completed the sentence: "The venom?"

"Yeah," Kenny said. "EightBall came about around the time we reconnected. You reminded me that I wanted to be around people, but I knew I wasn't ready, so I came up with a way to talk to people but not have them talk to me. Win-win. It had a slow start, the reviews were terrible, and the downloads were low, but over time it gained a small user base, and the people who used it used it a lot, so I was happy."

He showed Thurgood an app filled with message threads and a smattering of usernames that ranged from words to gibberish alphanumeric strings. It was so jumbled and slapdash he cringed.

"But one day, during some routine debugging, I noticed a glitch. Because of EightBall's text-to-speech function, it has access to microphones, so I can listen to people."

Kenny's thumb fiddled about, and then an audio stream started playing. Two or three people, possibly teens, were talking about some sneaker sale.

"Turn that shit off," Thurgood said. Where is this going?

Kenny exited the app and kept talking. "Listening to people's lives, I felt the automated responses the app gave them weren't enough.

So I tailored my messages, talking to them, counseling them, thinking about them. And you know what I realized?"

"For someone who hates rhetorical questions, they're basically the only kind of question you ask," Thurgood said.

Kenny continued. "I realized that this country doesn't deserve us, black people. For centuries it's tried to erase us. I say we settle up, reset this motherfucker."

"How the hell would we do that?"

"Well, as you know, all the libraries we trawled were organized differently, some not organized at all. The science is the science, but the metadata, the indexing, the tagging is a toss-up. And one day when I was trying to sort the cache, I noticed the formula for napalm. It shouldn't have been there, but it got me curious, so I started looking and found all kinds of nasty things. VX; sarin; 2,4-D; 2,4,5-T. We just wanted pharmaceuticals, but we pulled everything. Cosmetics, defoliants, aerosols, lubricants. So I got to synthesizing, and before you know it, I developed RST."

Kenny walked to the desktop and pulled up a pdf. Thurgood watched in disbelief as Kenny scrolled down the document, apologizing for blank columns, explaining asterisks, noting unknown variables, sourcing test subjects (What?). As the scroll bar shrank into a sliver, Thurgood's jaw nearly crashed through the floor. Kenny had created a material safety data sheet . . . for a weapon.

After the shock dissipated, the surprise became relief. His friend was having a mental breakdown, a far cry from what Thurgood had anticipated, particularly a betrayal or a religious conversion. Craziness was workable.

Kenny kept yammering: "The past week, I've been having some second thoughts. Who am I to set the agenda for a nation of millions? Some people might not want a reset. Or they don't want my reset. So I decided that I owe it to our people to let them decide. So all that to say I was thinking if we could talk to your distributor, we could move toward RST having a life of its own. Our people could choose their own path instead of me dictating it, which has started to feel a little grim . . ."

Thurgood revised his proposition as Kenny rambled. Craziness was not just workable: it was lucrative. If they could sell this compound as a demolition agent or a trash-disposal tool or a threat, they could build an empire.

Saliva greased Thurgood's gums as he conjured the deep-pocketed buyers on the other side of Kenny's brilliant, debased invention: companies, governments, conglomerates. The swollen numbers dancing across his mind's eye required letters rather than numerals. RST placed their enterprise in the realm of GDP, GNI, FDI. At that stratum, this deranged program of assisted suicides and eavesdropping became an afterthought. Thurgood cast them aside with the ease of a blink, negotiated them as settlements rather than original sins, growing pains to be delegated to the counsel and accountants he and Kenny could already afford, had already dispatched with NDAs and blank checks.

He stroked his scalp as he adjusted to the rush of thinking as a mogul rather than like one. As Kenny prattled on and the batch cooked, Thurgood could feel his thoughts coagulating into a light beam of lucidity, a sensation he hadn't had since hiip precursor fifty-four, a version they discarded only because of its attendant diarrhea.

The revelation struck him like an assassin's bullet. We are an empire, he declared to himself. This is why they were partners, he realized. Kenny's delirium sharpened Thurgood's finesse, stropping it into the scythe it was meant to be.

He raised his index finger into a shush then concluded the summit. "Say less. I'm your partner."

Kenny grinned from ear to ear and pulled Thurgood into an amoebic hug, squeezing his sides and drumming his back. The embrace felt intimate and familiar, the distant kind of unbridled fraternity that had birthed the lab and sustained it through fracases and fires. But when Thurgood revisited the moment, lying in bed after they finished the batch, caught the tail end of Adult Swim, then parted ways, he could only remember his erection.

FLICK OF THE WRIST

Baltimore slowed the video to a quarter of its original speed and pressed play. The clip opened with a blip of light and the muddy slosh of voices and noise crooked into mush. The perspective drifted up, down, and forward with wavy leisure, as if the videographer bobbed in calm waters. Baltimore had never been to a baseball game—the Dads found it dull, and she preferred the skin-baring uniforms of basketball players to the chaste potato sacks baseball players wore. But at a quarter speed, the game felt acutely alien.

A few seconds in, the camera ceased its drowsy swaying and settled on a distant figure at the mound. It lingered on him like a gaze, then zoomed, stretching his slender figure to the borders of the frame. A ball dripped from his right hand. (At half, three-quarters, and full speed, the drop looked more like the fall it was, but at one-fourth the air thickened, giving every motion a liquidity, a sluggishness.) Dirt poofed at his feet as the ball hit the clay, shrouding his ankles in a red cloud. As the cloud emptied, the boy's hand wormed into his pocket then slithered out, a vial in its crop.

Baltimore paused here. The sequence to come was the moment that she had fixated on ever since the videos appeared on all her feeds a week ago. She had viewed it from so many angles, at so many frame rates, with the volume muted and maximized, that she should not have to watch it. But there was something literally unmemorable about this moment; she could not store it for future use, could not re-create it as easily as she recalled the gossip of her classmates or the bemused smiles of the Dads when they paid attention to her in real time rather than scrutinizing her highlight reel of achievements and mistakes.

The video resumed. Another dirt cloud formed and dispersed at the boy's feet as his glove dribbled to the earth and his left hand met his right. The climax was quick and violent at all speeds. The vial emptied into the boy's mouth, and the boy emptied, a sheet of blackness disappearing his body, oil-slick prestidigitation. Baltimore could never press pause during this sequence. There was a majesty to the way he vanished, a grace to the completeness of the action.

The clip ended as Nigel brought the car to a halt at the edge of her school's parking lot. Baltimore tugged her earbuds into her hands and sighed. In middle school, Nigel would keep the car in drive and they would depart without ceremony. On the first day of high school, however, the year Vincent ran for and was elected DA, he began this ritual of stopping the car, getting out, and opening the passenger door. Why? According to the oft-cited advisors, the aggregate Southern voter, even in the business-friendly county seat of the city too busy to hate, needed every little reminder that a gay family was a real family. Ever since, for car trips brief and long, for official business and family business, Nigel and Baltimore performed to their invisible audience at the behest of their shadowy stage managers. Baltimore had always wanted to ask the advisors why opening a car door was seen as familial, but they were never around.

Baltimore kissed her favorite father and crossed the parking lot, the frisson of the clip wearing off. She watched it again as soon as she reached homeroom, which was empty. There was something momentous lurking in the interstices of this video, of this extraordinary incident, as the news called it. Every viewing brought her closer to understanding. She again watched the clip at quarter speed. Without sound.

It was his body, she realized, the way he strutted to the mound, hips a-jaunt, shoulders a-loose; the way he smiled; the way, in some recordings of the incident, the scoreboard loomed behind him like a monument. His death looked like such a flex.

But why? The answer was certainly not in his public socials, which had been ransacked and dissected by the whole world. Baltimore hadn't participated, of course. The online lives of everyone she knew were a ghost dance of light, shadow, and smoke. Athletes learned the steps quicker than most, especially if they had relationships or hobbies scouts might consider unsavory, like smoking or politics. Ugh, the only people Baltimore despised more than the advisors were the scouts. They were everywhere and nowhere. She'd secured a scholarship, so technically she was now free to spike her racket and fume at bad calls and decline the handshakes of the demoralized white girls whose breaths were heavy with defeat and slurs. But Vincent, counsel extraordinaire, suggested that perhaps she shouldn't. Perhaps a better scholarship might come along before classes started at Oglethorpe. Perhaps perhaps perhaps perhaps.

Baltimore hunched forward in her uncomfortable desk for another replay. She remembered it was senior skip day only after her third viewing, her memory jogged by the total absence of her peers as the first bell rang. Baltimore shot up from her desk. She was supposed to be at the BeltLine fifteen minutes ago.

Dr. Smollett teased her as she fled into the hallway. "You never struck me as the perfect-attendance type, Bali."

Baltimore met Meredith and Seth outside of a luxe dog groomer where a thoroughbred Australian shepherd was being decadently massaged in the window. The dog was a furry bust of indifference, its body stiff and its ice-white eyes locked on Seth and Meredith, who waved and jumped and danced to distract it. A smile tugged at the jawline of the groomer, but his professionalism was steadfast, his eyes and hands trained on the dog's dappled pelt.

Her friends didn't realize Baltimore had arrived until the dog directed its gaze past them, cocking its head as if confused.

"Damn, Bali," Seth said, somewhat out of breath. "How you both MARTA slow and ninja quiet?"

"Good morning," Baltimore said with finality. They'd already discussed why she was late in the group chat. She refused to dignify Seth's pathetic jokes.

Meredith was more accommodating, greeting Baltimore with a hug and the secret handshake they developed back in middle school, a ringer of finger taps, hand slaps, wrist pivots, shimmies, and movements English phonemes could not yet describe.

As usual, Seth tried to record the brisk sequence, but the shake was near completion by the time he retrieved his phone, and Meredith and Baltimore added a new riff. Seth was gang gang, of course, so his ignorance was nothing personal, and both Baltimore and Meredith were willing to teach him if he asked, but he didn't, so he didn't learn. Boys were dumb like that.

"I'm gonna catch y'all one day," Seth said. He showed them his latest sloppy clip, which was a viscid blur of fingers. It reminded Baltimore of the Maurice White incident, a comparison cut short by Meredith's sharper assessment.

"Trash," she declared with a clap.

The Aussie barked and mounted the shop window, its long, droopy tongue pendulating the glass. The worker shooed them away.

"That's the flick of the wrist that matters," Seth said as they ambled away from the shop. He was such a cornball.

"Why did we choose the BeltLine again?" Baltimore asked as three bikers narrowly avoided a collision a few feet ahead. Dressed in equally garish bike jerseys, moving in the same direction at comparable speeds, they seemed to resent their similarities. After nearly colliding into the herd of strollers that they would have seen had they not been so self-asserting, they were again angling for distinction, their bikes wobbling, their necks taut as they jockeyed to lead the pack.

"Because no one else will be here. Remember that time we skipped and we saw *everybody*?" Meredith said. They had skipped only once before this, so the exaggeration wasn't necessary, but yes, Baltimore did remember that day. They saw Eric and Andre at Walter's and Laura at Centennial Park; at Chick-fil-A they encountered the Ashleys (in fact, Ashli, Ashlea, and Ashlie were only phonetically Ashleys, a lesson Dr. Ingram explained back in freshman English, but spell-check liked the traditional spelling and the Ashleys were inseparable, so Baltimore let the error stand), and at AMC they ran into Devonte and Sandra. It was a good day nonetheless, but the cameos were un-expected—and deflating. Apparently their classmates skipped all the time! None of this answered Baltimore's question though.

"And that's relevant because?" Baltimore asked.

"Easier to get caught when you're in big groups," Seth said.

"Okay. Why don't we go to your house, then?"

"Can't. Mom and Dad are filming today," Seth said. At Seth's be-hest, Baltimore swore to never watch the reality show that Seth's parents starred in, but she did often wonder what kind of show required a mansion to be emptied of its residents. Meredith specu-lated they were porn stars.

Baltimore didn't have to ask why they couldn't go to Meredith's house. Her grandmother, a relic of a distant century, was always home, always ornery, and typically either cooking boiled peanuts or chucking them down her gullet.

"This still doesn't explain why we're here."

"We're here because it's so scenic!" Meredith said with a theatrical skip, planting herself a few steps ahead. "There's street art and vegan pizza and designer ice cream and dogs. So many dogs! Short and fluffy and chubby and—"

Baltimore groaned. "Okay okay okay, yes this used to be my favorite part of the city and yes I was annoying about it. I'm sorry." She really, truly, was. It turned out she liked dogs but not the snooty white people attached to them. "But you can roast me any day in any place. Why are we here on skip day?"

"Damn, Bali, do you read our messages or just skim through them?" Seth complained. Definitely the latter this past week, Baltimore thought. The mysteries of Valencia McCormick and Maurice White had eclipsed everything. Baltimore read the last few days of exchanges as they traipsed along the manicured walking trail.

The gang had been in regular contact. Meredith's younger brother and sister had cooked red beans and rice for her family and earned their grandmother's endorsement. Seth's cat had gone to the ER. Despite graduation being a week away, the Ashleys had grown their ranks after learning that Chandler's middle name was Ashleigh.

Class rankings had been released; Baltimore was twenty-two, Meredith twenty-one, Seth thirty-seven. The historical record showed Baltimore had responded to these updates with GIFs and replies, as well as issued her own dispatches ("finally found a vegan cheese that doesn't taste like ass"; "zendaya is GOD"), but she had clearly been in absentia. She heard why they had come to the Belt-Line before she read it.

Street wheels gurgled, purred, and thrummed against the BeltLine skate park's glossy concrete. Skateboarders and rollerbladers of indeterminate age dipped in and out of a bowl, posing on the ledge or soaring above it before floating back down. Skate decks skied over rails. Bodies hit the floor then sprang up undeterred.

Skipping to loiter at a skate park wouldn't have been Baltimore's top vote for senior skip day, but relative to their actual plans, which were becoming clear, it would have been simple. Good alibis were always simple, Vincent told her. Baltimore never knew if the mantra was a warning or advice.

They were at the skate park to meet Harrison, Meredith and Seth's dealer. He generally sold them weed and Molly, but the special occasion begot a special request. After small talk, Harrison gave them an address, a locker number, and a combination. Then he sent them on their way, the skate park as indifferent to their exit as it was to their arrival.

Traffic on the BeltLine was more leisurely now that rush hour was over, bikers giving way to strollers, scooters, and fanny-packed tourists. Baltimore scanned the thread for hints of what this locker might contain and found a message from Meredith reminding her to check Venmo. She checked, and apparently she had sent Meredith four hundred dollars. What in the hell had they bought? No wonder Harrison was so uncharacteristically cautious. He usually dealt right in the open, his hired muscle, two barrel-chested, thick-thighed goons, pausing their varials and pop shove-its to supervise the exchange from afar. Baltimore would never forget the day she saw Goon 2 chase a thief, catch the girl, and break her board in half with a single punch. The thief screamed she would just buy another one, but Baltimore never saw her again. Baltimore realized she'd also never see the message detailing the day's illicit substance again, given that gang policy was to delete said messages.

"I'm so pumped!" Meredith said as they stepped off the trail and entered an empty parking lot. "I don't even know how Harrison got access to this. We've been asking for acid for years and he's never come through."

"God's plan," Seth said. "I heard it's made by two dudes in an RV who roam the country." Meth?

Their journey ended in front of a yoga studio attached to a towering apartment building. They walked in and were directed to an empty locker room that smelled of vinegar and armpit hair.

Their purchase was in locker 17. Seth entered the combination and the door swung open. Inside was a crumple of aluminum foil folded inward like a dumpling. Seth removed it and peeled it open. At its center was a blue-and-taupe pill the size of a candy corn kernel.

"All that money just for one?" Baltimore said.

"Duh," Meredith said. She removed a small mortar and pestle from her backpack. Seth plucked the pill from the foil and handed it to her. Baltimore had seen her friends grind up Molly to add to water, but always in the privacy of a car or bedroom and never with a tool.

She watched Meredith deftly swivel and press the pill into a powder. Baltimore never had any interest in drugs. Her biological parents were addicts, Nigel told her when she was ten. When Baltimore turned fifteen, she asked to meet them and the Dads obliged, driving north to hilly Dalton. The carpet capital of the world was a waypoint between Atlanta and Chattanooga, where her biological parents had resettled after "way too much fun in A-T-L," in the words of her mother. Her father corrected "fun" to "sin," an appropriate revision given their full-throated embrace of their lord and savior. They apologized for their addiction; Baltimore declined their apology. They asked for money; Baltimore paid for their all-star specials. She did not meet her two biological brothers that day because they were at football practice, but through a social medium they connected (blood is thicker than water) then drifted apart (casual homophobia is thicker than blood).

She thought of her kin whenever Seth and Meredith rolled or rolled up or crushed down or whenever Vincent and Nigel downplayed the hatred they waded through. There was no way to know which of her choices and experiences would be adhesive, bound to her like a hex, and which ones would flake off, dead skin in the cosmic dust bowl. There was no way to know how the choices and experiences of others dictated her own, irradiating her future, leaching her entropy. Life was such chaos.

Baltimore thought back to Dr. Patel's class. Entropy could decrease, yes, and it often did. But it was never exhausted. It was redirected. Was that what Maurice White had done?

When the substance achieved the proper texture, Meredith dumped the mortar into her hand and sorted the grit into three lines. "Y'all ready for this?" she asked. "This is that ultimate. That *mm-hmm*. That *hiip*."

Ah. Baltimore giggled. All that stress over a drug with no side effects, a drug that she had read about and shared with her friends, hoping they'd embrace safer vices. She leaned forward, depressed her left nostril, and inhaled.

The high hit like a possession. Baltimore was admiring a stately magnolia tree when a switch flipped and she was experiencing her experience. Her thoughts were legible as a chyron, her sensations a fishbowl she could swivel and peer through. She saw that she fixated on the tree because it was beautiful and impenetrable, like she hoped to be. Its foliage stretched to the sky with opaque designs. Survival, yes. But also ambition. One day it would touch the heavens. She would too.

Seth and Meredith exhibited the same keenness. They all exchanged grins and strolled the Botanical Garden in collective concentration, their love for one another manifest. Hours passed in this state, the cedars and sweet gums and chatter revealing the secrets of their universe. Seth confessed that his parents hosted a cooking show and he wanted to join them someday. He might even be a better cook than them. He wasn't sure yet, his doubt as certain as his pride. Meredith divulged that she wanted to be a music producer and audio engineer, not an anesthesiologist like she'd told her parents and teachers and any adult who inquired about her future. She didn't like doctors. They were too rushed; she wanted more time, not less.

Baltimore's truth was more addendum than reveal. As they all knew, she hated tennis. But hiip helped her realize she haaaated it. She was tired of being ranked and quantified. She wanted to be nothing. She wanted to be Maurice White. Not dead, to clarify. Just in control. Free.

"Are you kids lost?" an employee asked as they lingered in front of an iridescent bush, relishing their newfound candor. The employee was perhaps a few years older than they were, leaning hard into the casual end of business casual with a neat buzz cut, an untucked polo, skinny khakis, and stylish loafers dotted with a luxury logo.

Baltimore processed his request. His question was a statement; the statement was that she and her friends were out of place. It didn't matter that he was also black and young, that they had paid their entrance fee, that they were quieter than other visitors, that bruh was also secretly stoned (she'd seen him vaping behind a hemlock earlier), that there was no place where they "should" be. How could three black teens, wealthy or not, skipping or in class, belong to anywhere in this stupid city, in this stupid country? Make it four teens, actually, because how real was the divide between her friends and this narc? If a pig came through on a Segway ready to protect and serve, what were the odds this guy would get a pass?

Baltimore and her friends said nothing as the fool waited for the answer to the question that wasn't a question.

"Ayy, Conrad," another Botanical Garden employee shouted from a kiosk. "Not them. The kids." He pointed toward a cypress tree where five children in matching uniforms were holding hands. "Oh," Conrad said and skulked away.

"I don't want to be here anymore," Seth said.

"Yeah," Meredith and Baltimore replied.

• • •

"Do you feel bad about locking black people up?" Baltimore asked Vincent. The hiip was dwindling, probably even exhausted considering she'd had such a small dose, but she remained charged, riding the lightning of the high.

"No," Vincent said. Baltimore focused on Vincent but felt Nigel's disapproving glare from across the table. She ignored him.

"Why not?"

"Why should I? I aspired for the job, I got the job, I do the job." He raised a hunk of glazed salmon to his mouth and paused before biting it, grinning. Baltimore couldn't tell whether the smile was a challenge or self-satisfaction. Vincent liked when she argued with him.

Nigel didn't. "Did this come up in school today? You know what your father does, and you know he's trying to do more. If he's mayor, he can do more for the city, more for the people."

"I didn't go to school today. Senior skip day."

Nigel frowned. He maintained perfect attendance for sixteen years of education. No doctor appointments. No sick days. No field trips. In third grade, Baltimore had promised him she'd carry on the tradition. She was glad she had been precocious enough to insist that sick days weren't negotiable.

Other than the unsanctioned skip from a few months ago, she had honored his request, technically. "It was on the school calendar," she said, which was true.

"So you, a truant, come to me, the district attorney, in judgment," Vincent said with theatrical flair. His amusement was infuriating. Baltimore plowed sautéed spinach into her mouth as she planned her riposte. This was not a game. Her dad's office led the state in plea bargains; never prosecuted cops; embraced the Georgia attorney general's draconian crusades against human trafficking and package pirates; took no stance on no-knock warrants, quick-knock warrants, body-cam audits, sentencing reductions . . . and that was just the stuff his main opponent in the mayoral race harped on before dropping out.

Vincent the man was even more conservative than Vincent the bureaucrat, chiding Nigel for getting manicures, measuring Baltimore's skirts to comply with school rules, brushing Malcolm's teeth so vigorously that the little bulldog would scurry when Vincent brandished the toothbrush. When the dog ran away during a Stone Mountain hike and a two-hour search came up empty, Baltimore was relieved. She missed him but knew he was happier away from Vincent's expectations. He had to be.

"It could be me one day," Baltimore said.

"What could be you?" Nigel asked.

"Gone."

"Is this about McCormick?" Vincent asked, his voice flat, business-like. "Bali, from what I understand, that girl was troubled. Classic signs of stress and depression that, tragically, got missed. She might have even wanted them to be missed, which happens. You know how our people can be about mental distress."

"Are they our people when you prosecute them?" Baltimore said.

"What I do—and do very well—put that food on your plate, those clothes on your back, and this roof over your hard head," Vincent said. He pointed his fork upward for emphasis.

Baltimore set her jaw, prompting Nigel to sigh loudly, the standard indicator that a needless family argument was underway. Baltimore knew he was on her side because he had a record from his days as a "companion," but she couldn't count on him to stand up to Vincent over dinner. He insisted meals must be neutral spaces, a holdover from the late Mama Ethel's holiday policy. Nigel could always count her table as a space where Uncle Tim's comments about sissies and fairies and his most hated quarterback turned sports analyst, Tony Homo, would be prohibited. Baltimore and Vincent often violated that mandate. They couldn't help it, Baltimore realized, hating hiip for making her pay attention to the things she'd learned to ignore. They were too alike.

Vincent read her pause as a concession. "I wish more innocents came through my office, but, sweetie, that's just not the case. Drivers run red lights on suspended licenses and hit cyclists and pedestrians. Felons carry guns they're not allowed to own, often with the identification stamp obscured, which is another felony. Idiot dealers sell to snitches and cops. Husbands get white-boy wasted and beat their wives to death. Sure, I claim them. But how many of them would claim us?"

Baltimore centered herself. Vincent, the bitter, haughty man, would not be moved. But he could be circumvented.

"I apologize for my questions and I love and appreciate both of you very much," she said with twee surrender.

Vincent hated submission. Saw it as weakness, cowardice, despite it being the logical outcome of his relentless dominance. Nigel, who flashed Baltimore a smile, knew it was the tool of the cunning. Baltimore rose, gathered the plates and silverware, and hauled them to the sink, which was packed with the previous night's dishes.

She was certain the hiip was out of her system, but the water and floral dish soap felt especially textured as she scrubbed away oil and residue, the solution rinsing over her skin in a bubbly skim that narrowed her attention to her sturdy hands. She hated her calluses as a child, but in recent years they'd become her favorite feature, giving her a sense of history, tethering her to her actions.

Was she convincing herself to continue playing tennis? Not quite. Her calluses were the product of so much more than the French nobility's favorite pastime: pull-ups, dead lifts, chapped library books aged by eager fingers, sifting through topsoil and beetles with Nigel. She had plans for these hands, for these niggas.

She dried her hands and headed to her bedroom, ascending the steps in threes.

Sprawled across her bed, once more she watched and rewatched Maurice White's death, the lingering hiip drawing her attention to the changing backgrounds rather than the consistent climax.

Bright screens.

Green field.

Deafening crowd.

White crowd.

Black players.

White players.

Black spectators.

White crowd.

White coaches.

Red Dawgs.

Crimson Tide.

White crowd.

Maurice White.

Baltimore paused the clip and exited the video player. There was nothing to see.

DEAD NIGGER STORAGE

Kenny didn't come to the Trap or DIY conference to lollygag on the astral plane. He was seated in an immaculate classroom of the Harriet Tubman Leadership Academy's Science Center because he had transactions to complete. One would be public. There was an industrial-grade PCR machine up for auction, and if Kenny and Thurgood could acquire it, they could boost RST production. The other deal was a private affair. At some point during this meeting of the Southeast's greatest scientific minds, a portal would form, and the RST in Kenny's pocket would slip into the possession of an EightBall user. The trick, of course, was for this portal to open and close without Thurgood knowing it ever existed.

The other trick, unexpectedly, was that Kenny had to return to the known world. He wanted to, truly. He'd planned on attending this tastefully casual biohacking conference long before his own biohacks pried apart a girl's body just outside this building. But Moses kept parting his attention. There were no posters of Harriet, thank God. Nor any wholesome murals or milquetoast plaques. The problem was that Kenny sensed her everywhere: within the spotless walls, beneath the off-white floors, above the vaulted ceilings, between his bated breaths. He suspected this unplanned immersion was due to the facility's aesthetics rather than its name. In parks, cities, and streets with namesakes, the honorees left him alone. He and Maddy had enjoyed a lovely honeymoon in Columbus, Ohio, for instance, despite Columbus being the scion of plunder and syphilis. And his love for the sandy creeks and spiny flora of Herbert Taylor Park peacefully coexisted with his contempt for the segregated lunch counter of Taylor Drugs. Only buildings made history feel so palpable, so encroaching, Kenny felt. It was the nature of enclosure. To seal a space was to control it. And a name was the most resilient type of seal.

Accordingly, as much as it pained him to indulge a charter school's pretensions, he couldn't sit inside Harriet Tubman Leadership Academy and not think about Harriet Tubman. Would the abolitionist approve of his plan to distribute the RST in his pocket to Zora, the woman from Jena, Louisiana, seated three rows ahead of him and Thurgood? Zora was going to kill herself, plain and simple. Kenny was going to enable her death, plainer and simpler. Would that conflict of interest preclude General Tubman from acknowledging him as a fellow fugitive? She might not even call him a compatriot. Not only had Kenny never been charged with or pursued for felony narcotics manufacturing and distribution, manslaughter, and destruction of public and private property, but he knew actual wards of the state. (He could open EightBall right now and listen in on the allostatic crinkle of the state pulverizing their lives into grist.) Even if Moses wanted him to embrace the label of *fugitive*, the game might not let her. And where would that leave Kenny? Were niggas allowed to decline compliments from Harriet Tubman?

These questions had no bearing on what Kenny knew he would do sometime between this plenary session on synthetic insulin and the breakout panels on bacterial mouthwash, homemade yeast colonies, and decorative mold. Nevertheless, the imprimatur of the building seemed to impose on his designs, to press into his inner space. Yes, that was it; named buildings branded. What Kenny felt was the quiet alarm of hair tugging upward right before searing metal scalded the skin. A futile warning, but a warning nonetheless.

Disaster inevitably struck. A half hour into the lecture, Harriet materialized, floating over the speaker's head in the form of the shawl gifted to her by Queen Victoria. Kenny had last seen the shawl in person at the National Museum of African American History and Culture, fossilized inside a display case. Now, as then, his brain speculatively mapped the bizarre logistics of the garment surviving its owner, her former owners, Jim Crow, minstrelsy, the Harlem Renaissance, McCarthyism, apartheid, Robert Mugabe, Michael Clarke Duncan, UPN . . . Was textile the most resilient technology? Kenny set that thought aside and watched the rags flutter in the spectral breeze. How did the preservers of that shawl know it constituted Tubman's history? Did they anticipate that the same government that sanctioned chattel slavery would one day honor the victims of the institution? Kenny found it perplexing that this object, by proxy, could evoke the woman it once adorned. Black history always came down to residue. Drops of blood, traces of humanity, leaked footage.

Too much to think about, especially with such a full docket. Kenny decided to recuse himself from fending for the race, extending his arm and slinging it back at full strength. The resulting smack was so hard his vision blurred.

It took multiple blinks for reality to flicker back into view. Every gaze in the room seemed to have settled on him. "Damn gnats," he said, holding up his hand.

The eyes returned to the speaker.

Thurgood tapped on Kenny's desk once the lecture was back underway. "You okay?" he whispered. Kenny couldn't discern whether his friend was surprised or concerned.

"Just a headache," Kenny said.

"Too much coffee?"

"Not enough."

Thurgood nodded and faced forward. Kenny followed, his cleared thoughts allowing him to appreciate the passion creeping into the speaker's presentation. The cost of insulin rose while the big three manufacturers' market share remained unchanged. According to the speaker's graph, the cost of producing insulin had been falling for decades. Yet in every year studied, the manufacturer's profits ascended. "Epidemic economics," the speaker called these trends. Every ailment was a market, and markets had two fates, a slide concluded: grow (trap) or fail (die). (Finally! Kenny had been wondering when the inevitable Jeezy reference would surface.) DIY insulin was a threat to the status quo. Not a disruption, either, for the market anticipated disruptions, had Jos. A. Bank bros on standby to throw VC and Bloomberg reporters at the slightest hint of change. DIY insulin would be a rupture, a break without warning.

Well said, Kenny thought as he joined the other audience members in applause. After some programming announcements, the lecture adjourned.

Kenny thought of Valencia and Maurice and Saskia as he and Thurgood mingled with the other attendees. His forsaken brood. He had outlived them all, his endurance bolstered by their exposure to this world, to him. Such perverse chronology, the past feasting on the future, the present stillborn into a void. He gulped a swig of free hard cider, the tart fizz rinsing away the phantom taste of blood. Doubt had no place on this timeline.

He discarded his cup and approached Thurgood, who was talking with the plenary speaker. Kenny knew their alliance was tenuous. There was too much money on the table for Kenny to be naive and Thurgood to be bashful. Someone would be hurt.

Thurgood had the woman cornered. "Has Big Pharma tried to buy you out yet?" Thurgood asked coarsely. Kenny offered them pieces of rosemary pita baked with homegrown yeast, hoping to sieve the tension.

They accepted the bread without pausing. "There's nothing to buy," the woman said. Up close the feeble glow of the energy-efficient lighting dimmed the sheen of her colored locs.

"There's always something to buy," Thurgood said. "Your silence, your brand, your audience."

The woman smirked. "You must be a pharmacist."

The three of them laughed. "You know what they say about pharmacists," Kenny said. "If they can't cure it with science, they'll cure it with money."

"Yeah? Let me guess, you're an underfunded researcher."

They laughed again. "In a past life," Kenny said. "Now I own and run a coffee shop over in Decatur, but I worked surfactants and esters for a spell, so I've seen a failed patent application or twenty."

"Oof, cheers to that," the woman said. She raised her bit of half-eaten pita, pantomiming a toast.

She turned to Thurgood. "But to answer your question, I'm here because official channels just didn't have the answers I needed."

"Dr. Halifax, I believe you but I don't. Come clean with me. Did they lowball you?" Thurgood said.

"Call me Monica. Okay, they did. Highest offer I got was five figures. That no-talent bitch Elizabeth Holmes ain't even have a degree and Theranos was drowning in cash. I'm not bitter though." She turned away to chew her bread. Kenny noticed the roughness of her hands as she smuggled the pita out of view. Lab results could be faked, but not lab work. She was definitely more than a suit. "But the payout was a formality. What really got to me was that at that level, we weren't talking health. The terms were purely economical."

Thurgood: "Yeah, so?"

Monica micro-sighed, a term Kenny coined during his years with Maddy. Thurgood's behavior prompted another coinage. He wasn't quite mansplaining, but his questions lacked diplomacy and, implicitly, respect. Manquizzing? Manbadgering? Manterrogating?

Yes.

Monica endured. "I just knew in those meetings that the more time I spent in rooms with lawyers and entrepreneurs, the less time I would spend in rooms like this."

Thurgood nodded in approval, nipped at his pita, then slunk off to greet a colleague he suddenly spotted across the room.

Man down.

"If you're going to tell me he's actually a pretty nice guy who takes care of his little sister and blind aunt, now's a good time because the breakouts start soon," Monica said. Kenny could feel Thurgood's glare sweeping across them from somewhere out of view.

"I don't mean to go off script, but I think we're better off discussing how before pharmacy school, he got an MBA," Kenny said with a wide, toothy grin. Monica laughed into his shoulder and walked away. She smelled of lavender and thyme.

Kenny met Thurgood at the door.

"Which session you going to?" Thurgood asked. During his exile he had rediscovered the art of subtlety, Kenny noted.

"Yeast, definitely. The bread was weird but good. It's in room 18."

Thurgood shrugged and gestured toward the hallway. Kenny stepped out first, walking a few steps ahead so he could text Zora. "Behind the pita bread," he typed briskly.

"Got it," she replied.

"You and Monica are quite a pair," Thurgood said as his stride lengthened, placing him parallel to Kenny. His phone was still open to EightBall. "Is she in on it too?"

Kenny halted. "There's nothing to be in on." He held out his phone.

Thurgood snatched it and flipped through EightBall as they stood outside room 18. Kenny's shoddy coding came through clutch. By design the messages were not time-stamped and the threads were listed alphabetically by screen name rather than by recent activity.

(The low ratings in the app store were very deserved.) Thurgood was searching for a skeleton key in a mass grave.

"You could just download the app, you know. I could give you admin privileges," Kenny said.

"I already have it." If this was true, he hadn't messaged Kenny yet. He must have chosen an indistinct handle, Kenny guessed. There'd been a few dozen downloads in the past few weeks, but most seemed to be bots. After a minute of fruitless scrolling outside the classroom door, Thurgood returned the phone. Let off with a warning.

Room 18 was filled to capacity. Biohackers liked bread and beer. Thurgood and Kenny swam to the rear. Zora entered a few moments into the lecture, joining them in the back, ignorant of their connection. Not a problem, but he hadn't expected her to hang around. Perhaps she just wanted her money's worth. Trap or DIY wasn't cheap, after all. Plus, she had a long drive ahead of her.

The session was interactive and jovial, but Kenny had to work. It was a full-time job averting Thurgood's gaze on his right while monitoring Zora on his left. Though she had ambitious designs for her dose of RST, she was capricious. There was a slim chance she'd drink the substance right here and besmirch Harriet Tubman's legacy. Kenny welcomed all insolence, but at this range, he'd be sucked in too, foiling both of their plans.

The speaker, a lithe Cuban man in a white Marlins jersey and orange nylon shorts, radiated charisma, keeping the room rapt as

Kenny remained alert. Kenny was astounded by all the adjectives that could be prefixed to yeast: nutritional, Jurassic, Mesopotamian, antediluvian. Zora was clearly impressed as well, her face bright and shiny like an untagged MARTA ad. Maybe Kenny had her all wrong. Wanting to die—no, planning to die—did not make her unstable. He'd narrowly walked her away from the cliff multiple times, but now, as then, she was resilient. Maurice and Valencia had been too. He strained to follow her example. She was so close. One swift grasp, one loving squeeze, and he could let her know that behind the murk of EightBall was another black body trying to retain form. He was not delusional enough to believe that he was her friend, but he wanted her to know that she was seen.

Did Thurgood see him? Kenny sized him up, his eyes moving so furtively a cop would be obligated to shoot. Thurgood appeared as engrossed by the session as everyone else, a status update Kenny found infuriating. His friend was so flush with control he could exert it in repose. This realization made Kenny's yearning to touch Zora orders of magnitude more intense.

He combatted the urge, his scalp stinging with heat, his pocketed hands cementing into fists. Tightness yanked his neck, clamped his ass. His reward, nine sweaty, vexing minutes later, was the cogency of exhaustion.

He did not fear for Zora or fear Thurgood, he realized. What he was experiencing was guilt. Patrice Connor, letter carrier, contralto, and mother of three, did not choose her fate like Valencia, Maurice, and soon Zora. Kenny had used her. She died so Kenny could confirm that RST worked. There, he said it. She was not a casualty; she was a calculation. Lord knew she needed the relief, the poor, overworked girl. But Kenny was not transparent with her; he told her she would go quietly in the night, not that she would implode in a gasp of oblivion. Kenny swallowed his regret himself and vowed to cease all deceptions.

He turned to Zora. She was gone. Good for her.

He checked on Thurgood, who was also gone. Not good.

Kenny pushed his way to the door. The hallway, redolent with lager and babka, echoed with the mirth from all the sessions. Kenny ran to an exit, shoving open a door and finding blank sports fields. Very triggering.

He turned around and rushed toward another exit, passing the mouthwash session, which smelled, curiously, like fingernail polish. The sweet, musky scent of a cigarillo greeted him on the other side of the door. Zora did not.

"You lost?" she asked as he tarried in the doorway, one foot in the school, the other outside.

"Yeah. I want you to know you don't have to do this."

She frowned at him with every muscle available on her bronze face. "You think I paid a $175 entrance fee and drove eight hours for kicks?"

Kenny was stunned. "No, I don't think that at all." He watched her take a drag of the cigarillo. She was completely uninterested in him and his motives.

"Then whatchu doing out here? All this secrecy and now you want to step out the shadows." She parked the cigarillo between her lips then removed her vial of RST. "I saw what this shit do on the news. Ain't no redos."

Kenny nodded and stepped fully outside, the door creaking shut. He pointed over the building, toward the sporting grounds. "This is where this started, in a sense. It's strange being here."

"How you figure? 'Cause you knew the girl?"

"I didn't know her. That's what's strange. I don't know you either, but here I am yet again playing matchmaker for death."

Zora smiled. "Damn, EightBall, you're depressing." She pocketed the vial.

Kenny laughed. "I don't try to be."

"Do you, man. I imagined you more as the hippie type though."

"I'm too angry to be a hippie."

"Yeah, but hippies love making their own supplements, they don't trust the government, and they love to take in strays." She shrugged in response to Kenny's blank expression. "Made sense in my head."

"So did me trying to talk you out of this. I had no right."

Zora cast away the cigarillo then smacked the ash off her hands with two quick claps.

"'Preciate that, EightBall. Bye-bye, now."

Kenny watched as she stalked toward the parking lot and climbed into a boxy Ford Escape.

When he returned to the yeast session, Thurgood was still gone. He showed up toward the end, an arm across his torso like a support beam, his face glossed with sweat.

"I'm going to stick to regular yeast from now on," Thurgood said.

• • •

Kenny installed the new PCR machine as Thurgood enjoyed a fruity Rwandan pour-over on the house. "Why coffee?" Thurgood asked, his comment punctuated with a loud, hearty slurp. "You didn't even drink coffee in grad school, which in hindsight is sociopathic."

Capitalism is sociopathic, Kenny thought as he examined the PCR machine's thicket of cables for the third time. This wasn't the first time Kenny found himself on his belly, squinting through a scrim of dust to avoid electrocution, burns, or death. The device was larger and far more sophisticated than its predecessor. Its backside was a stretched ligament of wires and inputs; setting it up felt like rigging an IED. (Technically, the PCR was far less likely to explode than half the shit in Thurgood's lab, but Kenny was a survivor, and survivors aren't known for their optimism.)

This wasn't the hard part either. Its quirky origins be damned, this was a used appliance; there was no guarantee it actually worked. Amelia had supplied plenty of venom to burn through if the learning curve with the PCR machine was steep, but Thurgood's patience might not be as abundant.

Thurgood insisted. "Seriously, why move into coffee?"

"I wanted to talk to regular people. I was tired of scientists."

Thurgood huffed. "I hear you, but that's a lot of money to pass up." Kenny heard him walk over to the PCR machine and set down his mug with a hollow thud. (He knew that Rwandan microlot had the jewels.) "How soon will things be up and running?" Thurgood asked. "I know those were your people, but today was a lot. I'm still recovering from that mold lecture. Believe me, the free beer wasn't the only reason that yeast lecture was packed. That mold guy is a fucking creep."

"You should have stuck around," Kenny said as he emerged from behind the PCR. He pledged to clean the roasting room more regularly as he stood and wiped away dust.

Kenny pressed the PCR machine's manual power button, causing it to growl awake. A soft light flashed from the touch screen as the software booted up. To Kenny's surprise, the interface was astonishingly neat, a dermis of smooth fonts and ordered menus. Apparently the upgrade in power and quality included a boost in UX design. Kenny swiped through settings, annoyance tinting his wonder. Big Chem had these kinds of resources and still managed to ruin lives?

Thurgood jittered with enthusiasm behind him. "Well shit, this should be a cakewalk. I've seen printers more complicated than this."

Kenny was unsurprised when that excitement narrowed into a column of force pressing into the small of his back.

"Turn around slowly," Thurgood instructed. "You forced me to do this, and I don't do nothing half-assed."

The gun traced an arc from Kenny's back to his navel as he swiveled to face his friend. Kenny's phone hung limp from Thurgood's free hand. Of course. Kenny had set it down when he brewed the coffee. The screen was dark, but Kenny knew Thurgood had seen enough.

"I thought we were a partnership? I thought the next step was making more, not distributing more?" Thurgood's tone was brusque yet affectionate, like he was reprimanding a dog too stupid to comprehend its disobedience.

Kenny brought him up to speed. "We are not a partnership. You want to get rich. I want to get free."

"Are you really condescending to me when I'm the one with the gun?"

"I don't fear death." Kenny meant it, but he was feeling more keen than candid. If Thurgood needed to kill him, he would have done it while his back was turned. This was a negotiation. Thurgood had presented his terms. Now it was Kenny's turn. Perhaps he could save his friend.

"I'd like to make you an offer," Kenny said.

Thurgood's eyes oscillated from the gun to Kenny's face and back. "You really don't give a fuck, do you?" Thurgood said. "Christ." The muzzle pushed into Kenny's stomach with gentle violence, soft as a forced kiss.

Kenny proceeded. "In a few months, every decision maker at Kingman is going to be in Atlanta for their annual board retreat. And they're staying at the Omni, which isn't secure at all. We can kill them, T! All of them. Help me pull this off, and you can make all the money you want."

"All the money I want?"

"Not a cent less."

Thurgood withdrew the gun from Kenny's abdomen then clobbered Kenny's temple. On a scale of copperhead to black mamba, the blow was Kobe in the 2009 finals. It didn't knock him over, but it certainly made the floor's property value skyrocket. Kenny eased down onto his ass and glared at his friend, his head tilted back to slow the bleeding. Now he really felt like a dog.

Thurgood embraced the role of master. "Kenny, this ain't about you and your stupid vendetta. We play this right, we could buy their companies and ruin them with the deletion of a spreadsheet cell. That's the list you should be making!" His voice was large and furious, swallowing the room.

Kenny focused on Thurgood's words. The rhetoric was inspired, but Kenny didn't like the logic. He had money. In fact, he had Kingman's money. A fraction of it, but who was counting? Thurgood misunderstood. Kenny had no intention of subjugating the people on that list. He was going to liquidate them.

Thurgood's tirade persisted. "You think you hate money, but look around you. This is what money buys. You switched careers at thirty-nine. Your house is paid off and you own a small business. You have a savings account and a community-garden plot. You think Maddy's cousins have that? You think you're liberating those people on this stupid app?" He shook the phone for emphasis.

"I don't think that at all," Kenny said weakly. He could feel his pulse with his whole head.

Thurgood scoffed. "Well, what *do* you think? Because I'm really confused, honestly. I can't tell whether you're crazy or grieving or just fucking stupid. You've struck gold and you want to be a murd—" Thurgood gripped his abdomen, then lurched forward, his head colliding with a roaster. He screamed. It was a primal, manic screech, so full-throated and outraged and piercing that Kenny froze and remained still as it dulled into a croak, then a gasp, then silence, Thurgood's body collapsing to the floor. Paralysis.

The foxglove should have kicked in earlier, but the delay had allowed Kenny and Thurgood to speak with candor. Some friends never got that luxury.

Kenny's head pounded as he rose and ambled over to Thurgood. Thurgood's barbs hurt as much as the pistol-whipping. Kenny corrected them, for the record and for himself.

Reparations was not murder, Kenny told his dying friend. And Kenny was crazed, not crazy. Aggrieved, not grieving. There was a compelling argument that he was fucking stupid, but what he felt was fucking determined. "Important distinctions," Kenny said. Kenny kicked Thurgood's gun across the room then lingered over his partner's body as his breaths grew slow and infrequent.

After a spell, Thurgood's eyes were blank and still. Kenny closed them then went and retrieved the firearm. It was black and heavy and cold. Kenny chuckled as he checked its ammo. Fully loaded. His best friend didn't do anything half-assed.

GEORGIA DEATH CERTIFICATE

A. BIRTH CERTIFICATE NUMBER					B. STATE FILE NUMBER	

DECEDENT'S INFORMATION

1. DECEDENT'S LEGAL FULL NAME (FIRST, MIDDLE, LAST)	1a. LAST NAME AT BIRTH (IF FEMALE)	2. SEX	2a. DATE OF DEATH (MO/DAY/YR)
Lester Lloyd Houser		M	May 5 2018

3. SOCIAL SECURITY NUMBER	4a. AGE (YEARS)	4b. UNDER 1 YEAR		4c. UNDER 1 DAY		5. DATE OF BIRTH (MO/DAY/YR)
		MONTHS	DAYS	HOURS	MINUTES	
770 XX XXXX	68	2	8			Feb 26 1950

6. BIRTHPLACE (CITY AND STATE OR FOREIGN COUNTRY)	7a. STREET AND NUMBER OF RESIDENCE	7b. ZIP CODE	7c. CITY OR TOWN OF RESIDENCE
Knoxville, GA	227 Houser Lane	30150	Knoxville

7d. COUNTY OF RESIDENCE	7e. STATE OF RESIDENCE	7f. COUNTRY	7g. INSIDE CITY LIMITS	8. ARMED FORCES
Crawford	GA	USA	☑Yes ☐No ☐Unknown	☐Yes ☑No ☐Unknown

8a. OCCUPATION	8b. NATURE OF BUSINESS	8c. EMPLOYER
Peach farmer	Agriculture	Self

9. MARITAL STATUS	10. SPOUSE'S NAME (IF WIFE, GIVE NAME PRIOR TO FIRST MARRIAGE)	11. FATHER'S NAME (FIRST, MIDDLE, LAST)
☑Married ☐Divorced ☐Married, but separated ☐Never Married ☐Widowed ☐Unknown	Agatha Melody Freeman	Lloyd Isaiah Houser

12. MOTHER'S NAME PRIOR TO FIRST MARRIAGE (FIRST, MIDDLE, LAST)	13. DECEDENT'S EDUCATION (HIGHEST LEVEL)	14a. INFORMANT'S NAME (FIRST, MIDDLE, LAST)
Morgan Penelope Walker	☐8th grade or less ☐9th – 12th grade; no diploma ☑High school graduate or GED completed ☐Some college credit, but no degree ☐Associate degree (e.g., AA, AS) ☐Bachelor's degree (e.g., BA, AB, BS) ☐Master's degree (e.g., MA, MS, MEng, Med, MSW) ☐Doctorate (e.g., PhD, EdD) or professional degree (e.g., MD, DDS, DVM, LLB, JO) ☐Unknown	Agatha Melody Houser

14b. RELATIONSHIP TO DECEDENT	14c. MAILING ADDRESS (STREET AND NUMBER, CITY, COUNTY, STATE, ZIP CODE)
Spouse	227 Houser Lane Knoxville, GA 30150

15. HISPANIC ORIGIN	16. DECEDENT'S RACE
☑No, not Spanish/Hispanic/Latino ☐Yes, Puerto Rican ☐Yes, Mexican, Mexican American, Chicano ☐Yes, Cuban ☐Yes, other Spanish/Hispanic/Latino (specify) _____ ☐Unknown	☐White ☑Black/African American ☐Samoan ☐Japanese ☐Korean ☐American Indian/Alaska Native ☐Asian Indian ☐Vietnamese ☐Other Asian ☐Chinese ☐Native Hawaiian ☐Other Pacific Islander ☐Filipino ☐Guamanian/Chamorro ☐Other ☐Unknown

17a. IF DEATH OCCURRED IN HOSPITAL	17b. IF DEATH OCCURRED OTHER THAN HOSPITAL
☐Inpatient ☐Emergency Room/Outpatient ☐Dead on Arrival	☐Hospice Facility ☐Nursing Home/Long Term Care Facility ☑Decedent's Home ☐Other ☐Unknown

18. FACILITY NAME	19. FACILITY ADDRESS (STREET AND NUMBER, CITY, STATE, ZIP CODE)	20. COUNTY OF DEATH
n/a	n/a	Crawford

DISPOSITION

21. METHOD OF DISPOSITION	22. PLACE OF DISPOSITION (NAME AND COMPLETE ADDRESS)	23. DATE OF DISPOSITION (MO/DAY/YR)
☑Burial ☐Donation ☐Removal from State ☐Cremation ☐Entombment ☐Other	Houser Peaches	05/10/2018

24a. EMBALMER'S NAME & CERTIFIED INITIALS	24b. LICENSE NUMBER
Otis Gunther III	88562671

25. FUNERAL HOME NAME	25a. FUNERAL HOME ADDRESS (STREET AND NUMBER, CITY, COUNTY, STATE, ZIP CODE)
Otis & Sons	34 Main Street Knoxville, Crawford, GA 30150

26. FUNERAL DIRECTOR'S NAME (PRINT)	26a. SIGNATURE OF FUNERAL DIRECTOR	26b. LICENSE NUMBER
Otis Gunther III	*(signature)*	6321547

PRONOUNCER

27. DATE PRONOUNCED DEAD (MO/DAY/YR)	28. TIME PRONOUNCED DEATH	29a. PRONOUNCER'S NAME AND TITLE (PRINT)
05/05/2012	7:42 AM	Boyd Hollister, EMT

29b. PRONOUNCER'S LICENSE NUMBER	30. ACTUAL OR PRESUMED TIME OF DEATH
872015897	overnight

CAUSE OF DEATH

31. Part I. Enter the chain of events—diseases, injuries, or complications—that directly caused the death. DO NOT enter terminal events such as cardiac arrest, respiratory arrest, or ventricular fibrillation without showing the etiology. DO NOT ABBREVIATE.		Approximate interval between onset and death
IMMEDIATE CAUSE (Final disease or condition resulting in death)	A Respiratory arrest	
	Due to, or as a consequence of	
Sequentially list conditions, if any, leading to the cause listed on line a. Enter the UNDERLYING CAUSE (disease or injury that initiated the events resulting in death) LAST.	B Adenocarcinoma	3 years
	Due to, or as a consequence of	
	C Lifetime pesticide exposure Family history	
	Due to, or as a consequence of	
	D	

Part II. Enter other significant conditions contributing to death but not resulting in the underlying cause given in Part I	32. WAS AUTOPSY PERFORMED ☐Yes ☑No ☐Unknown

33. WERE AUTOPSY FINDINGS AVAILABLE TO COMPLETE THE CAUSE OF DEATH?	33a. WAS AN INJURY OF ANY KIND INDICATED IN THE CAUSE OF DEATH FOR PART I OR PART II WITH THE DECEDENT	34. WAS CASE REFERRED TO MEDICAL EXAMINER OR CORONER
☑Yes ☐No ☐Unknown	☐Yes ☑No ☐Unknown	☑Yes ☐No ☐Unknown

35. TOBACCO USE CONTRIBUTE TO DEATH	36. IF FEMALE	37. MANNER OF DEATH
☐Yes ☑No ☐Unknown ☐Probably	☑Not Applicable ☐Not pregnant within the past year ☐Not pregnant, but pregnant within 42 days of death ☐Not pregnant, but pregnant 43 days to 1 year before death ☐Pregnant at the time of death ☐Unknown if pregnant within the past year	☐Accident ☑Natural ☐Could not be determined ☐Pending Investigation ☐Homicide ☐Suicide

38. DATE OF INJURY (MO/DAY/YR)	39. TIME OF INJURY	40. PLACE OF INJURY (e.g., Decedent's home, construction site, restaurant, wooded area)	41. INJURY AT WORK
Jan 6 2012	morning	peach orchard on property	☑Yes ☐No ☐Unknown

42. LOCATION OF INJURY STREET AND NUMBER CITY STATE COUNTY ZIP CODE
See above

43. DESCRIBE HOW INJURY OCCURRED	44. IF TRANSPORTATION INJURY
Fell down while applying pesticide	☐Driver/Operator ☐Passenger ☐Pedestrian ☐Other

CERTIFICATION

45. To the best of my knowledge death occurred at the time, date, place, and due to the cause(s) stated. Medical Certifier (Name, Title, License No.) (PRINT AND SIGN)	46. On the basis of examination and/or investigation, in my opinion death occurred at the time, date, place, and due to the cause(s) stated. Medical Examiner/Coroner (Name, Title, License No.) (PRINT AND SIGN) Patricia Downs, MD 7859 *(signature)*

45a. DATE SIGNED (MO/DAY/YR)	45b. HOUR OF DEATH	46a. DATE SIGNED (MO/DAY/YR) May 7, 2012	46b. HOUR OF DEATH overnight

47. PERSON COMPLETING CAUSE OF DEATH (NAME, ADDRESS, COUNTY, ZIP CODE)
Patricia Downs 94 Agency Street, Crawford County 31078

48. REGISTRAR SIGNATURE (PRINT AND SIGN)	49. DATE FILED (REGISTRAR) (MO/DAY/YR)
Jodey Barnes *(signature)*	May 28, 2012

Form 3903 (Rev. 09/2009)

This certificate does not constitute a certified copy without the appropriate certification on the back.

PARALLELS AND COINCIDENCES

Vincent twiddled the cord of his office phone as Riley Perkins asked, in so many words, whether a Blake mayorship would renew the existing body cam contract. The query truly was so many words, a protein string of caveats, provisos, conditions, and subjunctives. To obscure the dirty business at hand they had to turn their brokering into a complex arrangement of spouse chatter, Falcons players, and traffic gripes. There were no favors being exchanged here, just leaders of the community discussing the issues that matter, their joint vision for the city. So many words.

History would document Vincent's conversation with R. Perkins of SCRY Defense Systems as the 11:00 a.m. to 11:25 a.m. entry in Vincent's taxpayer-funded digital calendar, but Vincent knew that if he spoke too concretely or too loosely or too casually or too formally—if he made this one call too memorable—the episode might have consequences down the line. Perhaps a scandal when he ran for US representative, or poor optics as he cited the GBI's low case-clearance rate during a gubernatorial bid. Maybe even skepticism as he assured the police union he'd protect pensions as senator. Admittedly, these were distant possibilities—he wasn't even mayor yet—and crucially they were tied to histories that hadn't been written. But Vincent was a prosecutor. It was his job to make disparate connections not only real but also vital, compelling, true.

If he couldn't see himself in the Oval Office someday, recounting his days as an impassioned agitator seeking to end a pointless war, or a headstrong district attorney just trying to make the streets safe for the children, his daughter, how could anyone else?

After a few more rounds of end-to-end encrypted exchanges, the deal was done, and Riley hung up. Vincent unwound the phone cord from his finger and turned to his computer, where he opened his calendar. Five minutes until his next donor call. Nigel, a personal trainer to his superhuman core, told him to activate these tiny intervals of rest by thinking of things unrelated to the campaign, but Vincent's office was no longer a refuge for mindfulness and recovery (or a swift fuck). To combat those niggling, pesky reporters, who, in Vincent's humble opinion, were just wannabe lawyers, he'd transformed the space into a shrine to Atlanta, removing his floor-to-ceiling bookshelves and replacing them with a mural.

Vincent swiveled away from his computer and examined the massive artwork. For every Atlanta voter his advisors told him mattered, there was at least one head from their personal Mount Rushmore: Barack Obama, Martin Luther King Jr., Coretta Scott King, Samuel Cathy, Monica Kaufman, André Benjamin, Ciara Wilson, Steve Harvey, Mike Lazzo, Stacey Abrams, Tayari Jones, Radric Davis, Stan Kasten, Michael Vick. It was the tackiest, most incomprehensible mural he'd ever seen, but it continued to be fondly mentioned in every profile that had been published since the start of the campaign. Though they grew up in Seattle, his advisors knew Atlanta. Or their algorithms did. Or the coders who wrote the algorithms and sold it to his advisors did. Vincent had never asked. Frankly, as long as he got elected, he didn't care.

The phone rang. Vincent turned from the mural and peeked at his calendar. His 11:30 was Sandra Crow with the Atlanta Small Business Owners Association. She did not like him. Vincent steadied himself for her contempt by looking into the sea of faces, feeling nothing, intensely.

Activated?

"Hello, Vincent Blake speaking," Vincent answered.

As usual, Sandra did not waste time with small talk or niceties. He'd met her in person only once, months ago, at his campaign launch party. He was waltzing between circles of donors, one hand swirling merlot while the other popped cheese cubes, when he spotted her. She had no plate or glass and looked unimpressed and bored, which Vincent thought made her a prime target.

"On election night I promise we'll have a more inclusive spread," he said, thinking she was sober or a vegan.

"You've got to make it there first," she said. He wasn't surprised when he later found out she was a butcher.

Vincent survived the potshot somehow, probably with his smile, which he'd honed into a telekinetic armament. When wielded, it could loosen shoulders and re-holster police guns and reposition purses back into near-Negro orbit. The haze of wine and adrenaline fogged his memory of this heroic recovery, but he had endured then and would endure now. Making this a video call might have helped his chances though.

Fortunately, Crow was not carving into him as she had after he announced the crackdown on leash-law violations, or as she had after
he tweeted support for a curfew for the BeltLine. Today's mark was
the CDC, whom, serendipitously, he was scheduled to speak with
that afternoon. He decided to listen closely rather than scrutinize
Gucci Mane's face tattoos, which the muralist had recreated with
pointillist detail.

"They don't have the authority to declare an emergency!" Crow
said. Vincent detested her word choice but was tickled by her frus-
tration. It was a blessing for Crow's ire to be directed away from
him.

"They're just trying to get around the rigmarole," Vincent said calmly.
"Calling it an emergency grants them access to more funds with less
runaround." If he could end this call quickly, he could squeeze in
some donor calls before lunch. Hell, maybe he could even avoid that
other word.

"Well, outside the bureaucracy, *emergency* means *fucking emergency*,
and tourists don't exactly run toward emergencies. You do know
what month it is, right?" He felt foolish. Of course she wouldn't
call to rant for a half hour. This was about money. Summer money
in particular, one of the city's most critical lifelines.

"Sandra, most of the businesses you represent are food and retail.
Tourist dollars are icing on the cake. What's really going on?"

Crow sighed. "If you were more qualified, you wouldn't have to ask
me that, but Jillian's campaign nose-dived after that 'Send in the

troops' comment, and most of my board members like you more anyway, so I'll cut you some slack."

Vincent felt himself instinctively smile for control despite Crow being miles away.

"The board is worried about the so-called epidemic."

"Really?" Vincent said. "We barely closed during COVID-19. Tell them it's nothing."

"I can do that. But let's clarify. What are *you* telling me?" He hated how savvy this woman was. She was the only person who treated him like an elected official rather than an HR representative amassing inactions.

"I'm telling you that I don't know what is happening at the CDC, but I will find out and respond in kind."

The line clicked off.

Vincent eased his phone onto the receiver. He appreciated Crow's naked contempt, but he was increasingly skeptical that she was a Southerner. Faint twang notwithstanding, she had to have been imported from the Catskills or Lake Washington, somewhere without revivals and fish fries. Her manners gave her away, Vincent felt. She declined to pretend business and community relationships were more than transactions, was unafraid of the resulting social frictions. Vincent admired her somewhat. She seemed to peer into the empty heart of "friction" as a metaphor. After all, friction was the meeting of surfaces—not equals, not partners, not allies. Just skins. Just meeting.

Or maybe she simply embodied the New Atlanta, which Vincent could confirm was real. Atlanta was now a global city. It belonged to everyone with an open purse or an elastic credit line, and if their money said Southern hospitality could be slashed from the budget, mask off.

Vincent opened his door and peeked past the doorframe. The floor was still despite the steady encroach of lunch, which typically turned the office into a protest of aromas and shuffling feet. He caught the eye of Quinte, his executive assistant.

"Your one o'clock is in the area and wants to know if she can stop by instead of calling," they said.

"Who is it?" he asked.

"Dr. Ebonee McCollum, CDC."

"Absolutely. Order some coffee, from the good place."

• • •

Vincent made eye contact with Mike Lazzo as McCollum fussed with her computer. The lithe, long-haired television exec always struck Vincent as the mural's oddest figure. When Vincent asked his advisors what demo Lazzo represented, they shrugged, in so many words.

He turned to McCollum, whose movements were snappy and deliberate yet unhurried. Vincent couldn't read her. Either this visit was purely functional and she was here because bureaucracy necessitated perfect meeting attendance, no matter how redundant or extraneous the circumstances, or she was ready for war. Vincent prepared for the latter.

"Lovely to see you again, Dr. McCollum." Vincent said. "Where's your partner?"

"Like I told you at the briefing, Vincent, just call me Ebonee. Retta is doing fieldwork. But I'd be lying if I told you she's sorry she couldn't make it."

"I'd be lying if I told you I was sorry she didn't."

Ebonee swiveled her computer so that it faced Vincent. "On that unapologetic note, I'll let you know now that I'm not here to curry favor with you or do some kind of tit for tat. You see this?"

Vincent looked at a line graph labeled "Leading Causes of Death Reports: Census Region South." The CDC logo hovered in the left corner of the chart; "Official Use Only" watermarked the background.

"I see it," Vincent said.

"Great." Ebonee reached over the screen, and the page was replaced with another graph titled "Leading Causes of Death Reports: Census Region South, Georgia." A line labeled "suicide" sloped down from left to right. Nicely done. Vincent knew the script. He would read aloud what he saw, Ebonee would nod with satisfaction as he performed contrition, and at some point the humiliation would beget a transaction. Vincent wasn't too proud to beg. "Epidemic of suicide" was certainly more purple than the situation had warranted, as was the pageantry of the teacher and the classmate grieving onstage. Not his best moment, his advisors had reprimanded. But he didn't understand why Ebonee was in his office serving him his just deserts. She seemed like the emailing, I-want-this-on-the-record type. Plus, the school was already back up and running.

"I know you're too smart to think politicians don't occasionally stretch the truth, and you know I'm too busy to get hung up on some little episode of hyperbole, so what's really up?" Vincent asked. "If you'd come sooner, I could have put you in touch with the girl's family, but I didn't attend the funeral, so that door is definitely closed."

Vincent watched as Ebonee steepled her hands and stared over his shoulder. Perhaps she wasn't so smart, Vincent thought. He examined the graph as she regrouped. Heart disease is a motherfucker. A hundred thousand people's circulatory systems just shut down every year? Shit, cancer and respiratory diseases are up there too. Do that many people still smoke? Smog has been pretty bad the past few years. Perhaps that's a factor. Fourth was "unintentional injury"? What the fuck was that?

Vincent hovered the mouse over the odd category and turned Ebonee's computer back toward her. "May I?" he asked.

"Yeah," she said blankly. He spun the device back toward him.

Vincent clicked and got his answer. Unintentional injuries comprised poisoning, traffic accidents, falls, suffocation, drowning, fire, firearms, "unspecified." Essentially all the things his office would never address . . . His current office, that is.

The advisors' data showed public health didn't even crack the top twenty-five issues voters cared about, but maybe that was an opportunity?

Ebonee interrupted his thoughts. "I'm here because I don't think I'm investigating a public health crisis." Vincent overlooked the word.

"What do you think you're investigating? And why do I need to know?"

"The emergency announcement isn't official yet, but I assumed you would wind up being the face of the effort, and I just wanted you to know that we don't know what it is."

She said the other word, but Vincent knew his irritation was performative. What he actually felt was surprise. "Wait, then what are they going to announce?" he asked.

"That's being worked out by comms. Retta is at the scene of the latest blackout trying to find a connection. It feels useless though. All we have is a trail of vacancies."

Vincent's eyes darted between Coretta Scott King and Steve Harvey. "Another one happened?"

"Yeah, we've kept it under wraps, but a USPS worker over in Mechanicsville immolated herself, her truck, and about a hundred packages while on her lunch break a week before the death of Valencia McCormick. It was reported as a fire because it started with a smoldering crater being discovered in the lot. The fire department turned it over to us after the Maurice White video went viral."

Vincent was perplexed. She had shamed him for inflating one-off cases, yet she was doing the same thing. What was supposed to be his takeaway here? Keep off her turf? More importantly, what would he tell Crow? "CDC reports people die." He swallowed a giggle.

"Ebonee, level with me here. I just see a bunch of parallels and coincidences. What is the connection between this and me? And why am I talking to you instead of GDPH?"

"Like I said at the briefing, EIS is taking point while GDPH handles the mumps outbreak. As far as the connection between this and you, it's what you make it. At any given moment, another person could disappear. Your assistant, your daughter, your husband. This isn't abstract."

"Are you done?" Vincent asked.

Ebonee responded with an empty gaze then retrieved her computer, folded it shut, and packed it into her satchel.

"Wait," Vincent said as she slid her arm into a shoulder strap. He needed something concrete to deliver to Crow.

"Do you like coffee?" He called for Quinte, who appeared with two ceramic mugs emblazoned "Forever I Love Atlanta."

Ebonee refused the mug and rose.

"I love coffee, but I'm on the clock," she said. Vincent tucked his vexation and sized the woman up. Her posture betrayed neither accomplishment nor conviction nor delight. Her face was blank except for the electricity always dancing in her wide mahogany eyes. The rebuff was sincere, he realized. She worked hard.

"Next time," he said, raising his mug. She left, a grinning Quinte on her heels.

Vincent remained seated, the coffee's steam nuzzling his bare chin. The woman had really set up this meeting just to scold him, to insist that he could quote the stats but that without the CDC's guidance and expertise, he couldn't make the numbers real, make them matter.

Vincent met Michael Vick's gaze, shrugged, then reviewed his calendar. He had three more meetings.

THE SCENE

Retta broke away from a noxious chicken truck and streaked down an empty highway. She and Ebonee were less than an hour away from the scene. *The scene* was the term they had agreed upon as the rental-car company at Louis Armstrong International scrabbled through its inventory. Retta typically didn't like euphemisms, found them more patronizing than polite, but in this instance it was nice to have a sunny buffer of metaphor between what she said and what she knew.

The news was calling the scene arson. The web, depending on the social medium, referred to it as terrorism, voodoo, and Black Fyre Festival. Louisiana's governor called it a tragedy. Alonzo, a wise man, did not attempt to summarize it. Retta wished Floyd and Matthew, whom she should have spoken to when she returned from the scene, precluding a blitzkrieg of concerned messages and calls, shared Alonzo's reserve. They half joked that the scene would be a ritual sacrifice orchestrated by the Illuminati, an organization they both fully believed in. Whatever the case, Retta just planned to do her job.

Hence, *the scene*: a term that was perfectly neutral and modular and Bayesian. Retta and Ebonee agreed they would update the term once they saw the space for themselves. That was the epidemiologist way.

Ebonee was not awake to discuss what they would do if they were called to be more than epidemiologists. She was nestled into a ball, her face obscured by a canopy of goddess braids. Retta turned on the air-conditioning and rolled up the windows. Ebonee didn't stir as cool air loudly wheezed from the vents.

Seeing Ebonee's comfort inclined Retta to perceive her own, her body fusing into an antenna. The pine trees flanking the highway melted into a sage blur as she focused her perception on herself: her sciatica was a murmur rather than a siren; the calluses on her hands were not rigid puffs; her arthritic shoulders did not sing Whitney's greatest hits, disc two. She was completely at ease.

Perhaps the truck was a blessing in disguise. Retta had reserved a midsize sedan, but she ended up with a pickup truck the size of a carport. Retta normally would have contested such a slight, as she hadn't driven a truck since Ma and Pop crashed their Ranger. Bad vibes, she'd been dutifully not explaining for years. But the urgency of reaching the scene had expunged all that anxiety. And look at her now, whipping this behemoth like it was a BMX bike. Was that all it took to overcome death? One small change in habit? Retta bristled at her own hubris. Not only had she dove deeper into a profession that death routinely defied; she was becoming death's scorekeeper. She missed the doldrums of her practice.

"Everything all right?" Ebonee asked.

Retta focused her attention on the road. A moment later, a warm scented hand skated over Retta's right cheek, which was apparently wet. I'm crying? she thought. Ebonee's hand drifted to her shoulder and offered a gentle squeeze, a gesture of acknowledgment and empathy rather than inquiry.

After a few miles, Retta spoke. "What scent is that?"

"Some shit my little sister gave me. Queen Tone? I don't really understand the name."

"It smells good on you."

"I appreciate it," Ebonee said. "I've never even worn it before. I just wanted a little safeguard. These sites always smell so intense. They make me feel like I'm losing myself, if that makes any sense."

They arrived and parked, idling in the truck to ready themselves. The scene was mobbed with press and emergency personnel. Retta felt envious of the EMTs, journalists, and officers in their branded shirts and hats. The EIS didn't issue swag, in any sense of the word.

"Take this," Retta said, fishing a face mask from her purse, which was stuffed into a cup holder the size of a pressure cooker. She handed it to Ebonee, and they exited the vehicle.

Retta approached the police line and asked a muscular officer to notify Detective Bobby Ray Leonard that EIS had arrived.

"E, I, S?" the officer said after he babbled police talk into a shoulder-mounted radio. His thick hands rested on his thicker shoulders as if at any moment he might be called to pull rip cords from his bulletproof vest. "Let me guess. I'm great with acronyms."

"No," Retta said.

Retta walked away from Musclehead and scanned the parking lot. The industrial park that housed Zora's Natural Soaps was a smattering of loading docks, dingy storefronts, and new religious movements posing as churches. Retta observed the members of one such movement—Children of the Immaculate Christ—irritably interact with an aloof police officer. They seemed to want to enter their church.

"Fucking scammers," Muscles said without prompt. He had a mobile post, apparently. "I ain't never seen no church where every member looks like a fucking all-American. Look at them girls' backs. They make Ronda Rousey look like a crackhead. I think they're a militia."

Retta moved away from him again, focusing on Zora's, which had the manic foot traffic of a decapitated anthill.

Retta turned to Ebonee and gestured toward the steady stream of cops. "All these people in and out, there's not gonna be much to see by the time this detective shows up."

"I don't need to see anything," Ebonee replied.

"It's not the same as the video," Retta said, "which is in circulation because Zora streamed it, may I remind you. This is for our eyes only."

Ebonee huffed. "My eyes have had enough. My nose too. We've done this four times now, may I remind you. Ain't no new knowledge to be gained from staring into another black hole." She held up her phone. "Everything we need is in here."

"It ain't just a hole, and we ain't fucking cryptographers, so you need to chill," Retta said.

Muscles reappeared and lifted the police tape. "Detective Leonard's around back."

"Thanks," Ebonee said, pressing past him.

Retta followed, avoiding the gazes of the cops they passed, who seemed to all be trapped in a tense fugue state. Retta did not feel endangered, but she also did not feel secure, a common feeling when she was in the presence of the law. Perhaps the point of the police tape was to rein in the cops.

Homicide detective Bobby Ray Leonard was a chain combo of greetings and handshakes and mandates. Retta and Ebonee were not to touch anything, interfere with anything, or question anyone without his explicit permission. They were only here to advise and observe. If he got a whiff of anything more, they'd be sent back to Georgia. No disrespect to their expertise. They were probably very insightful, knowledgeable ladies, but an officer of the law had been killed. Though they already had a suspect, he spoke with urgency.

He paused to confirm Ebonee and Retta's understanding. They nodded.

Confirmation in hand, he led them to a low rusted door, then stopped at its threshold. Retta frowned at Ebonee, who had already put on her face mask. Their differences aside, they could both agree that guy was a massive prick.

Ebonee assumed an after-you pose, and Retta stepped through the door, slipping her own face mask on as she entered. The shop floor had the busyness of a janitor's closet and the openness of a luxury retailer. Shelves filled with neatly labeled ingredients lined the walls and grazed the ceiling; stainless steel workstations and sinks were splashed with colors and jagged scores; a massive fan thrummed above like an indifferent god. Floral, herbal, and chemical scents commingled without interacting—strangers awaiting introductions at a mixer. Retta checked her mask.

It was difficult to not think of the video LSP had sent her as she milled about its birthplace. The police had trimmed the clip, recorded by the dead cop's body camera, into a rewatchable nugget. In twenty-two seconds, a white man roped to a chair appears in profile, then offscreen the voice alleged to be Zora instructs him to "Tell them who you are." He identifies himself as a cop, to which she replies, "Wrong answer," then forces his mouth open and pours a brilliant black liquid into his throat. The video ends.

Retta stopped in front of a giant tub of lye to gather her thoughts. The instinctive question was why was this happening, but she'd asked that at every scene. She'd also wondered who was putting these people up to this, another dead end. She was an agent of health, not justice. She'd once thought the two pursuits were intertwined, but lawmen never felt like kin. At the scene, at the fusion center, and at home in Metter, they obsessed over bodies and nothing else. Catch them, manage them, punish them. They looked at these bodies, often scrupulously, but never through them, around them. That narrowness was the actual thin blue line, a strained squint misunderstood as deep focus.

"We're lucky this shit didn't spread and explode," Detective Leonard said.

"Lye isn't flammable," Retta said. She pointed at the lye tub's label. "Don't feel bad; it's a common misconception."

"I know how lye works, Doctor. I meant whatever that witch gave my partner. You got any intel on that? I know you're here as an observer, but feel free to share what you see. The State of Louisiana has its own public health agency. Your offer was one of many, if you understand what I'm saying."

She did. "I've seen nothing you haven't."

"Well then, I guess that there's the end of the CDC and LSP collaboration. It's been great working with you."

Retta looked for Ebonee and walked to her, Leonard's gaze on her back. Ebonee was stationed in front of a framed photograph of Zora and a flank of women. They were shot in portrait, standing with their chests puffed like spring robins, their arms crossed or akimbo. Ebonee's mask dangled from her fingers as she stared at the photograph, apparently unfazed by the smell.

"We've got to go," Retta said. "There's nothing here."

"No, this is something," Ebonee said, pointing at the photograph.

Retta examined it. Just looked like proud black women, frankly. They appeared healthy and youthful, but that also struck Retta as inessential.

Retta returned the friendly squeeze Ebonee had given her in the truck. "We need to go."

Ebonee obliged and they filed out.

"What did you see?" Retta asked as they approached the rental vehicle. Her face mask felt like a shield as they swam through the throng of reporters, which had grown since they viewed the scene.

"I saw a busy next couple of days."

"Amen to that," Retta said, documenting the deflection for further review. They climbed in the truck and proceeded to the hotel with the windows down, wind screaming between them.

The Garvey Inn & Suites received them indifferently. The unrushed receptionist, the drowsy elevator, and the heavy door to her room resisted Retta's urgent need to forget another day of wearying travel and bewildering death. She tried to decipher Ebonee's reticence as she tucked her bonnet behind her ears and sank into a sea of pillows, but exhaustion and the pleasant image of Ronda Rousey uppercutting Leonard and Musclehead nudged her into sleep.

• • •

Ebonee plopped beside Retta at the hotel breakfast bar. "I've never seen a breakfast bar taken so . . ."

"Indulgently?" Retta said, lifting up her Bloody Mary.

Ebonee grinned. "Is this how you do it on your girls trips?"

"Not quite. First of all, this is virgin, and second, I'm usually swatting away a married man or two."

"Well too bad; you had me excited for a second. Thought I was gonna get to be mama bear today."

Retta's thick hurricane glass hit the bar with a thud. "Mama bear? I ain't nobody's mama."

"You say that, but I don't think you believe it."

"I'll stop treating you like a child when you stop acting like one." Retta took a generous gulp.

"I'm not the one who threw a tantrum and pissed off our only contact."

"Well, I'm not the one who pissed off me. Are you going to explain what you saw yesterday?"

Silence.

"This is what I'm talking about. You don't respect me." Retta waved at the bartender.

"I'm not dissing you. I'm trying to protect us. Because we're way past public health."

"Changed your mind, ma'am?" the bartender asked, his hand extending toward Retta's drink.

"Do you have to say *ma'am*?'" Retta asked. "I'm fifty-two. What's wrong with *miss* or *madam*? *Ma'am* makes me feel like somebody's auntie." The bartender froze, mouth taut, hand cupping Retta's drink.

Ebonee chimed in. "She's fine for now. Thank you." The man bowed and slipped away.

"You know you are somebody's auntie, right?"

"You don't get to decide who gets protected. I'm just as deep in this shit as you. I should get a say. You think I don't also feel overwhelmed and pressured? Scared? We both know this is somebody's vendetta. And I'm just as lost in it and fascinated by it as you are."

Ebonee fell silent again then placed her phone on the bar. The rose-gold device sparkled against the black slate bar top like a pearl in loam. Ebonee did not interact with it; the way her gaze rested on her lap, she seemed to be avoiding it. Retta swirled her nearly depleted drink, wondering whether she should order another one.

It had been quite refreshing, a word she had never associated with a Bloody Mary. Her tongue scoured her gums and teeth. Was that mint she detected? Maybe marjoram?

"What the hell are you doing?" Ebonee said.

"I'm appreciating my drink. What are you doing? We've got contact tracing to do."

"Contact tracing? But this agent isn't even infectious." She paused. "Oh, that's the work-around." She fiddled with her braids. "You know, without the LSP escort, there's a chance we run into Leonard or the Department of Health. Are you willing to take that risk? You know they love any excuse to say 'states' rights' down here."

"It's either that or you stare at your fucking phone all day while I get ma'am'ed." She stopped and looked closely at Ebonee's phone. "You're still using that app, aren't you?"

"Just for research. Let's go."

Retta added the latest deflection to the tally and closed her tab.

Moments later they were on the road, en route to the home of Marley Carter, Zora's aunt. The drive to the woman's trailer was a straight shot from the hotel: a right out the parking lot, a left onto a dirt lot, with a heap of trees and factories in between. Retta had forgotten how functional country roads could be.

Retta stepped out of the truck and sized up the small lot. Verdant flower beds and manicured bushes softened the abrasive smell of industry, which made Retta's breaths feel heavy and final. She stood back as Ebonee knocked on the screen door. A woman spoke from inside, her voice faint and unsteady like a weak radio signal. She declined to identify herself and had nothing more to say, she said with exhaustion. Ebonee immediately turned away and headed back to the truck. Retta remained. "Your garden is beautiful, ma'am," Retta said. No response. The woman kept her word. Retta returned to the truck.

Their next destination was the residence of Susan Eggers, an employee of Zora's Natural Soaps. She lived far from Carter, on a shady cul-de-sac at the end of a winding gravel road. They parked in a long crooked driveway pocked with cracks. Retta tapped on the screen door of a squat bungalow, the smell of hot oil and cornmeal mixing awkwardly with the fishy must of a nearby creek. A silver-haired, butterscotch-skinned woman appeared behind the screen door dressed in an apron, a tank top, and bunched sweatpants. A gleaming black spatula extended from the hand that wasn't on her hip.

"Can I help you?" she said.

Ebonee replied. "Yes, we're with the CDC, looking for Susan Eggers."

"This about Zora?"

"It is, ma'am. Can we come inside?"

"You gon' have to. I'm cooking." Susan opened the door, and Ebonee and Retta were led into a cramped kitchen where floured fish fillets lined a linoleum counter and oil crackled inside a Dutch oven. Susan seated them at a round table with multiple saltshakers corralled in its center. "Where y'all from?" Susan asked as she retrieved golden fillets from the stove and placed them on a rusted drying rack.

"I'm from South Georgia, ma'am," Retta said.

"I'm from Atlanta, ma'am," Ebonee said.

"Y'all sure say *ma'am* a lot," Susan said as she dunked new fillets into the oven. Retta frowned at Ebonee, who was looking at Susan. "Also, I meant where are you coming from. I'm guessing Atlanta. That's headquarters, yeah?"

"Sure is," Ebonee said.

"I had a lot of family move to Atlanta after Katrina and then even more after Jena Six. Y'all remember that?"

"We do, miss," Retta said. (Yeesh, *miss* was awkward as hell, she thought.) "I didn't live in Atlanta at the time of Katrina, but my church had a clothing drive, and I had some neighbors who took in some family. As for the Jena Six, I'm from a small town. We never came up with a name for ours, but we got more than six."

"Mhm," Susan hummed as she delivered two tall glasses of iced tea to the table. Flour smudges gave the glasses an awkward murk. It smelled great though. A sip confirmed it was infused with sugar and lemon.

"So what can I do for you?" Susan asked. "Y'all ain't the police and I ain't no snitch, so don't ask me nothing you don't got no business asking."

"Of course," Ebonee said. "We want to know about the Black Guard."

Susan glared at Ebonee then turned toward the stove. "Let me finish up this breakfast. My husband has to go to work soon." Retta avoided looking at Ebonee; they'd discussed the questions they'd ask whoever came to the door, but the "Black Guard" hadn't come up. Retta let the chips fall.

Susan moved fish from the pot to the drying rack then from the counter to the pot, the gargle of the oil the kitchen's sole sound. Then she removed plates from the cabinet and set the table for four. Guess we're joining them for breakfast, Retta thought. Susan moved about the small space nimbly, drawers opening and closing, measuring cups and pots filling and emptying with a casual rhythm. After a spell, Susan's bustle was punctuated with a shout. "Earl, breakfast is ready. Get down here. And make sure you're dressed. We got guests."

Retta and Ebonee sat still. Contact tracing was a delicate enterprise. Participation was voluntary and necessarily begrudging. Retta understood the hesitance. It was easy to question the value of public health when it required such arbitrary and awkward invasions of privacy. Why would anyone be eager to talk to a stranger about the time they caught vaccine-resistant gonorrhea on vacation? Or the frat kegger where they contracted mononucleosis? Or the monthly orgy that was also a conjunctivitis hot spot? And those were just the ailments that could be blushed away, not the ones that produced lesions and scars and corpses.

A tall, thick man with a molasses-brown complexion stomped into the kitchen in worn gray coveralls. "Smells great, baby," he said as he examined the multiple pots and pans Susan had enlisted for breakfast. He opened a cabinet and removed a syrup bottle and a massive bottle of Qrystal hot sauce. "Who y'all?"

"They're with the CDC," Susan said.

Earl whistled with delight. "That creek got runoff in it, don't it? Finally, we can get the fuck out of here." He shook Ebonee's and Retta's hands with fervor.

"I'd be happy to put you in touch with a friend at the EPA, but we're here to inquire about Susan's employer, Zora's Natural Soaps," Retta said.

"Oh," Earl said as he sat down at the table.

"We were asking about the Black Guard," Ebonee said. "When we were in Zora's shop, I recognized the insignia in a picture on the wall. I took a history class on black self-defense groups in the South a long time ago," Ebonee said. "A few things stuck."

"Some things you can't learn in a class," Earl said.

Susan cut in. "He's our newest member," she said as she placed serving plates on the table. Heapings of fish fillets, cheese grits, and corn cakes formed a ring around the salt. "That's why he so mad."

Retta watched Earl and Ebonee fidget about as the table filled, the room tense until Susan sat. Earl filled his plate and quickly began to slather hot sauce across his food. Retta and Ebonee followed. Retta was surprised that Susan and Earl didn't say grace. They seemed like the type.

Susan halved and quartered her food into bite-size pieces as she spoke, rarely stopping to actually eat. "The Guard goes back a few generations. My grandmother was in it, along with Zora's aunt and mother. We supposedly formed after a lynching, but no one knows which one."

"How often do you meet?" Ebonee asked and took a generous bite of a crispy fish fillet.

"As often as necessary. These days, we mostly focus on handling guns. Storing, shooting, cleaning, licensing."

"Been in this county fifteen years and I ain't hear nothing about it till three years ago," Earl said as he refilled his plate. He sounded more amused than upset.

"Used to be ladies only," Susan said. "Started allowing the men 'cause they was getting jealous." She reached over and pinched Earl's ear.

"So why are you still active?" Ebonee asked.

Susan paused her cutting. "Just maintaining."

"I see," Retta said aloud, more for Ebonee's understanding than her own. "What's your mission?" God, why am I talking like Ebonee? Retta thought as she prepared a bite. She revised her question. "What would happen if you disbanded?"

"Same things that been happening," Susan said. "Our county loves to fine people that they know ain't got no money. They'll charge you for sewage in your yard that their damn burst pipes put there. For not showing up in court on a date they set in the middle of the day. For not registering the clunker sitting in your driveway that you can't afford to fix. For illegal fishing at a spot with no signage—they go put the sign up after you get charged, of course. And licenses ain't cheap." She sighed and brought one of her many morsels to her mouth. "The Guard just reminds everyone we're not alone."

"Did Zora act alone?" Ebonee asked.

Susan scoffed. "Now I told y'all I ain't talking about nobody's business but my own."

Earl rose from the table, his plate spotless. "I gotta get on to the shop," he said. "Y'all ain't park behind me, did you?" Hint, hint.

Retta furnished the keys. "I think we did. Ebonee, can you move it?" Ebonee emptied her plate then took the keys and followed Earl out. "You're an excellent cook," Retta said as she sopped up her last bit of grits with a corn cake.

"Thank you," Susan said. She rose and began clearing the table.

If Retta wanted to salvage this excursion, this was her only chance. She thought of her own foray into radicalism as Susan bustled about. It was decidedly cosmetic, a semester-long adoption of "organic" as the organizing principle of all her consumption, overly permissive embrace of kente cloth, and countless heated discussions about the revolutionary potential of slam poetry. She had been on the verge of a deeper transformation—she loved Anne Moody and Angela Davis, and some bell hooks texts were loitering somewhere in her attic—but when she went back to Candler County after spring semester with her hair plaited and her face undone, she felt plain. She had become more normal instead of more distinct. That wasn't the purpose of college.

But maybe she'd underestimated plainness. Susan had cooked for a stranger, spoken freely of a controversial militia, and done the work of organizing her people against terror—all while living a normal life.

Retta asked, "Between me and you and nobody else, what did the cop do?"

Susan poured cooking oil into a large porcelain cup. Retta watched as the mixture eased out of the Dutch oven, hot and fluid as a revolution. Susan was patient, cautious, like any good cook.

Retta matched her cadence, saying nothing, thinking little as Susan cleaned dishes, wiped surfaces, emptied glasses.

When Ebonee returned, Retta directed her to the table with an authoritative finger.

Susan kept tidying up, kept taunting. Her silence was interrogative: How far are you willing to go? Retta didn't know, but she had left her house, her state, her soft hotel bed with its deluge of pillows. Pretty damn far, she felt.

"I don't trust you," Susan said as she stopped moving. She leaned onto the refrigerator, photos and magnets scattering around her shoulders. "But you're the only ones who can find the person who pushed Zora this far. She's had a rough couple of years, but she wasn't raised like that. When she wanted to kill herself, she would tell me and I'd come collect her guns." Susan whispered as she wiped tears from her cheeks, "The Guard has a system."

Retta offered a tissue. Susan waved her away.

"I'm not asking for your sympathy," she said. "I'm telling you to put a bullet in that motherfucker."

Retta grimaced. She was not an assassin. Nor was Zora a victim. Manipulated or not, the girl, like the dead cop, whatever he had done, had made a choice. Choices had consequences. Retta's eyes rested on the linoleum counter, avoiding Susan's gaze. All Retta needed to do was lie, a quick fib to lubricate the moment, end it.

But she couldn't speak. Inertia stalled in Retta's throat, sauntered through her thoughts. Deep in the engine of her mind, in the humid nook of vengeances plotted but unconsummated, Retta knew she too hated this phantom puppeteer. Dragging her away from her work, wasting rare talent on death, distant from consequences and corpses. Far too distant. A bullet might be too merciful.

The moment passed.

"But what's done is done," Susan said. "That cop had it coming to him anyway. We got a lot of people who did time around here. For years, Lancer would hire them for odd jobs over the county line. Raids on drug dealers, shakedowns for loan sharks, things like that. Convicts were cheap labor. Money was too good to turn down, so a lot of these knuckleheads took it, but then they got trapped. Lancer would take videos of the gigs, threaten to tell their POs, 'gift' them guns for protection, all kinds of low-down shit. Zora's brother got caught up like that, pulled over with a gun with bodies on it. Doing life at Angola now, so I guess Lancer's life is a fair trade."

"Shit," Retta said.

"I know," Susan said. "I look forward to seeing the CDC solve this one."

They all laughed.

The visit concluded with filled Tupperware and hugs and intel on the best local spot for crawdad étouffée, but Retta resented the enduring lack of closure. Four scenes, five bodies, two trips out of state.

"Worried about how we're going to return those containers?" Ebonee asked as they idled in the truck. Retta had turned the key and nothing else. Too many paths stretched ahead.

"No, no," she said. "Just thinking about what to do next. It's still early. Maybe I should apologize to Leonard."

Ebonee laughed. "Or you could not do that and we could hit the flea market we passed yesterday, the pool, the crawdad spot, and the bar. In that order. I think we've done enough for today."

Retta's foot eased off the brake.

Hours later, Retta began to toast to Ebonee's lifesaving itinerary, but her glass was empty. "One more round?" she asked Ebonee, back at the hotel bar.

Ebonee's head rested on the bar, but her right thumb ascended upward. The girl couldn't drink to save her life, but she was trying. She always tried.

As the bartender prepared their drinks, Retta focused on the muted television screen, which displayed a cable news program awash in colored banners, skinny text, and a chyron.

The closed captions, delayed as always, were lapped by the images, which kept changing. A black man's face. Helicopter view of a house. Somewhere in the suburbs. Is that Atlanta? Retta wondered. The face appeared again. The man was rather handsome. Young too. Well, younger than Retta.

Retta focused on the captions:

```
GBI CONFIRMS SUSPECT
IN BLACKOUTS HAS BEEN IDENTIFIED
AND FOUND
DEAD IN ATLANTA HOME.
```

Tumbling Stone Magazine
July 31, 1998

"The Bomb Breaker"
by Marshall Hunter

BATON ROUGE, Louis. — Detective Bobby Ray Leonard is inked like a sailor, tattoos streaming down his muscled arms and across his chiseled back. On an unseasonably warm July day, we're swimming in a cool, still water hole he's asked me not to identify because it's the one place in Baton Rouge where no one can reach him. He was a Navy SEAL in a past life that he's recently turned nostalgic for. "Back then I took orders rather than gave them," he tells me in his molasses-thick drawl. The water is his refuge.

You'd think capturing Manuel Noriega and clobbering Saddam Hussein would be enough action for one lifetime, but when Leonard came home after six years of duty, he went straight to the Louisiana State Police academy. Now he's the state's top investigator of bombings and arson. In the week I spend with him, shadowing him as he consults on cases across the state and country, attends trials, and processes an endless stream of paperwork, this swim is the only respite he takes. In his words, it's the only rest he can afford. We idle for just an hour. He's got a court date.

He didn't intend to become the bomb breaker, as he's known in law enforcement circles across the country. His parents, Robert

Leonard, MD, and Rachel Leonard, Esq., strong supporters of education, were floored by his decision to join the police, disapproving until his second year on the force. When Rachel Leonard retrieved the *Times-Picayune* off their wide porch one morning, her son's choice finally made sense. "There was a large disarmed bomb on the table of some kind of dinky shack, and he stood behind it, grinning like it was Christmas day," she recalls from her small practice in downtown Baton Rouge as we drink tea so sweet it'd make Scarlett O'Hara blush.

After eight months undercover, her son had foiled a neo-Nazi plot to bomb an African American fraternity house at Louisiana State University. As we head to the sentencing hearing for a member of the Aryan Hammer, the group that he infiltrated, he takes me to the start of the case that changed his life, and perhaps his state, forever.

*

The Aryan Hammer, one of Louisiana's many neo-Nazi militia groups, recruited Leonard inside a Veterans Administration hospital, a common hunting ground for such groups, which are active across the state.

It was his day off and he was visiting a comatose friend when he was approached by Joseph "Bear" Campbell, a barrel of a man who loved to spin a good yarn—always with a tragic white protagonist. That day, Bear told Leonard the story of Peter White, a red-blooded American infantryman who got an early holiday after a grueling tour and came home to find his wife in bed with two other men. Black men. He beat the men to death and turned himself in.

At White's trial, Campbell said, the serviceman pleaded not guilty, and his counsel argued that his reputation and impeccable service record proved this episode was uncharacteristic. But none of White's commanding officers or fellow soldiers would take the stand. He received a life sentence.

At the end of White's story, Campbell nodded at Leonard's incapacitated friend. "This could be you one day."

Leonard saw both the bullshit and the opportunity in Campbell's pitch. He's six three, blond, and more brick than the Thing, so it wasn't his first time being solicited by neo-Nazis. He's their type, down to his solemn azure eyes. But it was the first time he thought they might be his type too.

As we weave through traffic on the way to the courthouse, Leonard picks apart Campbell's pitch. One soldier beat two men to death then turned himself in? He's seen enough of military life to know the plausible versions of that story. That soldier would have shot the men. Or shot himself. Or assaulted his wife after she dismissed her partners. Or bowed to karma as his wife's arrangement of limbs called to mind his first night in Manila with his brothers-in-arms. Leonard took Campbell's card with a knowing smirk.

Leonard wasn't flirting with white nationalism, he assures me. He was just a beat cop that wanted to make detective. Not only did the detectives at his precinct not have to wear uniforms, showing up to work in slick suspenders, stylish panamas, and minimal oxfords;

they were respected: in the union, in the community, by the FBI and ATF. Leonard wanted that.

He was respected as a veteran, but obliquely: on holidays, in uniform, with other veterans. The detectives reaped the full benefits of their service: higher pay, more vacation days, free spaghetti plates and hurricanes at the local haunts. Magazine profiles?

"That's a new one, I reckon."

His first day back at work after meeting Campbell, Leonard talked to his sergeant, who was intrigued and paired him with seasoned detective Richard Spicer. The sergeant trusted Spicer to quickly find out whether Campbell was a standard idiot deadbeat like most neo-Nazis or something more sinister.

Spicer, who is the only other person Leonard ever told about the watering hole, died at home earlier this year after choking on an andouille sausage. Leonard declined this profile multiple times because a late-night host joked about his partner's death a few weeks afterward. I tell him that's entertainment, not journalism, but he doesn't care. He hates all publicity. The only reason he's yakking to me, he reminds me multiple times, is that it's the best way to show his fellow bomb breakers what they're up against.

*

Leonard didn't start off so hot. The Hammer investigation began as a reconnaissance mission. Leonard set up a meeting with the neo-Nazis and they bit, giving him the address of a rock quarry just past the Baton Rouge airport. Spicer sensed early on that these neo-Nazis weren't posers, case records show. Quarry workers typically had access to explosives, the premier neo-Nazi means of carnage and mayhem.

"Like their namesake, all neo-Nazis are cowards," Leonard says with contempt as we idle at a red light.

His first encounter with the Hammer was tame. After Leonard parked in an unfinished lot, Campbell and two muscle-bound enforcer types beckoned him into a trailer. When he emerged four hours later unmolested, Spicer knew they were onto something.

"Tiny organizations like the Hammer are vulnerable to infiltration, so they are very suspicious of new recruits," says Leonard's new partner, Richard Lancer. "The fact that he got in so easily told me that we had the right guy, and that the Nazis were trying to make a move."

The neo-Nazis explicitly asked Leonard in that first meeting what he knew about explosives; it was clear they were aiming for the sky. Lancer, a former corrections officer, joined the investigation soon after and used his network of informants to train Leonard in the ways of neo-Nazis.

He learned all the slurs and the talking points about protecting white women, jobs, and culture, embracing white heritage, and restoring white pride.

"It's all bullshit, so it's easy to remember," Leonard tells me as we sit in his car, folders spread across the dash. We've arrived at the courthouse early, and he wants to refresh his memory of today's case. These days, it's one of many. He finds his report from six months into his investigation, when he had almost had his cover blown. He declines to speak about it on the record.

His report is less coy. The bombing he'd eventually foil was not imminent, though it appeared that way at first. The Hammer onboarded him swiftly, enthralled by his combat experience and technical expertise. With help from Spicer and an old police-academy buddy, he expanded his government-issued radio repair skills into deep knowledge of improvised explosives, building them and detonating them on the expansive wooded property of the Brooks brothers, two former linemen who were the only Hammer members bigger than Leonard.

After two months of training and occasional interrogations, the program abruptly stopped as the Hammer life shifted from race war to fraternity. Instead of backwoods creeks and utility sheds, Leonard found himself at cookouts, dive bars, and strip clubs. The sudden casualness sowed doubts. Beneath the theater of hate and vengeance, might the Hammer be just a social club? He wasn't sure. Even worse, he began to like his marks.

Campbell was a joy when he wasn't hawking white superiority, it turns out. He'd been a miner and an oiler throughout Texas and had a well of colorful stories. The other guys also weren't so bad, Leonard recalls.

I see these men at the hearing. They don't look like Nazis to me; they look lost and rudderless. But I'll take Leonard's word that they're the bad guys. The court certainly has. Lancaster Brooks is sentenced to forty years in prison. Despite the decisive victory, Leonard streaks past the African American family whose son was a member of the fraternity the Hammer targeted, not even stopping for a handshake.

He's got more bombs to break.

*

Back in Leonard's office, which is flush with binders, we revisit the turning point in the case. The women of the neo-Nazi circle were an even greater challenge than the men. Leonard's cover depended on him not being particularly intimate with the Hammer's dozen or so members, which was easy, "Because Nazis aren't soldiers," Leonard says. (All soldiers can relate to one another, he claims.) But the women swooned. Leonard speaks of this attention with humility, noting that if he were more attractive than the average neo-Nazi, it was probably only because he doesn't smoke and maintains his SEAL regimen of daily runs and regular weight training.

He's certainly a stud, but he was also swimming against the tide. Neo-Nazis are small fringe groups, explains anthropologist Kierstin Stephens of Xavier University, who studies white nationalist groups in Louisiana. She's quite the Aryan herself, her eyes frost blue and her blonde locks creamed-corn yellow. "Unless they have strong, binding norms, small communities can be very disrupted by newness. Think of the way small offices or businesses or classrooms can drastically change with the addition or loss of one person, especially if that person is charismatic or in a position of leadership, like a teacher or manager."

Leonard's coyness almost tanked the operation. When he rebuffed one particularly insistent Nazi-lover because she was close to Campbell, she threatened to tell the group about the time she had seen him at the movies with a black woman. Leonard had been two counties over, but apparently that wasn't enough. He was blown. "Officer exercised poor judgment in personal life," his report records tersely in his neat manuscript.

He told Spicer and Lancer of his mistake, and they began plotting to extract him without incident.

But then something extraordinary happened. We'll call it Chekhov's threesome.

Campbell came home one day and saw an unfamiliar car in his driveway. Concerned, and always paranoid, he called Leonard, who arrived a few minutes later. They circled the perimeter and saw Campbell's worst nightmare through a back window. His Aryan queen was tangled up with two black men in the master bedroom. And she was visibly, audibly, enjoying herself.

Campbell turned away in disgust and told Leonard to follow him to another quarry a few towns over, where they stole dynamite and other incendiaries from an unmanned and unlocked warehouse. Leonard is still dismayed by how unguarded it was.

"We just pulled right up like it was a goddamn drive-through," he says. Then they drove off. Fearing for the woman's life, when Leonard and Campbell parted back in town, Leonard called Lancer and told him to collect her before the neo-Nazi could return home.

Leonard's Roman jaw softens as he recounts the absurd prophecy come true. "It was such a custom-ordered snub, like he was Job and God allowed Satan to make a fool of him. I still wonder whether it was a setup of some sort. It was so perfect. Like a miracle almost." A smile breaks at that last line. He's enjoying this trip down memory lane.

The woman, whose name we are withholding because she's now in the federal Witness Security Program (commonly known as witness protection), confirmed the encounter took place as described but denied any third parties arranged it and declined to put *Tumbling Stone* in contact with her paramours.

"When the universe gives you a break, you take it," Lancer says. He dismisses my questions about his network of informants possibly playing a role in the ménage à trois deus ex machina. "Seduction can't be arranged," he says, a take Samson, Shakespeare, and Ian Fleming would surely dispute.

With Chekhov's blessing, the investigation ramped up. Soon after the frictionless heist, the Hammer returned to scouting, visiting black churches, day care centers, neighborhoods, recreation facilities, and restaurants to finalize targets. To Leonard's surprise,

Campbell didn't ever seek the woman, instead focusing the group's efforts on growing their arsenal and their ranks.

Leonard split his time between an unemployment office, where Campbell tasked him with finding new recruits (he refused to solicit soldiers), and Campbell's basement, which Spicer and Lancer had miked.

In late April 1993, Campbell finally gave the investigation legs. One night, he was visiting a university campus to acquire some marijuana from a student dealer, and he saw a gaggle of gorgeous Aryan women emerge from an African American fraternity house, their bodies flushed with pleasure. It disgusted him so much that that same night he assembled the Hammer for an announcement: on June 19, 1993, which is a holiday commemorating the Emancipation Proclamation for some African Americans in the Ark-La-Tex area, the Hammer would come down.

Leonard had never heard of Juneteenth (nor had this writer), but he knew he had a winning case. Between the holiday, the target, Leonard's story, and the scouting of black locales, the Hammer could be charged with every hate crime on the books.

The next day, Leonard, Spicer, Lancer, and a task force of state police officers and US Marshals rounded up the Hammer without incident.

Leonard instantly was crowned a hero, the local press fawning over him and his colleagues greeting him with applause his first day back to work. Leonard had earned their respect, and his supervisor nominated him to take the detective test.

But he refused to bask. As he prepared for the exam and for months of testimony, he began to sift through police records about local bombings.

*

Baton Rouge, like many Southern cities, has burned for most of this century, racialized violence razing homes and sometimes neighborhoods. David Duke's failed presidential (1988) and gubernatorial campaigns (1991) brought this sordid history to national attention, but for longtime residents it's a fact of life. From the many statues honoring the Confederacy to parishes named after Andrew Jackson and Jefferson Davis to the neo-Nazis and Klan chapters, Louisiana is awash in blood and hate.

One area of the state drew Leonard's eye. In Iberville Parish, to the south of Baton Rouge, a string of cases stood out: for seven bizarre months, white homes and churches had been bombed. No deaths or injuries were reported, but the case fascinated Leonard. Could there be black militants flying under the radar?

As the Hammer trials got underway, Leonard made detective and was immediately put on homicide with Lancer. Homicide brought no shortage of work and more bullets than bombs, but in his limited spare time, Leonard kept returning to Iberville. The lead investigator on the Iberville bombings was Delroy Hawkins, an African American, Leonard learned as he dug deeper.

I ask Leonard why Hawkins's race mattered to him as he rummages through files. "They're few and far between in my experience, but there are cops who have been outed as white supremacists. Why wouldn't that be true for a black cop? Crazy leap, I know, but it's just due diligence. Gotta consider all angles."

To scratch that itch, Leonard arranged to meet Hawkins. The former detective had retired to New Iberia, an hour-plus southwest of Baton Rouge, so one Saturday Leonard hit I-10 West, snaking through the verdant Atchafalaya National Wildlife Refuge and hooking south on LA-347, an emphatically less beautiful stretch.

The meeting was tense. Hawkins welcomed Leonard's tenacity but disliked his naivete. "No one takes to a fool's errand like a fool," Hawkins says from the neat living room of his row house in downtown New Iberia. "He's chasing racists through bayous when there's racists walking distance from his desk. I told him that. And I told him a black supremacist was the kind of phrase only a cop would take seriously."

Hawkins does not have a flattering view of the police, especially detectives. "They get the most resources to do the least thinking," he huffs as we drink an exotic black coffee redolent with citrus and incense. He holds up his mug. "Take this, for example. This brew comes from the best coffeehouse in the state, which I shit you not is in Plaquemine. I never knew because I was loyal to a diner by my precinct. Every damn day, I walked past this world-class spot that's won awards and where I've now befriended the owner. Detectives spot routines because they follow routines. And routines lie."

Leonard found his elder prickly but encouraging. Though Hawkins stood by his cases, he did not deter Leonard's investigation. "He seemed like the kind of person who learned through failure, so I gave him everything he needed to get high marks," Hawkins says.

"He didn't believe in me at all," Leonard tells me as we continue to sift through case files at his desk. It's dusk now, and the station is quiet and dim as the shift changes. Night looms. Leonard finds the files for the case that made him the state's bomb czar and breaks out in a grin. "But I believed."

*

Leonard returned from Iberia determined to best the grumpy retiree. Where Hawkins saw cold cases with no bodies and no value to terrorized black communities, Leonard saw a lack of initiative. So what if white neighborhoods and structures weren't bombed as often as black ones? So what if known neo-Nazi organizations outnumbered black militant ones twenty-five to one? The facts were the facts. Bombs are unlawful and chaotic. If the bomber changed tactics or missed a target, anyone could be hurt. Black or white.

His success with the Aryan Hammer case helped his superiors look past his shaky logic. Leonard's supervising lieutenant gave him free rein as long as he prioritized homicides, so Leonard spent his ever-diminishing free time revisiting the principal findings from Hawkins's cases.

It was obvious a single party was responsible. From July 1987 to February 1988, a bomb a month—seven in total—went off across

Plaquemine, Louisiana, bringing down two Episcopalian churches and five residences, and spooking residents. The pattern was discerned after the fourth explosion. Each explosive was placed by a load-bearing structure, in daylight, then detonated with a fuse. And all the bombings took place on a Saturday—the seventh day of the week.

Hawkins had logged all of these odd symmetries but was stumped by the motive. He agreed that bombs are for cowards (and claims to have taught Leonard the phrase, which Leonard denies) as well as communicators. But these bombs' maker was the silent type.

There was no clear reason the churches and homes had been targeted; the bombers never sent a communiqué to the local paper or left any evidence at the scene. And the targets had little in common beyond a shared zip code. Plus, both the houses of worship and the domiciles were politically inactive and could cite no known adversaries or antagonists.

Hawkins squeezed some gambling dens and weekly card games a few times after the bombing campaign ended, thinking 7-7-7 represented some kind of aleatory cipher. But no dice. "I did the work, and I did the extracurriculars," Hawkins says. "You get only so many billable hours in your career to accomplish nothing."

Leonard pushed ahead, immersing himself in the town rather than the case files. Cruising and camping around the well-off side of Plaquemine in an unmarked vehicle, he learned the community's rhythms and cadences. The morning was a relay race: as cars full of white families exited the residential areas, car pools of domestic workers entered it, African American women in pressed uniforms vanishing into Greek Revivals and Creole cottages. Many of them smoked cigarettes, Leonard observed.

In tandem, nearby chemical plants began to rumble awake, smoke drifting out in puffs, then plumes, then thick, sinuous rivers that grayed the sky. By afternoon Leonard's car seat and clothes smelled of dust and chalk. Early on in his research, he would grab lunch at local shacks and pubs, hoping to converse with locals, but he found the town's current too strong to swim against. People ate, paid, and left.

Leonard decamped to the black side of town, where the time signature was harder to keep. The smoke never dissipated here, sitting atop the sky like cappuccino foam. Workers and residents slumped off buses and out of cars at all times of day, the streets never empty, the people never the same. No patterns emerged: they wore linen suits, designer jeans, work uniforms, discount sneakers, fourteen-karat gold chains, counterfeit designer watches. Their hair gleamed, bobbed, drooped, swished. Poor and rich looked alike, lived together.

Cops were just as irregular, gliding through streets at odd intervals and varying speeds, leaping from cars with and without warning.

"The only consistent thing over there was garbage collection," Leonard says with a wink as he spreads three mug shots across his desk.

A trio of sanitation workers turned out to be his men. Leonard noticed them when he resumed surveillance on the white side of town, the weeks of chaos heightening his attention to order. Brothers LeMarcus and Quentin Cartwright and their friend Nathan Toussey were fixtures among the domestic workers. On the days they swept through the neighborhood, the women would line the alleys and curbs and wave at them as if welcoming back soldiers from service.

What could garbagemen have done to earn such reverence? Through one of Lancer's informants, Leonard found out they did odd jobs across the community: masonry, carpentry, electrical repairs, construction. These were common skills for a blue-collar worker in a working-class town, but Leonard was intrigued. He pulled some strings then some records.

The brothers had been pinched but not charged for burglary a decade ago. At first, Leonard shrugged. A decade's a long time, and after seeing the Plaquemine police department ambush janitors and high school students in the street, he wasn't particularly impressed with their acumen.

(A Plaquemine Police Department spokesperson disputed this characterization.)

But then he looked into Toussey. Toussey was a former Army Ranger who served in Cambodia and Grenada and had a background in demolition. Bingo.

Leonard examined the sanitation department's attendance records. Though the men normally worked Saturdays, on the Saturdays of the bombings, they weren't in. Leonard had his first lead, but it wasn't enough for an arrest and certainly wouldn't secure a conviction. He had no fingerprints, no eyewitnesses, and a glut of physical evidence scorched to hell—no case, in other words.

He circled back to the seeming randomness of the targets, looking at the properties themselves rather than the occupants. A new pattern emerged. The church lots, he found out, were once black cemeteries. And the houses were all sites of reported lynchings. The bombings were shaping up to be acts of revenge.

What Leonard couldn't put together, though, was the emphasis on seven. By his count, Plaquemine had far more than seven reasons to piss off African American rebels. Why these targets? And why no deaths? He'd never heard of a black supremacist protecting white life.

The puzzle came together as he watched the trio, whom Leonard had started to tail, collect garbage. "It was like ballet the way they moved down streets and alleys. Instead of start, stop, start, stop, it was just one fluid motion," he says. Seeing the brothers Cartwright pirouette from house to house as Toussey kept the truck at a perfect creep, the compactor gnawing on glass and banana peels, he joked to himself that they would make excellent bank robbers. He didn't laugh.

Nor did he breathe. Nor did he drive. He put the car in park, turned it off, and stared ahead, as he's doing now. This time-stopping sensation is clearly the feeling he cherishes most about his line of work. He'd cracked it. The trio blew up the houses they'd robbed. The sevens meant nothing.

To close the case, he contacted the churches and the victims and had them compile a list of heirlooms, jewelry, and rarities that would catch a thief's eye but couldn't be duplicated or counterfeited. Then he got warrants for their apartments. On the days the warrants were served, Leonard's persistence proved fruitful. While cash and jewelry were expectedly long gone, the brothers were hoarding a Fulani clay bowl and a Maasai shield previously owned by the Jefferson family. And Toussey was in possession of a Rhodesian bullwhip, a silver-plated shell casing from one of the bullets that killed Black Panther Fred Hampton, and a bonnet once owned by Harriet Tubman. (The owners of these items have requested their names be withheld to prevent future thefts.)

African American leaders weren't as enthused about this bust as they were about the fall of the Aryan Hammer. The Baton Rouge chapter of the NAACP called the case "pure rigmarole" in a press release. And echoing Hawkins, the Black Guard, a community group out of LaSalle Parish's Jena, called the case a "distraction." But Leonard remains proud of his work. These cases have not only inspired the Louisiana legislature to pass more hate crime provisions; they've been credited with increasing interest in specialization across the state police force and are the basis for a new explosives-training curriculum at multiple police academies across the state. Where the previous curriculum emphasized technical knowledge, the "Breaker" approach is holistic, combining criminal profiling, forensic science, and pattern analysis. Preliminary reports from the Criminal Investigation Division, Louisiana's top law-enforcement agency, indicate that in one year, the Breaker approach has already increased the state's clearance rate for arson and bombing incidents by 8 percent.

Leonard shrugs at his accomplishments as I list them, his mind already making room for the next case. "Anytime I get to prove that there's consequences for actions that harm people and communities, I'm content," he says as he files the mug shots away. Seconds later, another binder thuds onto his desk.

THE LEVELER AND THE REVEALER

Maddy watched with fascination as Kay-Kay ladled grits onto a crisp of bacon then scoured them off the strip without breaking it. Her young cousin made utensils of everything, a habit that had turned each meal of her visit into an exhibition. When the grits were exhausted, Kay-Kay bisected her biscuit and used a half to scoop up eggs and bacon, again clearing the surface of her implement but not consuming it.

"I hope this ain't how you eat pizza," Maddy said.

Kay-Kay grimaced. "I hate pizza. Tastes like hot foot and it gives me gas."

"You might be lactose intolerant."

"I'm too young for that."

Maddy laughed. The girl considered all manner of illness and affliction the province of the elderly. When they spoke about poor Maurice the previous night, Kay-Kay rebuffed all talk of stress or depression. That was old-folk stuff, she insisted. He had talked to her every day before the final game. He was a conveyor belt of jokes and prank videos and music. Everything was fine. Actually, leading up to the game, things were exquisite. He was Gucci. Radric, even. What happened was a fluke, she insisted. A stunt gone wrong, perhaps. He was too young for all that.

Recollecting that conversation, which stretched past midnight, made Maddy aware of its toll. She had slept poorly, sweating despite the chill of her zealous air-conditioning. She eyed Kay-Kay's mug with envy. The sole old-folk stuff the girl approved was coffee, which she saved for last. It was best lukewarm, Kay-Kay explained, parroting Kenny. Heat was a concealer. Once it faded, you could access the true soul of the cup, she said, holding the cup to her nostrils before taking a swig. Calvin, her father and the source of her nutmeg complexion, had instructed Maddy not to give the girl coffee, but Maddy failed to pass that message along to Kenny, whose roastery Kay-Kay had visited twice while Maddy was at work. When the girl hauled back four pounds of beans to Maddy's apartment, the matter was settled. Maddy no longer drank coffee, but she knew she couldn't just toss the epicurean beans out. Nor could she return the beans to him. Not with what she knew.

Kay-Kay interrupted her thoughts. "You want a cup, cuzzo? You look like you need it. And I'm getting really good at the Chemex method. Try it?" She pushed her cup toward Maddy.

Maddy fanned it away. "I'm too young for that."

"You funny," Kay-Kay said, her megawatt smile lighting the room.

Maddy stood and gathered her plate, which she realized was still full. She stared at the spread, which was so untouched the food looked laminated.

"Don't worry about that," Kay-Kay said, shooing her away. "I'll clean this up while you get dressed."

Maddy nodded and left to take a shower. She scrubbed herself with ferocity, her strokes heavy and abrasive, like she was paring her skin rather than cleansing it. She stopped when her arms grew sore, a vague disappointment setting in as she accepted that her anger was exhaustible.

Kay-Kay entered her room as Maddy was finishing her makeup. "One or two?" the girl asked, displaying a charcoal maxi in one hand and a vermilion sheath in the other.

"Kay-Kay, I thought you said we were going to the aquarium, to lunch, and then to the park?" Maddy took the sheath and held it at arm's length. "This is a freakum dress."

"A what?"

Maddy chuckled. "It's just not the vibe I had in mind."

Kay-Kay sighed. "Cuzzo, when you told me to come visit you, you said this would be my summer getaway and yours. But you didn't even take off like you said. I only see you at night, and you always tired." She swiveled around, arched her back, and dispensed a single twerk. "If I wanted to keep all this to myself," she said, "I woulda stayed in Birmingham."

Maddy laughed and handed Kay-Kay the maxi. Then she stepped into her closet and retrieved a bodycon that she'd last worn at a probate. "Okay, but I better not appear in your story."

. . .

"Why you and Kenny don't talk?" Kay-Kay asked as they walked around Piedmont Park, dodging strollers and ogles. To make "freakum Friday," as Kay-Kay deemed it, complete, Maddy had snuck the girl some moscato at lunch. Ever since, the girl had become a living comment section, embodying every element of the format, from the unsolicited nosiness to the repetition. She'd asked about Maddy and Kenny's relationship at least five times in the past hour.

"We don't need to talk. We've moved on."

"Maurice would hate that. If y'all were together, I bet you could solve what happened to him."

Maddy scowled at the girl.

"Don't look at me like that," Kay-Kay said. "Y'all used to be like this." She stopped walking and interlocked her fingers. She was so tipsy that the abruptness of the halt rocked her whole body. She looked like a tree bowing to a gust.

Maddy placed her hand on Kay-Kay's waist and guided her forward. "Why you don't ever ask me about me?" Maddy said as they staggered past picnickers and nappers. "This the first time you've left the state. You know how many states I been to?" The girl was leaning on her now, her head resting on Maddy's shoulder. "Forty," Maddy said. "Mm-hmm. Gonna see the rest before I turn forty."

"That's so cool, cuzzo," Kay-Kay said, lethargy on her breath.

"You wanna travel with me when you graduate?"

Kay-Kay whimpered. "Cuzzo, you really tried me. I told you I don't want to do school. You were the one who told me not to go if they not giving me no money." She straightened up and unadhered herself from Maddy's shoulder.

Maddy immediately missed the girl's warmth. "I did say that. Sorry for pushing."

"It's okay. Maurice used to say the same thing. He said he wanted to be like you."

Maddy halted. "Really? He said that about me? I always thought he preferred Kenny. Seemed like everyone did."

"Yeah, I used to think you were stuck-up driving that Mercedes. But he told me about all the things you did for the family. Birthday presents, graduation gifts, bail money . . . my abortion."

Maddy froze. "How long have you known about that? How did he know?"

Kay-Kay's dimples sprouted. "Cuzzo, we bamas, but we not stupid! You the only one in the family with the bankroll. You the plug!"

Maddy rolled her eyes and reeled her cousin in for a hug. "How was it?" she asked, holding the girl tight. "They treat you okay?" They were in the middle of a walkway, people streaming by in a current of shoulders and insults, Pomeranians and terriers brushing their ankles. But she couldn't let go. She wouldn't.

. . .

Maddy tapped on the glass a third time, ignoring Kenny's confused gestures. She understood that the door was unlocked, that Black Sublime was open. It was actually quite patronizing for him to think there was some sort of misunderstanding. The lights were on; spirited jazz leaked through the door; two customers sat on opposite ends of the bar, steam drifting from their mugs.

Maddy watched Kenny's mouth open and close in consternation. He must have been saying something persuasive. His customers enlisted in the effort to invite her in, scowling, waving, flailing, their arms flags in wind. She turned her back to the shop. Waited.

Kenny emerged a few moments later, his apron undone, his brow reaching for his hairline. He stood a respectable, post-marriage distance from her. They filled the space between them with focused inquiry. Why didn't she call? Would he be free after he closed the shop? Why wouldn't she come in? Had he talked to Thurgood's parents since the news dropped? Was she thirsty? Was he sober? A consensus emerged from the cross fire.

Maddy returned to her car. Rolled the windows down. Listened to a podcast about *Cowboy Bebop*. She reminded herself to revisit the series soon as she watched people trickle in and out of Black Sublime, some of them heading straight for their cars, others taking selfies in front of the store or browsing the plaza's other offerings.

Around dusk, Black Sublime went dark. Kenny appeared haggard as he approached her vehicle but brightened when he got in. Always a showman. Maddy started the engine and pulled off. They hadn't agreed on a setting for their summit, but she drove straight to a familiar café on Marietta Street. They'd both frequented it before they dated, to attend concerts and events. It was neutral.

As the squat plain building came into view at the end of a block of parking lots, she was surprised to see it. It seemed like the kind of place the city had committed itself to erasing. Perhaps it was toward the bottom of the queue. She had no doubt there was a queue. She'd been to a few of Vincent Blake's fundraisers.

They parked on the street. A homeless man lobbed a crude compliment at her as they approached the café on foot. Kenny threatened him. His sincerity was disarming.

They walked in and seated themselves at a table near the small stage, which was bare except for a snake den of wires bathed in pink and blue light. Maddy appreciated that Kenny didn't pull out her chair; he never had, as she preferred, but Maddy wasn't sure how divorce would affect their dynamic. Until now, most of their time together as divorcees had been mediated by family, friends, or lawyers. Alone, uncertainty abounded. At Maurice's funeral, he mentioned he'd picked up coding, but she could also see him going the men's-rights route. Divorce tended to intensify men's attraction to martyrdom. The server took their drink orders and informed them there was an additional fee, per person, if they stuck around for the performances. He didn't specify who was performing. Maddy thanked the man for the intel and removed the venue from the erasure queue. This joint would thrive in New Atlanta; its commitment to the shakedown had helped it survive Old Atlanta.

She turned her attention back to Kenny, who was not his usual chatterbox self. He was thinking he might have to kill her too, she guessed.

Maddy asked him about the bodies: Thurgood, the girl and the women and the cop, and their nephew. "I want to understand," she said. "I need to understand."

Their drinks arrived before Maddy could read him. Long Island iced tea for her. Sweet tea with bourbon and peach schnapps for him. Kenny buried his eyes in his glass. Maddy clarified, "I'm not here to save you. I just want to know why."

"Oh." Kenny found a weak smile then tipped his straw toward his lips. Sucked. "Oh," he repeated, his cheeks flushing red and his eyes meeting hers. She saw no regret in his expression, no empathy. She slapped him. The blow moved every head in the room except his, cutting through first dates and neo-neo-soul and pickup lines from the toxic depths of *Rules of the Game*. Maddy gripped her cold glass to assuage her stinging palm and to steady herself. Everything was fine, she told the two burly bouncers that had appeared at the table. Kenny agreed, his copper-toned face blank save for the bright outline of Maddy's palm.

"I almost killed you," she whispered as the spotlight waned, her voice a croak. "I thought about pouring lime around your bed while you were sleeping, then waking you with a water gun, watching you burn. I considered taking you out for a drink, then dropping thallium in your beer."

Kenny frowned. Watching true-crime shows, they had always joked thallium was for chemists who didn't respect their peers. It was such a tightly regulated substance that only chemists had access to it, so if it were found in a body, it would be flagged by a peer. It was the laziest, most self-defeating route a homicidal chemist could take. Maddy found it insulting that that was the scenario that disturbed him.

She glanced at his sweet tea. "But I can't deny that my family had pressured Maurice since he was young. Even now, no one will admit that he was overwhelmed. By us." Kenny glared at his drink, then grabbed it and gulped it down, leaving a heap of ice.

"Do you have anything to say to me?" Maddy asked.

"I'm thinking."

"What's there to think about? You owe me an explanation. You owe Kay-Kay."

Kenny grinned. "Did you actually acquire thallium and lime?"

"I did."

"Good."

"Good?"

"Yes. If you could kill me, you could kill them."

"Who is 'them?' Are you on the venoms again?"

"The Kingman board."

"Is this an invitation?"

"It is," Kenny said. "Making RST requires a salt by-product of hiip, and hiip won't be made anytime soon now that Thurgood's lab has been seized."

"RST . . . black stuff. And hiip? You and Thurgood made it?"

"Yes," Kenny said. "There's seven board members at Kingman Coke. And their parent company has twenty-four members. And their parent company's parent company—"

"Can trace their ancestry back to the fucking *Mayflower*. I get it. But what are you building with all these bones?" Maddy's grip tightened around her glass.

"If I do it right, there won't be any bones."

"You're avoiding my question."

"I reject its premise. I'm here for the demolition. I can't waste any more of my life on reconstruction."

"I'm here for you."

"Thanks, but the last time I checked, we were divorced."

Maddy took a deep swig from her tea. Her palm had cooled, but her head was on fire. She turned her attention to a cute bearded worker with a nectarine of an ass. He was setting up microphones on the stage, his hands quick with skill and confidence, his chest leading his body. Kenny used to have that kind of self-possession. "We're divorced because you thought a child was the best we could do," she said.

Kenny leaned forward, resting his face in his palms. His sobs were inaudible over a stagehand purring, "Testing, testing, testing," into microphones. Maddy excused herself to the restroom. When she returned, Kenny had regained his composure.

"Did Maurice know it was you?" she asked.

"No," he said emphatically.

"Good," Maddy said, more to herself than Kenny. A presumed stranger goading her nephew's self-destruction felt less horrifying than a family member doing so—even though that was exactly what had happened. She snuffed her percolating wrath and latched on to one of the million other thoughts pinballing against her skull. "What happened with Thurgood?" she asked.

Kenny explained the pirate library, the creation of hiip, EightBall, and his and Thurgood's final moments together. Strangely, the content of his story was less unnerving than his bitter delivery. Kenny's passions typically burned bright. The man before her was a jet stream of cold conviction. He scared her.

"He was going to kill me," Kenny said, emotionless. "He thought I was crazy."

Maddy smiled politely and thought, That doesn't bode well for me.

Kenny's face sank into contemplation. "I thought about your question while you were in the restroom. Thurgood asked me a similar one, before he . . . before I killed him." He paused. "I think we're providing feedback. And it doesn't matter whether they react to it or understand. It matters that we act."

"But why act this way?"

"Is this my plan or yours?"

"I don't know."

"There have to be consequences," Kenny said as he swirled his empty glass. "Those last two months of your pregnancy were hell, and no Kingman exec ever has to think about it. Every day your sister and mother drink and bathe and breathe in their negligence and Kingman persists." He dug into his pocket then placed a tiny glass vial on the table. Its contents were so jet-black that the blue and pink stage lights seemed to bounce off it. "Thurgood saw this and wanted an empire. I want to roll out the guillotine."

Maddy glanced nervously around the space. She had no clue how the RST worked; seeing it out in the open and knowing the magical thinking the substance had fomented in Kenny and Thurgood, corroding their minds, their friendship, made her wonder if she was next—to die or to be bewitched. The compound felt unbound from reason and causality, sorcerous.

Maddy nodded at the vial. "Why didn't you use that, to, you know? It would have been less messy. You created a crime scene. The news said a snake was on the premises too."

"I wasn't sure how it would interact with the foxglove."

"So you're at least more scientist than mad. That's good."

He plucked the RST from the table. "Any more questions? I'm shocked you haven't berated me for leaving the lab equipment behind. You hate waste."

"No, it makes sense," Maddy said with a canned coolness. "No time to haul all that, and it would be obvious if things were missing. You've left EightBall running, right?"

"Yeah, they'll remove it from app stores, but if they ever find the servers, I don't want them to know they've been shut off."

"How do you pay for the servers?"

"2Coinz, the 2 Chainz crypto. 'TRU' encryption, goes the motto."

Maddy groaned and summoned the server to confirm they wouldn't be staying for the performance. He snatched away her credit card. Maddy ignored his insolence, dwelling on her own. She had come to this table in the name of vengeance and understanding yet had eked out only a slap, a morsel of both. She'd expected to have so much more to say, to demand, but familiarity overtook her. Or maybe it was recoil. Their split still rocked her. How could a marriage survive Athens keggers, Ann Arbor winters, New Jersey traffic, Towson segregation—but not a pregnancy? Their love was chemical, they would say to each other with a wink. It was a nonsensical phrase coming from two chemists—everything was chemical, technically— but it restored mystery to love, affirming its liquidity. They'd planned to fill Saskia with their corny affection until she frothed with joy, but the chance never came. Liquid snakes.

Kenny offered no new terms, reneged nothing, as Maddy drove back to Black Sublime. His commitment to death unsettled her. She could barely grip the wheel. Maddy pulled into an empty parking lot where skateboarders streaked across the asphalt, their spinning wheels a thick gurgle.

She kept the car in drive as she spoke, as if she had one quick thought rather than a flood of feelings. "This can't be about consequences. Remember when they offered the settlement after showing us up in court four times? Remember how that wide-headed Karl Rove–lookin' motherfucker called us over and said, 'Congratulations, they only call me in for the VIPs'?"

"I do."

"Then you know these aren't people in the business of feedback, even among themselves. You could kill the whole board of directors and they'd just hire a new board. Are you supposed to kill them too?"

"If the new board makes the same kinds of choices, yes."

Maddy drummed the dashboard so violently her foot slid off the brake, lurching the car forward. "No no no no no no!" she screamed as she stopped the vehicle.

She put it in park and steadied herself. "Blood is fickle, Kenneth. We have more to contribute to the world, to ourselves, than high turnover at a single company."

Kenny steepled his hands and inhaled deeply, leaning back into the seat. While he pondered in that elusive way of his, Maddy turned her attention to the kids circling the lot, thinking of an online video of skaters swarming on a cop car that had plowed into a crowd of protestors. They wailed on it until the windows were crooked smiles and their decks splintered into jagged planks. When their boards gave out, they mounted the vehicle, kicked it, shook it, until the cop fled the cruiser. Maddy still remembered the goose bumps the clip gave her. Until that moment, she had forgotten the ecstasy of collective revolt. Its openness. Had forgotten how it felt when she and twenty-five coworkers walked off her job at Old Navy and fell in formation with a red wall of Target employees participating in the same action. Her manager, Phyllis, tried to pull her aside, telling her, "This isn't for people like you," as if Maddy's education made her job less shitty. That was the problem with Kenny's plan. It was a closed feedback loop, offering no ways in, or out, or forward.

Maddy put the car in drive and eased onto Ponce. She had found her terms. "In exchange for me agreeing to produce RST in my work lab, you will agree to the following. We will send RST to organizations and individuals who share our outlook. We will seek other chemists who can make it and distribute it in our absence. And we will not, under any circumstances, target a Kingman manufacturing plant or board member."

Kenny didn't speak until they were back at Black Sublime. "Are you sure you don't want to come in?" he asked as they pulled next to his truck. "It's not on the menu, but I stock that Ceylon you like."

Maddy leaned over the console and kissed him, her lips lingering longer than she intended. She collected herself and eased back to her side of the car. She needed to go pick up Kay-Kay from the movie theater.

"I assume that was a yes?" Maddy asked.

Kenny nodded then unbuckled his seatbelt, staring ahead.

"Second thoughts?" Maddy asked.

"No, I'm just realizing how much you must have trusted me to allow Kay-Kay to see me, knowing my role in Maurice's death."

"You're not the only fool in this relationship, Kenny. Good night."

REAL NIGGAS JUST MULTIPLY

blacksublime: you look better than I anticipated. sexy, in fact. certified right swipe

blacksublime: you look so innocent in these photographs they've assembled for this briefing. after louisiana I had imagined you as a combination of negrodamus and the invisible man, casting spells in your basement, your chest a well-floured surface of snow-white curls. your bunker, lit by candles burning purple flames, was filled with books. not even rare books. you had barnes and noble classics, multiple editions of encyclopedia britannica, assorted works by donald goines and toni morrison, seize the power, coming of age in mississippi, a bible, a qur'an, game of thrones. you were cultured but normal

blacksublime: you didn't look it though. I always saw you as bald, with intense eyes and a harden beard. you once bore a halo of curls, but age caught up with you, so you redirected your radicalism to your chin. some of it. you always wore a kangol. you'd once thought it was too on the nose, too "i'm officially an old black man," but you visited japan once and saw the brand was having a resurgence among the cool kids. so you dusted it off. you try to keep up with the times. or rather, you try not to let the times reveal who you really are

blacksublime: I doubt you're gone, frankly. it's a doubt that flies in the face of a mountain of evidence collected at your alleged house, gleaned from your alleged lab, extracted from that alleged fit body of yours

blacksublime: you're not looking so good. they found you in your kitchen, belly up like a lizard in the sun. anonymous tip that they can't trace said your front door was open. said your cul-de-sac smelled like chemicals

blacksublime: always a funny word, that. chemicals are those things we can't quite graft to our perception of the world, that exist outside our sense of propriety and order

blacksublime: like now, phil, short for philistine between you and me, just told this room of law enforcement, epidemiologists, researchers, and elected officials that you were a bomb maker. "bio bombs," as he put it. exhibit a is a chemical library of defoliants, incendiary agents, corrosives, nerve and asphyxiating gasses, and blights that was found on your computer

blacksublime: scary shit!

blacksublime: but the cache also contained formulae for apple cider vinegar, baking powder, toothpaste, mouthwash, acrylic paint, lemonade, shampoo, hand soap, deodorant, perfume

blacksublime: so many ways to frame you

blacksublime: the cops, haters of effort, lovers of certainty, are following their instincts

blacksublime: phil is shaking with enthusiasm as he describes how you were captured, which is the part everyone wants to hear. cops don't often stumble upon a dead black body. they're usually on the scene, midwifing the passage

blacksublime: I'm obvi feeling a type of way, but I admit phil is a good storyteller

blacksublime: he sets the scene so well I can see it. two local cops showed up, he says, pushed through your foyer, and found . . . a snake! (which, wtf? you really think you're a pharaoh, huh?) the parties quickly exchanged blows. the snake nipped one on the ankle; his partner shot the snake between the eyes. warriors that they were, they continued to clear the house, announcing themselves (yeah, right) and watching for more snakes (definitely). they found you snow-angeled on the marble tile, cold as an orphanage (phil's words, not mine. he's really embracing the spotlight)

blacksublime: GBI got roped in because after the cops called in an ambulance, they ventured into your yard and met another surprise. you'd booby-trapped the lab. your slingshot missed because cops know how to clear doors, but one of the cops used to work vice. and you know how vice cops do

blacksublime: not content with surviving a copper-head bite, wannabe herc doubled down. went to the vial that had flown past his head and smashed it with

his boot. then your compound splashed onto his bite
and that was that

blacksublime: mucous membranes . . . that's how it
works. we finally figured it out

blacksublime: that's about all we figured out. the
vice cop's heroics very conveniently ruined all your
surveillance equipment . . . coincidence or nah?

blacksublime: I can't call it. what's being emphasized
today is that your choices killed not one but three cops.
no mention yet of the others

blacksublime: I bet you feel the same way I do

blacksublime: we don't know what else you made in
the lab, but we'll know soon. we have your standards

blacksublime: strange to think you were just a dealer.
did Valencia and Patrice and Maurice and Zora know
exactly what they were buying? or did you manipulate
them?

blacksublime: I'm going to say their names again.
VALENCIA. PATRICE. MAURICE. ZORA

blacksublime: 4 lives. 4 people. 4 emptied vessels of
family and time and love

blacksublime: 4 vessels YOU emptied

blacksublime: remember that. I will

blacksublime: I hate how little mention they're getting
in this briefing. the officer that died at your house and
the cop zora killed are the only victims they acknowledge as people. the partner of zora's mark is here, a
few seats away. he's got one of those uber-southern
names you think only exist in faulkner. he's mean as

hell too. I met him back in jena. we didn't hit it off. I
read up on him afterward. he used to be louisiana's
premier investigator of bombings. bagged some nazis
blacksublime: not the ones he knew, tho
blacksublime: here, he's interrupted the briefing every
time someone called his partner richard instead of dick
blacksublime: "his name is dick!"
blacksublime: looool can't make this shit up
blacksublime: I envy how good cops are at giving
death a single face. such coherent terms they use.
victim, hero, patriot, terrorist, monster. it's a real art with
them
blacksublime: for me, it's just a bad habit
blacksublime: just like talking to you. I kinda want you
to still be out there
blacksublime: I shouldn't tell you this, but you took
the messiness out of death. made it smell better, look
neater, feel

Ebonee stopped typing, remembering her promise to herself to re-
sist willed ideation. She focused her thoughts on the present: I am
happy. I am present. I am . . . being quoted? No, but there were
screenshots of EightBall on the giant smartboard behind Phil. She
blinked at the gaping screen. Once. Twice. Three, four, five. Shit!
She stuffed her phone between her legs like she was taming a flared
skirt. She had promised Retta and Alonzo that she was rid of the
app. If they had seen her, she'd be so, so fucked. She faced forward,
trying to sense them without drawing their attention. The phone
warmed her thighs.

Seconds passed, then minutes. Phil walked the assembly through the steps the GBI had taken to (not) locate EightBall's servers. Ebonee eyed the screen so intensely the Parallax Corporation would have hired her on the spot.

After she realized no one had accosted her or planned on doing so, her anxiety leveled off and she focused on the presentation. Seeing the app's minimal interface on such a massive screen was sobering. What had felt sleek and foreboding in miniature was dingy when scaled up. There was no flair or spark to its plain fonts and empty margins. In fact, on this massive screen in this auditorium jointly funded by the Chick-fil-A Foundation, the Robert W. Woodruff Foundation, and the Vincent Blake Campaign, the app's slapdash aesthetics were obvious. It had clearly been cobbled together in a fugue of Red Bull and YouTube tutorials, perhaps even copied and pasted wholesale from a template. Ebonee suppressed a giggle as Phil again riffed on Thurgood's boundless evil genius. A joyous one—all bubble, not a single quivering nerve. Was anyone else privy to the kayfabe? Did they also enjoy it?

That's inappropriate, she told herself. She was getting too comfortable again. It was so easy. Ebonee reached between her legs, unlocked her phone, and deleted the app. She was free.

The presentation moved past EightBall to slides detailing Thurgood's motive. Ebonee paid close attention. This was the point of bifurcation, all the information she and Retta weren't privy to once the investigation had become decisively criminal. She doubted the profile of Thurgood would be any better than the GBI's other conclusions, but knowing the official spin would help her better craft the definitive account. Retta said parrying true crime with true health was a fool's errand and Retta had been right about a lot lately, but fuck it. Why not go for broke? Must every public health finding only be useful to the public health community, bored science journalists hunting for evergreen stories during a news drought, and sci-fi authors fishing for prompts? Not if Ebonee could help it.

As expected, the GBI came on strong. They presented Thurgood Houser, the "black biobomber," as a terrorist accelerationist hellbent on inaugurating helter-skelter. He recruited stressed, despairing individuals into his network and used them as guinea pigs for the chemical abominations he hoped would give blacks an advantage in the coming race war. Recovered phone records from two of his "gophers" showed him to be paternal and vindictive, encouraging violence against the people who harmed his recruits and against themselves. Mention of self-harm was routine, as well as solicitations to meet in person, where he would share his cocktail of death and encourage carnage.

By day he was a warm and elusive instructor who students say was nurturing yet distant. In interviews, his pupils, especially black ones, disclosed that at happy hours and other social gatherings, he was prone to discussing generational wealth and beating the system. A few reported being implicitly recruited to make some extra money, though none of them bit. A standard for one street drug, hiipower, was found in Houser's home lab. He was likely trying to reproduce the rare drug, which has a street value in the tens of thousands per gram.

By night, the bodacious black biobomber bent on boogaloo, balkanizing Van Buren's bold bulwark into Babylon, breaching Buchanan's bulkhead bearing broadsides and berkelium Berettas Buffalo buffalo Buffalo buffalo buffalo buffalo . . . Ebonee stopped doodling, gathered her things, and left the auditorium.

She found Retta seated on a bench near the elevator.

"That was work," Retta said.

"Yeah, they don't pay me enough."

"You ready to get this interview over with?"

"Over with? I thought you said she was promising?"

"Will you allow me my exhaustion, just once? In six weeks, we've interviewed twenty people, fielded three times as many tips, and just watched cops literally argue about 'dick.'"

Ebonee grinned. "I'll allow it. Today. I can lead this one."

"Thank you. I'm going to go grab a bite since we're running ahead of schedule. See you in the conference room."

· · ·

Retta and Monica Halifax entered the conference room in spirited conversation. Ebonee took in Monica as they seated themselves and wrapped up whatever they were talking about. The woman was the most casually dressed person Ebonee had ever seen in the fusion center. Glinting Dahlia bites tugged at her full lips. A sleeveless striped smock billowed over meaty, tattooed thighs. Pedicured, oblong toes peeked over the midsoles of her gladiator boots. One side of her head was freshly shaved, the other a thicket of crisp locs with tips dyed seafoam.

"Dr. Halifax, you look like a fucking goddess," Ebonee said.

Monica blushed and offered her hand. "Monica. Before we started raving about Jean's Famous Sandwiches, Dr. Vickers—I mean, Retta—told me you had quite the eye for detail."

Ebonee shook her hand, ignoring her urge to bow. "Ebonee. Don't mind her. She's just feeling generous today. I'm a mess."

Retta overruled her, imitating her voice. "Don't mind her. She's bashful. Always. She's the one who got this ball rolling. CDC wouldn't even be involved without her drive."

Monica nodded with admiration. "Own it. I'm tired of bashful women." The tip of her tongue slid over one of her piercings.

Ebonee smirked. Of course the goddess was a flirt. Worship was a two-way street.

Ebonee stayed on course. "Well, first off, we appreciate you talking to us. We know you already talked with the GBI during their investigation, so bear with us if we repeat any questions. As we told you when we reached out, this conversation is not tied to a criminal probe. This inquiry is scientific in nature, and its findings legally can only be used to make public health recommendations. Understood?" Retta produced a form that outlined the bounds of the interview and placed it on the table.

Monica reviewed, signed, and handed the document to Retta. Ebonee watched her face scrunch into contemplation, wondering what she was thinking. After a spell, she spoke in a solemn hush.

"I know it's just basic courtesy, but thank you for giving me time to review this. I've been in so many rooms like this, with women, with men, with papers of consequence, and felt rushed and pressured. I've certainly never been thanked for being present."

"That's no problem at all," Ebonee said.

"I also had worried you would be just like the GBI. They were obsessed with Mr. Houser's personality. What he was like. His demeanor. I tried to tell them I didn't know. I spoke to a lot of people at the conference. Him, his friend, students, colleagues. It was a busy day. I only came forward because I thought I could tell them about the PCR machine he won. But they didn't care about that at all."

"His friend?" Retta asked.

"Yeah, well, he had two friends. One I didn't speak to. The other was a weird guy. Very personable, but quirky. Worked in coffee, I think?"

"Really," Retta said.

Ebonee reached for the recorder since the interview seemed to have begun. Monica's praise made her stop short of pressing it. More consent couldn't hurt.

"I'm beginning the recording now," she said, eyeing Monica. The woman nodded, then Ebonee clicked the record button and stated the date, time, and subject.

Ebonee decided to stick to the script despite Retta's interest in the friend—clearly Kenneth Bomar. "So we'd like to ask you about the PCR machine, which, we agree, is something overlooked in the criminal probe of Thurgood Houser. It's actually exactly why we wanted to talk to you. What's its significance to what he was doing?"

"PCR machines have many uses, but their main value in the DIY community is thermal cycling. Depending on what we're making, a PCR machine helps us control the reaction. We can better regulate temperature at certain points of a reaction, tamp down volatility, and finely dictate how ingredients interact in terms of volume, time, and lots of other variables, depending on the quality of the machine. It's an essential device for any compound with substances with vastly different reactivities."

"Because it allows precision?" Ebonee asked.

"Exactly. For DIY drug manufacturing, and by *drug* I'm referring to any substance designed to induce a specific pharmaceutical effect, a PCR machine gives commercial lab–level control. That's very, very important for tech transfer, if a DIYer hopes to scale up their production at some point. Which is a lot of DIYers these days, unfortunately. Fucking VCs have really changed the community . . ." She paused. "Sorry, straying off course a bit. Ultimately, precision is an ethical concern. We don't want to ever provide a drug that produces effects the patient isn't anticipating. Especially since we're already trying to address ills done by the pharmaceutical industry. That trust is our greatest resource."

"Tell us about the machine Houser won at the auction," Retta said.

"Sure. It was a Genentech Veloci750, a high-end model used by a lot of top drug companies. It had the works. Touch screen, terabyte RAM, some preloaded recipes. It was the kind of device only a high-level chemical engineer with industry experience would be able to do anything with, honestly."

Ebonee nodded. "Our analyses of the blackout compound show it consistently contained copperhead DNA as well as amphetamine salts and caffeine. Assuming Houser didn't just sell it off, could a Genentech make something out of these?"

Monica closed her eyes and ran her fingers through her locs. Ebonee assumed she was thinking, but she looked like she was reciting a desperate prayer.

"Yes, that's very possible. I had to take a moment because this reminded me of a controversy in the community a few years ago. Some mithridate, who we do have a small number of in our community, became a cult hero for a few months after he died from a cocktail of black mamba venom, heroin, liquefied keto pills, and four thieves vinegar. Called it warrior blood, I'll never forget. Posted it online and it was all the rage for a bit. I don't know why so many people look up to incompetent scientists."

"Do you think Houser was incompetent?" Retta asked.

"What? Absolutely not. He induced the same pharmacology in six individuals. Small sample, but for a novel home-brewed drug, that's impeccable. It must have taken years and hundreds of trials to come up with it. My company makes insulin, which is a common drug made through a standardized process, and we had hiccups first starting off."

"I don't think so either. Just wanted to play devil's advocate," Retta said. "Last question from me. How much power would the Genentech need? It didn't show up at Houser's lab."

"Really? Wow. It would have to be in a warehouse or some other industrial setting. It's a big boy. Did you check his school facilities?"

"We didn't check anything. That's the GBI's purview," Ebonee said. She clicked off the recorder, then rose and opened the door. "That's it from us. Can I walk you out?"

Monica took her hand.

Retta was fumbling with the accursed Keurig when Ebonee returned to the EIS floor, Monica's business card in tow. Ebonee resisted the temptation to tease her colleague and instead approached Retta and jingled her keys. "Really? You're that certain Bomar is getting over on us? I thought I was the stubborn one."

Retta glowered at the K-Cup in her hand then tossed it into the trash. "Your treat," she said.

• • •

"So you do like the coffee?" Kenny said as Retta and Ebonee entered Black Sublime. As usual, the cramped shop was empty as an unsold casket, but Kenny's tone was spirited, like he was addressing a packed big top. "I thought you were just being nice."

Ebonee beamed. It comforted her to be somewhere untouched by the chaos of the past months. Kenny was characteristically chipper and hospitable, the GBI probe be damned.

"Do you still have that coffee I had last time?" she asked.

Kenny pointed at a small dry-erase board that contained two lines of neat text. She read the first one aloud. "Gujo Koodie?"

"That's it! Single origin, grown in Kenya's picturesque Aberdare Range. Light, citrus body with hints of peach and a melon finish. Turn up!"

Ebonee chuckled as he twirled and spun with Motown flair while he began to prepare her coffee. Was that a shimmy? He was showing off.

Retta was unimpressed. She seated herself. "Espresso," she said flatly.

"Dr. Vickers! Nice to see you under better circumstances. Even better to officially serve you. Don't think I didn't see you take some coffee home after the wake. How's your investigation going?"

"It's not really an investigation at this point. More an act of witness," Retta said.

"*Can I get a witness?*" Kenny bellowed.

"Can I get a beverage?" Retta replied at a much lower volume.

Ebonee sat down and pulled her chair close to Retta. The woman was going through it, her face sunken like she was back at that hotel bar in Jena being called "ma'am."

"You got anything other than coffee back there?" she asked Kenny, nodding toward the door beyond the restroom. She spoke over the clatter of beans being ground.

"Say that again?" he asked.

His mask of hospitality seemed to slip, his smile shifting from warm to ceremonial. A trick of the light perhaps. She raised her voice. "I asked if you have anything other than coffee back there."

The warmth returned. "Nothing I want to give to the CDC!" he said.

She laughed and let him work. His command of the tiny space was balletic. He bent, pivoted, reached, every movement fluid. Ebonee watched him prepare their drinks step-by-step, but her pour-over and Retta's espresso seemed to materialize.

"Why did he do it?" Retta asked as Kenny served them.

"Why did who do what?" Kenny said.

"Why did Quentin Tarantino cast himself as a racist in *Pulp Fiction*?"

"I've read that he was trying to—"

"Don't be fucking dense."

Kenny's face swished into a scowl. A candid one, the contempt unobscured. "I'm not even sure what he was doing. Are you?"

"Do I look like I know?"

"Someone once told me answering questions with questions was evasive."

"Someone once told me evading questions was evasive," Retta said. She sipped her espresso, holding the tiny mug below her lips, which quivered. "This is divine," she said. It felt like more of a declaration than a compliment.

Kenny said nothing.

Ebonee concentrated on the citrusy, peachy, melon-y bliss that was her pour-over. Retta was being prickly, but it was true that Kenny was suspicious. Friend of Houser, relative of Maurice White, coffee roaster, former chemist—his fit to Monica's profile was hand in glove. GBI had looked into him and he came up clean though. No phone calls to Houser or White, no EightBall, alibis provided by his ex-wife and family. This PCR business was alluring but flimsy. In fact, it was the kind of tenuous connection the GBI would make. Ebonee couldn't let Retta embarrass herself.

"Retta, you're tired. Let's just settle up and get today over with," Ebonee said. She slid her credit card to Kenny.

Retta slurped her espresso, left the mug on the counter, then rose without a word. Planted herself by the entrance.

"We've had a rough couple of weeks. Paperwork, interviews, meet-ings, data sets," Ebonee explained as Kenny rang her up. "We're just trying to make something useful from this mess."

Kenny returned Ebonee's card and addressed her quietly. "Join me, and you'll die with dignity."

Ebonee held his gaze as she nervously tapped her credit card. She had so many questions. Why did you do it? Why me? Are you okay? She managed one.

"Do you have a PCR machine?"

"Do you have a warrant?"

Ebonee knocked over a glass carafe and ran to the back of the shop, pushing open the door to the storage room. She flipped a light switch and saw the room was windowless and spare. It smelled of heat and dust and metal. Large, bulging burlap sacks leaned against a wall, uncooked beans peeking from the folds. Two black-and-silver roasters sat in the middle of the room, bedecked with tubes, knobs, and basins. A desk and a workbench covered in twist ties and sealable paper sacks lined another wall. For bagging roasted beans, she guessed. The garage door rattled as vehicles rolled by outside. Ebonee strolled around the room, witnessing it, documenting it. There was no PCR machine.

The door remained ajar and the room still and solitary as she accepted this finding. Tears traced her cheeks. Cold thick globs. Her year of magical thinking had exhausted itself three months in. From the time she'd seen that first stupid black hole on her timeline, she'd been convinced she was one interview, one closed door away from unmasking the forces of evil in the town square. Rinsing the monster in light so bright and hot it cleansed. Maybe even deterging herself.

But there was no town square. No purifying light. There was just this cell and its dim fluorescence. Ebonee left the room and closed the door behind her. Kenny had already swept up the carafe and was behind the counter. Just another day. Ebonee left him a tip and exited the shop.

"What just happened?" Retta asked when Ebonee stepped outside.

"I asked him if he had a PCR machine."

"He's already moved it."

"I saw."

Retta sucked her teeth. "The GBI's already cleared him, so there's no point in turning him in. We have other options though." She unzipped her purse and thrust her hand into its depths. Ebonee knew what was inside.

"Are you fucking kidding me," Ebonee said. "What the hell is that for?"

Retta spoke without moving her hand. "Self-defense, persuasion. Depends on the day, really."

Ebonee turned around and peered through Black Sublime's front window. Kenny was leaning on the counter with his arms crossed, watching them, his face plastered with a simper. She felt proud of her choice to delete EightBall. "You know he's not afraid of death, right?"

"It's scarier than a report."

Ebonee stepped off the curb and sat on the concrete, looking out on the parking lot, which was flooded with pigeons. "I often think about killing myself. I don't know why, but it occurs to me as often as hunger or thirst. It's just a part of me."

Retta removed her hand from her purse and sat beside her. "I'm sorry," she said, resting her head on Ebonee's shoulder.

"Don't be. I manage."

"How? I can't imagine."

"My sister. Alonzo. My parents. A therapist. An uncle. You. Most days aren't so bad."

Retta stiffened. "And this man deserves to walk because he's also got a death w—" She caught herself. "Because he's suffering."

Ebonee playfully nudged Retta with her shoulder. "I don't care what he deserves. I just know we've seen things no one else may ever see, and it has to matter. We can't throw it away just because it's unfair or because it pisses us off."

"Us? Since when were you mad?"

"I've been mad this whole time. He's made death look so pretty." She carefully lifted Retta's purse and held it in front of them. "So easy."

Retta exhaled loudly then took her purse and stood. "Thanks for the coffee," she said.

HARBINGERS ABOUND

Maddy half listened as the guide led her and Kenny across the forested grounds of the serpentarium. She'd never been comfortable around reptiles. They were too quiet. Insects buzzed and whirred and advanced, announcing themselves, asserting their right to space. Birds, whose chirps and twitters resounded throughout the expansive menagerie, were even more candid, always singing their freedom.

Reptiles idled. Stock-still unless occupied or disturbed, they seemed to absorb sounds rather than produce them, a silence that struck Maddy as entitled. It was as if they were waiting for humanity to die off but too proud to declare outright war. They were that certain they would inherit the earth.

Maddy looked into the beady eye of a black-and-pewter diamondback, no exception to her rule. It lay still in its dirt enclosure, corkscrewed in the shade, unblinking. It did not rattle. Maddy kept walking, remained on alert.

She wasn't afraid of snakes. Her grandfather had made sure of that, teaching her to recognize the worm snakes, rat snakes, and pine snakes that littered the four acres he'd never, ever let go undercounted. His father's father had bought that land. Her mother had sold it.

He caught and killed snakes if he ran into them too often, hacking them with a machete. Maddy always looked away when the blade hit. "If they scare you, they control you," her grandfather said of the creatures. He applied the mantra to animals, people, institutions, emotions.

Maddy could still remember the day he let her weep into his firm shoulder, despairing over her middle school boyfriend getting burned alive in his house. She had held in the cry for days, feeling guilty for barely reacting to her grandmother passing in her sleep two years earlier. She had loved the squat, peculiar woman and her commitment to neatness and etiquette; decades later, she was still ironing T-shirts and socks and keeping her elbows off tabletops in Estelle Laremie's honor. But she shed no tears for the woman.

Nor did she have tears for little stillborn Saskia. She felt more exhausted than sad, though she never told Kenny that. His postpartum depression was all-consuming. Telling him it was his alone seemed cruel. She now knew she should have been crueler.

Maddy studied the facility map. They were approaching the pit viper range. She shared this intel with Kenny, who grew visibly excited. His year of injecting poisons, their last year together after eight in love, had been the year of the snake. He brought home Medusa, his first copperhead, fellowshipped with other snake lovers online, and read and reread herpetology journals like they were copies of *Ego Trip* excavated from a sawdusted attic. It was bizarre to see someone so knowledgeable and detail-oriented fall prey to the fervor of mithridatism. He truly believed that being bitten by Medusa once a week and later harvesting her venom and mixing it with cinnamon, vinegar, salt, and spring water (this was the most absurd ingredient, she felt), then injecting it into his forearm, would fortify him against endocrine-disrupting compounds and environmental racism and, ultimately, America. Maddy's mother called it "home-brewed snake oil," though she never stopped calling him her son.

Her poor sister, whose son was now gone because of Kenny, joked that Kenny's masculinity was literally toxic. Maddy had laughed in the moment—Ivy Lynn had a wicked comic delivery—but over time she realized her sister was wrong. There was an intense femininity to the way Kenny's body and mind changed in response to his injections and bites: swollen limbs, pus-gushing sores, cracked skin, mood swings cycling between euphoria, rage, delirium. His appetite fluctuated too: one week he'd want nothing but nuts and fruits like a bird; the next he'd want cakes and cookies and burgers. He reminded Maddy of her pregnancy.

Kenny pointed out a moccasin the color of sage and sand that had wound itself around an overhead branch. Maddy agreed that it was majestic. She asked the guide if snakes ever attacked visitors. It was a bit of a mood-killing question, but she needed to clear her head. They were here to rob the place, after all.

Snakes are snakes, the woman said. "Poetic," said Kenny, still entranced by the moccasin.

Maddy asked the guide when the day's milking would take place. Soon, she said. The woman glanced at her wristwatch then hopped to and led them to the milking area, where a crowd had formed. Families, mostly, with a few couples and individuals. Their guide was the day's milker, it turned out. She slipped into this other role without ceremony, like a teleworking new mother pivoting away from a Zoom call and baring a breast. Maddy watched closely as the woman entered a small arena, disappeared behind a card-protected door with a single bolt lock, then emerged with a large snake with a bronze pattern and a crimson tint. Neither she nor Kenny knew the species.

Some kid did though. It was an inland taipan, an Australian snake. More poisonous than a black mamba, the pale, bony kid said, impressed. Maddy noticed that he stepped back after he identified it.

With the snake's head pinched between her fingers and its body stretched like a deployed tape measure, their guide explained that milking was important for producing antivenoms, which were the only reliable tool against snakebite. The serpentarium shipped the harvested venoms to hospitals and research institutions all over the world. The guide estimated they had perhaps fifteen gallons of venom in all on-site, from over forty species of snakes.

Snake Kid was awed but concerned. How did they protect all these important venoms? The serpentarium was so open and unprotected. Maddy smiled. "You can always count on kids to ask the questions adults can't," she whispered to Kenny. He was wearing cologne, she noticed. It smelled like boiled wood and hand soap. He was helpless without her.

The guide claimed they left a snake on the floor every night as a guard. The kid stepped forward.

Maddy suppressed a laugh. Long before Kenny helped him kill himself, Maurice had been a dinosaur kid. He too had oscillated between respect and fright for his reptilian muse.

The milking began, the guide arranging the snake's slender head on a stopper and pressing down its fangs, lifting its head, and repeating. Maddy scanned the arena for cameras as the woman narrated all the ways the venom could destroy a human body. Kidney failure, brain damage, paralysis, cardiac arrest. Worse than smoking, Snake Kid's mom summarized. She seemed like the kind of person who never wasted a teachable moment.

Maddy spotted no cameras nor any signs threatening surveillance—which meant either the devices were well hidden or the owners of this place reasonably didn't fear getting pinched. She'd find out tonight.

The gallery shelled its peanuts as the venom accumulated. Bird Kid, so named because she whisper-huffed, "Snakes are fucking evil," when the guide confirmed that yes, snakes ate birds, was especially outspoken. Snakes didn't even fuckin' fly, she pointed out. Nor did they fuckin' sing. Weren't even fuckin' pretty. All excellent points, Maddy felt, though she recalled seeing a few pretty ones with her grandpa. She convinced him to let them go.

Bird Kid's father's aggressive response to her profanity nearly drove the group apart, the crowd variously praising and scolding him for spanking the brash girl. Maddy was glad she would never have to pick a side in the national whoopins debate. She was probably pro-choice, more out of a sense of not wanting white people to tell her how to raise a black child than any particular beliefs about child-rearing.

The guide bridged the divide by noting that birds and snakes had a common ancestor. A shrewd move, but Bible Man, a proponent of intelligent design, disagreed. Maddy took Kenny's hand and led him back to his truck. She hated listening to fools talk; they were all evangelists.

They returned that night in balaclavas, carrying a cooler filled with dry ice and a crowbar each. They left with every venom on-site.

WHOLE LOTTA BLACK

Kenny cradled the gun in his hands, conscious of its emptiness. He dwelled on its light, hollow frame, its gray corrugated surfaces, its bulbous chambers and purple sights.

He'd never get to train this water gun on Saskia, spray her as she, her friends, and her cousins doused him, a cross fire of giggles and joyous screeches. This toy would never make an appearance at a birthday party or cookout or kickback. Would never co-conspire with hyperactive kids, rabid with fun, to drive up water bills, soil pricey sneakers, sully intricate braids.

Kenny slid on his latex gloves then placed the gun on the table he'd set up under his backyard deck. Then he perched the device so that its unsealed reservoir faced upward and stuck a funnel in it. He stopped to wipe his brow. The shade under the deck was a reprieve from the merciless July sun, but the taut gloves and his long sleeves made up the difference. He picked up a sealed vial of RST and looked at Maddy.

"You're sure ABS plastic won't react with RST?" he asked.

"Of course I'm sure. Called up the manufacturer myself. Tested it too."

"And the screws and glue?"

"The whole kit and caboodle. You know it's my job to test things, right?"

"Really? I've known you, what, twelve years? You've never mentioned your job. Never."

"Well, I'm the director of quality control at the biggest producer of cypermethrin in the state."

Kenny placed the vial on the table. One more round of safety checks couldn't hurt, especially with Maddy's innovations. Through her after-hours tinkering at her work lab, she'd quartered hiipower's production time, showing via equation, then proving via synthesis, that Kenny and Thurgood were wasting energy. And through her experiments in Kenny's basement, she'd already mastered the PCR machine. Kenny wished he'd had her aptitude and company all along. They could have saved some lives. Patrice, specifically. Thurgood, definitely. Maybe his own.

He nitpicked further. "Okay, how do I know those new venoms are going to have the same effect as Amelia's?"

"You don't. Next question."

"How do I know the pressure from the water gun's pump mechanism won't aerosolize the RST and burn my eyes or, like, incinerate a mosquito caught in the line of . . . liquid?"

"It's on the MSDS."

"It is?"

"Yes, you tested this on your own. Page 1. Chemical and physical properties. Page 4. Stability and reactivity. Inert at atmospheric pressure. Page 8. Toxicity to microorganisms. Unknown. Fish. Unknown. Invertebrates. Fatal. That answer your question, or would you like to continue stalling?"

Kenny sighed and uncapped the vial he had set aside. Tipped it into the funnel. Dropped the funnel into a bag of rice. Sealed the reservoir. Mounted the gun. Aimed at the free-range chicken carcass dangling from the mayhaw tree fifteen feet away. Hesitated.

If Maddy still wanted to kill him, surely she would have struck by now, right? After her tweaks, she had the process; after the heist, she had raw materials; and now she had the substance itself. She wouldn't arm a person she planned on offing. Right? She was smarter than that. Smarter than him, certainly. And even he would know better than to arm the opposition. He wished Thurgood had been smarter.

"Something wrong?" Maddy asked.

"No, just thinking about Thurgood." He squeezed the thick trigger and watched a jet of RST stream onto the target. A blink later, there was no target.

Maddy's recipe worked. They returned to the house to stock up.

...

Despite the tedium of pipetting, pipetting, pipetting, making RST
was a simple process.

First, they took the template, the base cocktail of DNA being duplicated, and dropped it into a plastic reservoir tip via a micropi-
pette. Kenny's template was venom.

Next, the primer: coffee grounds. Kenny'd do anything to reverse
that cursed year of injections, trauma, and divorce, but without
its crushing juxtapositions, he'd never have thought of this bon-
kers mash-up while idling in Thurgood's lab. Before the settlement turned coffee into his workspace, he'd drank coffee in all
his workspaces anyway. It was the one beverage every lab from
Norcross to Fort Detrick to Ann Arbor let slip past safety protocols. Scientists, technicians, engineers, government auditors—
perhaps even science itself—needed the beverage. Why not turn
the beverage into science? he asked himself one night while staring at a coffee cup and calculating how many cups of coffee he
could purchase with his blood money. All that cash just to fuck
off. He couldn't.

Kenny missed being strung out on those poison cocktails. Though
they left him scatterbrained and aching, they were pure experiences. Fleeting and numerous as those altered states were, they
were concentrated. Macrodoses of sensation and imagination.

He had learned to leave that era behind for the sake of his sanity
and his people, but sometimes, as on the night he invented RST,
he could tap into it. Could so thoroughly summon the kiss of the

needle and the warm hellfire of the mithridatium that his salivary glands pumped spit and his breaths grew short, his mind hastening. He feared he'd reach for the real sauce whenever he did this, but he was stopped by the comfort that this chaos lived in him, that he didn't need an external source to access his pneuma, his self. It was quite the revelation to learn he could live with his despair, tucking it behind his canines in anticipation of an exposed neck, rather than constantly spitting it out.

That's how Thurgood lived, preaching his prosperity gospel. It was strange how niggas could know that the United States of America does not negotiate with niggas but still spend their lives trying to barter. Wasn't much of a life at all, Kenny thought.

Where was he? Pipetting, pipetting, pipetting. Ah! The enzymes! They were the deglazer, pushing the template and primer to combine and not just dick about. With them, the primer would anneal with the template and duplicate its DNA with the help of the nucleotides, the building blocks.

Kenny always found it funny that this nanoscopic process was described in grandiose, architectural terms, as if the universe were maintained by tiny masons with miniature wheelbarrows, trowels, and mortar pans. Eating their sack lunches on Lilliputian scaffolding. Building life brick by brick.

His grandfather had been a bricklayer. Kenny called him a mason once. The septuagenarian leaped from the throes of his dementia and slapped him. Everyone took Kenny's side because he was a kid and had been forced to sit by the old man because they were both messy eaters, but their support made Kenny feel worse. It was Thanksgiving Day, an occasion the man probably didn't even remember, he was eating with people he half recognized, and he got scolded for insisting on a little respect. Slap didn't even hurt. It was one of those Three Stooges slaps, staged to look intense, but soft. Funny, even.

Maddy's slap was far more painful. It had shocked him; it was the first time she had struck him. He had never seen her hit anyone. Look at her now, transferring fresh RST doses from their droppers to vials. A killer. He opened the PCR machine and removed the finished batch. Maddy smiled as he delivered it to her workstation. He could live in that moment forever.

It passed. After fourteen hours they had stockpiled enough RST to part ways. They split the bounty down the middle then took turns sledgehammering the PCR machine.

Once it was a pile of bits and shards, they swept the debris onto a tarp, then hauled the load outside. The feeble deck light dimmed as they approached the back fence. By the time they reached the edge of Kenny's property, lightning bugs were the only light, drifting in and out of the hot darkness. The rubble hit the earth with a dull jangle. Maddy breathed heavily. It had been a long walk.

Kenny tossed a dead mouse onto the pile then stepped back and aimed. Maddy's labored breaths melted into the chorus of cicadas and the distant moan of a freight train as he waited for light. A lightning bug flared orange, and he shot at the mouse. It vanished in a whisk of blackness. The sizzle of the grass reminded Kenny of the bloom.

As they headed toward the house, Maddy commented that the yard, which was splotched with black grass stains from all the mice who'd met similar fates, looked like it had cavities. "My mighty works," Kenny said.

When they reached the house, Maddy halted in front of the basement door. Faced him, her body so close he could feel her heat. Kenny tightened his grip on the gun.

"We can break the NDAs. I haven't spent a dime," Maddy said.

"You mean that?"

"Yes." She pulled his hand into hers. Caressed his fingers. Peeled his index finger off the trigger, then his hand off the grip. Took the weapon and placed it on the ground.

Her offer was genuine. "We can go on *Good Morning America, Dateline, 60 Minutes, Tom Joyner*—"

"*The Breakfast Club*?"

"Wherever we'll be heard. We don't have to shoulder this alone. You don't."

Kenny considered her proposal, imagined them weeping on phones and tablets and gas-pump televisions across the country. They'd look contrite and respectable in their Sunday best as they explained how, in her third trimester, Maddy went to Birmingham to stay with her mother. Her job provided generous maternity leave, but the baby and Atlanta traffic and her small, shrinking bladder were turning routine errands into *Sonic* levels— the really challenging ones, with water and floating platforms. Going home to Birmingham would allow her to decompress and spend some time with her extended family. Unfortunately, her mother's humble rambler and her sister's Section 8 home and her aunt and uncle's bungalow were all in the shadow of a coke plant whose excretions hung over the neighborhood like thought bubbles and coursed through the soil like rhizomes. Maddy's divorce lawyer would probably counsel them to use different metaphors, but this was Kenny's imagination; he was allowed bias. The excrement made its way into the people of that neighborhood, too, bestowing them with extraordinary gifts like asthma and colon cancer; some people even went bald, like Jadakiss. Didn't lots of Americans live near coke plants, the interviewer would devil's advocate. Yes, Kenny would say. And don't the EPA and OSHA regulate emissions, the interviewer would continue. Yes, Maddy would say. But, she'd inform their inquisitor, regulations applied to companies whose emissions harmed people, which niggers weren't. Oh my, DJ Envy would remark, You two are niggers? I hadn't even noticed; you're so articulate and well-dressed. Are you sure you haven't got some Cherokee in you somewhere? Is this nigga serious, Maddy would ask. He was. Persistent too. But what about your degrees and money? Still no luck? Nope, we're just

Drs. Nigger now, Kenny would say to the camera. Then the show would cut to commercial. Cheerios. Good for cholesterol.

Obviously, only *The Breakfast Club* would allow an interview this unhinged, but the premise held throughout the multiverse. On every channel, in every format, from every angle, if Kenny and Maddy went to the press, they would look like simps.

"This isn't about being heard," he said. "We can't be."

"You're such a man," she said.

"There's worse things to be."

"Dead?"

"I'll find out."

"I think you already know."

Kenny's gaze dropped to the gun between them. They'd gotten along so well together the past few weeks, traveling to the serpentarium, barbecuing with the Tusks on the Fourth of July. He'd been close to leaving Kingman alone for good. But they wouldn't keep their hands off this family. At the kickback, cousin Skeet told him he had been headhunted by a Kingman recruiter and had been working at the plant for three weeks. How could Kenny overlook an obvious act of war? Maddy told him to let it go, but that's what they wanted. If he didn't break the cycle, who would? She said nothing the entire ride back to Atlanta.

He looked her in the eye. "I'm just trying to play my role. Every king deserves a coup."

"What does the coup deserve?" she asked softly.

Kenny picked up the gun. He was tired of this conversation. "To win."

Maddy stepped into the house.

SLAY/KING

Kenny wanted to end the Kingman board retreat before it started. His plan had been to leave his posh hotel room, walk in on the board's initial session, and not walk out. There'd be severe collateral damage since the retreat was being held on the fifth floor and RST probably burned through steel, but Kingman had a sterling credit line. They could afford a few more bodies.

The CNN Center's paramilitary security came for his body though. The day before the retreat began, three linebacker motherfuckers caught Kenny browsing the empty conference room and swarmed, pummeling him with body blows until he had the chance to reveal he was a guest. While they didn't apologize, they explained they were cracking down on unauthorized access to meeting rooms after two Vincent Blake campaign staffers had thrown a party in an unlocked ballroom a week earlier. That didn't explain why they had to shuffle around Kenny's viscera, but he let it go.

He escaped to his room, flipped the do-not-disturb sign to don't, and lay down to rest.

He woke up three days later in a puddle of excretions. All of them. Their combined texture was worse than their combined smell.

Kenny rolled out of the sludge and looked at the clock. It was just past midnight. He needed Jesus, but he ordered room service. He felt empty. The soiled sheets corroborated the feeling.

He cleaned up as he awaited his meal. First, he opened the window to the balcony. Then he showered until his skin cracked from the heat and astringent hotel soap. Afterward, he gathered the sheets, walked them outside, and chucked them into the city. He lingered as the bedding tumbled down to the street. The humid air cooled his skin.

Someone knocked on the door.

Kenny robed himself, turned off the lights, and peered through the peephole. "I'm naked," he said through the door. "Can you just leave this in the hallway?" The man obliged and disappeared from view. Kenny retrieved the pushcart.

He devoured his thirty-five-dollar burger and fries like they were the $7.99 plus tax they were worth and checked his phone. It had somehow clung to 1 percent for days despite last being charged before he checked into the Omni. He had four missed calls: his mom, his mom, a purchaser of his beans, and his dad (probably his mom). He located his charger then plugged in his phone and realized the date.

The retreat had ended that day. Holy fucking hell.

He had hours before the seven men and women whom he'd vowed to kill would disperse to the ethereal and inaccessible nowhere

where all rich people lived. All his sacrifices and plans undermined by goons with fists like cinder blocks. He focused.

He logged into LoopedIn, where the Kingman board members were very active. So active that Kenny knew the seven men and women like lovers. Teuton brothers Isaac and Joseph Walker, routine visitors to strip clubs and Sunday school, were the Jesus freaks, emphasis on both. 3D—Duke Davis O'Donald—red-blooded fracking magnate and gun nut, was the brute. The world's last living Cro-Magnon often boasted that he'd taken guns to every US state on the continent and the District of Columbia despite having a concealed-carry permit in only North Carolina. (Kenny never understood what exactly made this a boast; soldiers and criminals carried guns everywhere too . . .) Sheryl Bonhomie, local news anchor turned self-help guru turned anti-vaxxer turned crystal miner, was the ideologue; she always capitalized *white*, even when it was just a color. Grace McKaren, founder and owner of regional cupcake empire Daughters of the Confectionary, was the emotional core of the board; she formally denounced the United Daughters of the Confederacy following a summer of reckoning but continued to cater the hate group's annual cotillion, as she had done for two decades. Leonidas Seamus Finnegan Jones, a black man whose closest friends were white, an apparent accomplishment, had no characteristics of note besides being rich and having four names (which wasn't even notable if you knew, like, one Nigerian or Francophone). And then board chair, Raymond Kingman, spoiled twat and heir to the Kingman fortune, was the blowhard. He insulted the EPA so much he'd condensed the agency's name to one syllable. (Kenny couldn't pronounce it.)

Kenny's fake profile gave him access to everyone except Kingman, who only looped with premium members, which Kenny was not. Kenny scrounged the other board member's feeds, which were rife with updates, shares, and pictures. Surely some stray like or geotag or overshare would reveal where they were or where they were going. They were all rich enough to flaunt their status without having to protect it. Not quite unadulterated fuck-you money, but still, fuck you.

The Brothers Walker gave him his lead. Earlier that day, they recorded themselves buying golf clubs and attire at Lenox Square Mall. Kenny didn't recognize the store, didn't even find it plausible a golf-supply store could survive at Lenox, but he'd once heard a fellow barbershop patron propose opening a gun store at Lenox, so the frequent shootings could at least benefit someone. That made sense, kinda! Why not golf?

Kenny's lead led everywhere. Metro Atlanta was overrun with country clubs; might have had more country clubs than rappers, frankly. How in the fuck was he going to figure out where these nobs were headed? He scoured the feeds of the other members. Nothing of note.

As he saw all the executives and vice executives and managers the board members looped with—their descendants, essentially—Kenny thought of Maddy. She'd been right about his plan being futile if he wanted to destroy the company. There was no way around that.

Should he just end things now? He removed his water gun from his bag and pressed the barrel into his forehead. Closed his eyes and breathed slowly, imagining the completion of the act as a kind of fellowship. People died in hotel rooms all the time. At least half of all celebrity deaths were in hotels, it seemed. Elected officials and political leaders, too, followed the trend.

His thoughts turned to his parents as he felt his head pound with heat and indecision. He thought of the Tusks, too, the most patient and enduring people he knew. He never understood why he had to resent living when he had so much to live for, when others had survived so much worse. He refused to categorize his deviance as a defect—what reasonable person wouldn't choose death when black life was so pernicious, even when niggas "made it out" or whatever the fuck his status was? Kenny never, ever felt unreasonable. He just wished his yearning for absolution didn't feel so incompatible with the people he loved. He'd never know.

His phone chimed. He dropped the gun and picked up the device. His dad again.

He answered. "Hey, Pops. Everything okay?"

His mom spoke. "Yeah, we just made a bet about which of us you liked to talk to more. Looks like your dad won."

Kenny laughed heartily.

"I love y'all both equally."

"Boy, don't bullshit me. I know you love me more." She chuckled. They'd clearly been playing tonk and drinking, their Saturday ritual for ten retired years.

"You gonna visit us soon? After this business with Thurgood, I'm praying for all you angry young men."

"Don't worry, Mama. I'm no Thurgood."

"I believe you, but tell that to the Lord, not me. You wanna holler at your father?"

"Sure."

True to form, his parents had an audible sidebar before his father took the phone. His mom sensed something was wrong, told his dad to find out. Kenny regretted that he'd never taught them how to use the mute feature.

His dad's baritone thundered through the phone. "Son, I don't need your love like your mama do, but I do need some."

"I got you, Pops."

"Okay. I'm gon' remember this the next time you say you're too busy to fish."

"I won't say that, I promise." He paused, appreciating the steel of the promise, the alien, umami rush of ironclad certainty.

He couldn't celebrate too soon though. There was still work ahead. "Speaking of fishing, what's the fanciest golf spot in Atlanta? I've got a friend in town who asked."

"Son, I know you making good money with your fancy coffee shop, but ain't you, Maddy, or nobody you know got Marietta Estates money."

"He says he wants the crème de la crème. You sure that's the spot?"

"I'm damn sure. You remember my partner K.D.?"

"Of course. You're getting old, Pops, not me."

"He used to say Marietta Estates is where the wind gon'. You better take your little homeboy and his new money down to Topgolf."

"Old man, what you know about Topgolf?"

"I know it don't cost top dollar and they ain't got slaves."

. . .

Thunder crackled as Kenny walked toward the Atlanta Country Club shuttle parked beyond the Omni's canopy. He'd been able to confirm the board had a reservation for transit to Marietta Estates. Less clear was whether he'd be able to hitch a ride.

In the seconds it took for him to reach the vehicle, the rumbles begot a feral downpour. Kenny knocked on the door as the rain pounded the street. The bus driver, a fellow black man, was unmoved by

Kenny's plight. As Kenny rapped on the door, water pummeling the earth, the man eyed Kenny with annoyance, dismissing him with emphatic waves. After thirty seconds in this deadlock, Kenny ran back to the canopy. The driver clearly thought Kenny was homeless.

It was a reasonable guess. Though Kenny wore a double-breasted mustard suit over a black pima tee, with tar oxfords, a Cuban link, and an off-white messenger bag, he had been up all night. Surely he looked it as much as he felt it. He steadied himself, remembering how close he was to completing his mission, and stepped into the rain again.

He walked slowly this time, like he was unbothered by the rain. Tink, tink, tink, he tapped with his fingernail. He offered the driver a smile. His favorite Black Sublime customers were all tappers rather than knockers. The small act of smarm always spoke to Kenny, made him feel like less of a servant. He hoped the driver was kin. He didn't want to kill him.

After a spell, the door eased open and Kenny stepped inside, water streaming down his face. His drenched suit felt heavy as a pelt in the bus's hot, staid air.

The man halted him with an outstretched hand. "Sorry, boss. Can't be too careful these days," the man said from the driver's seat. A knife lay across the man's lap like a favored pet. He had an accent. Kenny guessed he was of Central African origin. He didn't know any Central Africans, but he knew West Africans, East Africans, North Africans, and South Africans, and he'd never heard this particular lilt. The math was simple.

"I understand, and I appreciate your caution. Cautious men live longer."

The man eyed Kenny's messenger bag. "I don't have any cash."

"Great. I have a job for you."

"Thanks, boss, but I already have a job." He drummed the steering wheel.

Kenny pointed at a tip jar lodged in the cup holder. "I see. Pays so well you have to rely on the generosity of strangers?"

"Is that not what you are?"

Kenny opened his bag and removed a glob of Franklins. Thirty-five thousand dollars. "For now." He handed the man the cash.

The man took it like a beating. He counted it twice, mumbling the growing total as bills slipped through his fingers. Then he stared out the window. Glared at the tip jar. Huffed. Sighed. Tapped his feet. Shook his head.

Kenny stood still the whole time, water drizzling down his legs. He too had been strong-armed into a life-changing settlement before. He was on this bus because he now knew such transactions were reversible, but that wasn't the kind of information one just bandied about. The man would have to learn on his own time, make his own mistakes.

Kenny offered some explicit reassurance. "I promise you won't endanger your family. Or lose your job."

"I'm from the Congo. We go to war over broken promises."

"How's that working out for you?"

The man chuckled and pocketed the money. "So what's the job?"

Kenny told him and was offered a seat in the front row. An hour later, Kingman's top brass boarded the bus in a parade of umbrellas, dandy garb, cart bags, and luggage. If Kenny had seen them on the street, he might've thought they were starting a colony. Everyone stepped past Kenny without comment except 3D, who stopped and asked him if he was lost. This was a private shuttle for a private party, he declared. Kenny noticed the way the man's hand hovered near his holster.

Kenny ignored the question (no) and responded to the decree. "Don't mind me. I'm just an auditor. As far as you're concerned, I'm not even here."

3D grunted and sat down behind the driver. "Let's go," he said.

The driver pulled off onto a lifeless downtown street. Kenny faced forward, focusing on curbing his glee. In fifteen to forty-five minutes depending on traffic and the distribution of churches along the route, some of which would be emptying at this hour as others filled, he could die proud.

The board bickered about the Omni's so-so shrimp and grits and limited hot sauce options. The Bentworth in Charlotte was far more accommodating, Bonhomie said. For esteemed guests such as her, the waitstaff brought out their illegal Oaxacan sauce made with rattler fangs. Jones didn't respect such pageantry. The Lauriol in Biloxi was to the point, offering in-house sauces made fresh every day. McKaren agreed but noted that the Sucre Plantation in New Iberia had the best all-around hospitality. She could just feel the history in the air, she claimed.

3D took no sides in these debates, his hand loitering near his hip as the shuttle hit traffic. Kenny rested his hands flat on his thighs. He was being watched.

As the shuttle slowed to a creep, he became a curio.

"So how do you like auditing?" 3D asked.

"I absolutely love it," Kenny said. "It's fascinating seeing into the hearts of companies, popping the hood and really seeing the engine in detail. It would surprise you how many companies are cutting corners."

"What's the worst thing you've ever seen as an auditor?"

"Ooh, that's easy. There's a coke plant in Alabama that for forty years has been pumping all kinds of toxins into the soil, air, and water. The workers at the plant and the people who live near there suffer from asthma, high blood pressure, throat cancers, stillbirths, eczema."

"Things like that sicken me. I bet it was a mess in there, spiritually and organizationally."

"No, actually. That's why it's the worst. The business is running as intended. When workers get sick, they fire them. When the community complains, they settle with them. They actually have a fund for it. It's a well-oiled operation."

"What about their leadership? I'm former military. We had a saying. Poor leadership produces poor outcomes. P-L-P-P-O. Write that down."

"Their board comprises some of the top business owners in the region. From what I understand, it was their idea to create the settlement fund."

3D sucked his teeth and turned away. The shuttle had finally reached the highway. It picked up speed as it descended the on-ramp, quickly making it to the HOV lane. Traffic was smooth, exits streaming by.

The storm passed by the time they hit the surface streets, where, as planned, the streets hit back. The driver attacked the many potholes littering Windy Hill Drive like they owed him money, rocking the passengers to and fro.

After a particularly nasty lurch that made the Walker brothers yelp for their lord and savior, the shuttle slowed and pulled into the half-empty parking lot of an office park.

The driver cut the engine then stepped off and circled the vehicle.

He returned with bad news. "Flat tire!" he announced, sticking his head through the door like a sitcom neighbor. He was going to make some phone calls, he said. He walked off.

"Should've audited the goddamn bus," 3D growled at Kenny. The Brothers Walker asked that their lord's name please not be used in vain, riling up the rest of the group. Kingman was especially irate, tearing into 3D for choosing, in his words, the world's most ghetto golf course. Kenny suggested they all step off the bus for fresh air. Maybe someone could call a rideshare? The group accepted this suggestion—with a condition. Kenny would call and pay for the rides, not them.

"My pleasure," Kenny said.

As soon as they were all out the shuttle, Kenny sprayed the fuckers. The single stream of RST cut through the air and then through them, catching 3D in his agape mouth, Kingman in his armpit, and the rest in their stomachs. They liquefied instantly, sloshing to the ground in a gelatinous, arrhythmic splat. Kenny stepped back but couldn't look away as the group's collective goo gobbled up parking-space markers and discarded fast-food cartons and crabgrass, a column of steam rising into the air. The asphalt burned black as hate in their absence, sinking, cracking—then surging, like a tide. Kenny and the driver, who had retreated behind the cover of an SUV, were knocked off their feet as force rippled through the ground.

Kenny stood and watched the reaction sizzle out, car alarms blaring around him as the liquid slowed its death march, a fragrant haze drifting from the black crag. The smell was overpowering, tickling his throat and numbing his gums. This was the most RST he'd ever used. Standing in its aura, its smoldering heat dancing on his skin, its scent greasing his sinuses, he felt quenched. He held the gun at his side, his nibbling inclination to turn it on himself slightly dulled.

His time would come. He had one more promise to keep. He waved to the driver, who was watching him from a distance. The man shook his head, muttered something in French.

"We had a deal," Kenny shouted back.

The man stepped from behind the SUV with his hands up and began walking toward Kenny.

"Don't be dramatic. I told you what I was going to do," Kenny said. He handed the man the gun. The driver studied it, his face a watercolor of horror and wonder.

"I'm going to go get the clubs. Remember, you want complete de-niability. Drive to another parking lot and recite your alibi until it's truth. Your angry passengers grabbed their gear and stormed off in their UberX as you waited for a tow truck," Kenny said. "The cops will try to grill you, but you don't know anything."

The man glowered, and Kenny went to retrieve the clubs. It took a few trips, as the clubs were heavy and cumbersome. But Kenny felt spry. He stood in the center of the pile and told the driver to step away.

The man waddled backward, the gun dangling from his pinched fingers like a banana peel. He was scared of the device. Not quite warlord behavior, Kenny thought.

Kenny directed the spooked man. "That's far enough. Just aim at me and squeeze the trigger. I'll be gone in a blink. The gun is worth more than the money I gave you, but I suggest tossing it in. If you keep it, it keeps you."

The man raised the weapon and planted his feet. "I don't understand why you are doing this," he said. "Is there no other way?"

"Of course there are other ways. This is just the one I choose. That's freedom, right?"

The man's finger drew back.

CRABS IN A CENTRIFUGE

There was a woman sitting in Maddy's bedroom. Maddy couldn't see her in the darkness, but she could smell her. She lay still, parsing the woman's scent. She smelled of sweat and cheap, dark-roasted coffee. She'd been working, Maddy guessed.

"I'm awake," Maddy announced as she sat up. She didn't want to startle the intruder.

Maddy adjusted her bonnet and reached for her bedside lamp. She brushed her clock by mistake, the snooze button filling the room with barely censored trap music. She turned it off and saw it was 3:13 a.m. She turned the light on. Maddy recognized the invader.

"What can I do for you, Dr. Vickers?" Maddy asked. The woman sat comfortably in a chair imported from the kitchen, her legs and arms crossed. Maddy was more alarmed by her relaxed posture than the gun in her hand.

"You're a hard sleeper," Retta said.

"You're a hard worker. I didn't know epidemiologists made house calls."

"I used to be a small-town doctor. Some people are more comfortable when you visit them at home."

"Is that why you're in my bedroom?"

"It's one reason."

"What's the other? Working on your bedside manner? It's not great."

"I'm looking for your ex-husband."

"We're not in touch. We take the divorce thing pretty literally."

"That wasn't the case two weeks ago, when you were at his house all weekend. But I'm a divorcée, too, so I'll cut you some slack. Fuck him. Where's the compound you two made?"

"What compound?"

"Dr. Tusk, I spent the night stripping his house floor by floor, so please don't make me stay here longer than I need to. I've never liked cleaning up blood. It's why I no longer fish or hunt."

"You a country girl?"

"I am. I prefer the speed of the city though." She stood and ripped off the sheets. "Where is it?"

Maddy placed her hands behind her head. "Dr. Vickers, you've got me cornered. The compound is in my oven."

"After what your husband pulled on those cops at Thurgood Houser's home, excuse me for not believing you."

"Ex-husband."

"Like I give a damn. Up." Retta waved the gun toward the hallway.

Maddy swiveled her exposed legs over the bed and stood, keeping her hands behind her head. She walked toward the kitchen slowly, Retta one step behind her. When her feet went from carpet to linoleum, she stopped and asked Retta to turn on the light. She obliged.

The kitchen was in disarray. The dishwasher and cabinets were turned out. Spices, utensils, and Tupperware cluttered the counters. The fridge door was ajar. Damn, I am a hard sleeper, Maddy thought. "You did all this but didn't think to look in the oven?" Maddy said.

Retta scowled. "I'm sorry, I never got around to taking the CDC's how-to-strip-a-home course. I've been kinda fucking busy, actually." She spat onto the linoleum between them. "Open the fucking door."

"Are you sure?"

"Bitch, do I look unsure?"

Maddy opened the oven and removed a tray of RST. She turned toward Retta with triumph and stepped back.

"See what paranoia gets you, Dr. Vickers? If I drop this tray, you, me, and everyone in my apartment complex will die."

Retta froze, her body still except for her eyes. Maddy watched the reddened orbs dart up and down the barrel of the gun, ease over the tray, sweep across the room. The woman was processing.

"Well, I fucked this up," Retta said after a spell.

"You did. Put your gun on safety and slide it toward me."

The woman sighed then acquiesced, relinquishing the weapon and plopping onto the floor. Maddy removed one vial of RST then placed the tray on the counter. She joined Retta on the floor, sitting cross-legged. Utensils tickled her lower back.

"Why do you even want this? Money?" Maddy asked, rolling the RST between her fingers.

"Peace of mind. That shit is vile."

"It's supposed to be."

They sat in silence. Maddy realized she had probably spooked the woman. She didn't care. "Have you ever mourned the death of a complete stranger?" she asked.

"Yes."

"How did it feel?"

"It felt like I had lost a part of myself."

"Which part?"

"Excuse me?"

"Which part of you?"

"Nothing in particular," Retta said. "It just hurt everywhere. Like I was watching a well-done horror movie."

"How long did that feeling last?"

"It varied. Last time I felt that torn up was on a work trip to Jena, Louisiana. There was this proud old woman who broke down because a younger girl she kind of mentored had killed herself. I felt responsible. I still do."

"Because you couldn't help her?"

Retta started to stand. "Can you just let me go? I don't see how we can sit here and talk like long-lost acquaintances when you're holding a building hostage. You're a coward."

Maddy opened the RST vial and wafted its smell toward Retta. "Sit. You lost the ability to make demands when you showed up with a gun."

Retta frowned and returned to her butt. "I felt responsible because I'm really good at my job and it doesn't matter."

"Right. People die anyway. More accurately, people are killed anyway. No need for secrets here. I know Kenny killed that Louisiana girl." Maddy closed the RST vial.

Retta gestured at it. "This compound is what, reparations?"

Maddy laughed. "We can't give ourselves reparations."

"What's the purpose of this compound, then? Revenge?"

"Clarity."

"For whom?"

"For us, obviously," Maddy said.

"What's so unclear?"

"Do I really have to answer that for you? Don't you study death?"

"I used to, before you and your ex-husband took me away from helping people." She paused, corrected herself. "Helping us."

"Us?"

"Don't say that skeptically, like you and me are any different. I met your family. There was more Goodwill than J.Crew in that funeral home."

Maddy chuckled. "I'm not skeptical. I'm just listening to you figure yourself out. And sure, I know that my individual success hasn't done anything for my family. You wouldn't be in this room if I hadn't figured that out."

"Maybe that's why I'm here too."

"I can't let you go on a 'maybe.'"

"Okay. Then let me go on a promise. Let me walk out of here and I'll never bother you again."

"That easy?"

"Girl, this ain't at all easy."

"Okay, I'll let you go if you promise never to forget that everything they've ever done to us is present."

"Present?"

"Present. In the water, in the soil, in our bodies." Maddy stroked her stomach. "I thought I was safe, having a kid. I knew the type of companies I worked for, the kind of substances I worked with. Read all the MSDSs, subscribed to *Science and Nature*, read the disclosure forms. I thought I was safe. But there is no safety. The shit was in me."

Retta stretched her lanky arms like wings and yawned. "So you're saying we, our people, are a crime scene?"

"That's not how I'd put it, but it's not inaccurate."

"Honestly, Dr. Tusk, that's the first thing you've said that makes sense." Retta lunged for her gun, springing toward it hands-first. Maddy kicked the weapon away then grabbed a knife she felt behind her and plunged it into Retta's skull. The weapon smoothly slid through skin and bone, like a chopstick through hot oil. Retta spasmed for a few seconds then grew still. Maddy sighed then got up and began collecting provisions to dispose of the body.

When the woman was loaded into her trunk, Maddy left her building and headed toward Memorial Drive. It seemed a proper burial ground, though it took her an hour to find a suitable plot. She rode in silence, her attention on the road and its metamorphic landscape. She drove past Daddy D'z BBQ Joynt and its brick-size cornbread, past the bail-bonds service owned by a former Civil Rights Movement leader, past Stone Mountain Park and its Confederate kitsch, past six AutoZones, eight Waffle Houses. She shuddered whenever the body shuffled in the back. Had she acted in haste? The gun might not have even been loaded. It too rattled back there. And where had the woman parked?

She drove on. They were both beyond questions.

She stopped at a cemetery in Between, a town that was a literal preposition. Drove until the main road ended and the wheels hit grass. She turned the car off and stalled in her seat. She was a killer now, but she felt the same. Was she always that way? Or was this feeling just the stiff aegis of self-defense, protecting her from the world's judgment while confining her to her own? A cocoon. She scooped the RST vile she'd brought along from the cup holder and held it in her palm, felt it conduct her heat. The substance seemed duller in the darkness. Maddy stared at it with intrigue, feeling for the first time that she could see through it, that she could contort its chaos. She got out of the car.

When the corpse, the weapons, and her least favorite rug had sizzled away, she headed home. She tuned the radio to an AM news station, wondering if Kenny's big fat kill would belong to him or to the world. Surely he was dead if his house, once her house, too, could be ransacked. The news offered no insights, the broadcast a mix of weather updates, sports scores, and paid messages from the Vincent Blake campaign.

Maddy pulled over and called Kenny. Straight to voicemail. She returned to the road and drove with urgency, her thoughts turning to the RST in her oven. There was no telling who else Vickers might have been in contact with. She needed to off-load her supply immediately.

Maddy's speed drew the attention of a cop, who pulled her over near the former site of the Tupac statue where the dead rapper had been rumored to appear before aggrieved fans. The officer asked Maddy, "Why are you here?" a question Maddy imagined Tupac might ask, not his fans, but the statue itself, given he liked rhetorical questions and, to Maddy's knowledge, spent so little time in Atlanta. Maddy told the woman she was here, between Between and Atlanta, because she'd had a rough night and was driving to ease her mind. The cop shrugged and sent her off with a warning. "Get home safe, ma'am. All lives matter," the woman said in the cadence of a salutation. Maddy thanked the woman and drove off, speeding once the cop had shrunk into a speck in the rearview mirror.

At home, she prepared all 399 packages of RST in one sitting, using the guest book from Saskia's funeral when she ran out of organizations whose politics she admired, many of which understandably didn't have a known address. She used Ebenezer Baptist Church as a return address. Even atheists liked Ebenezer Baptist Church.

After two fill-ups and five hours of driving, illegally parking, dashing to public mailboxes, then repeating, Maddy returned home and slept the best sleep of her life.

Morbidity and Mortality Weekly Report

Recommendations and Reports / Vol. 78 / No. 2

Recommendations for Maintaining Corporeal Integrity Among African Americans

Ebonee McCollum, PhD[1]; Lauretta Vickers, MD[1*];
Alonzo Colón, MD[1]

Affiliations

1. *Epidemic Intelligence Service*
* Whereabouts unknown, assumed deceased. Please direct any tips or leads to 1-800-CDC-MMWR.

Summary

This report provides CDC recommendations to health care providers regarding the corporeal integrity of African Americans,[†] who have recently shown increased susceptibility to blackouts: fatal, self-willed discharges of allostatic loads in response to environmental and epigenetic stressors. Using field reports, clinical trials, and toxicological profiles, these recommendations analyze and detail the pathology of blackouts and provide guidelines for diagnosis and intervention.

CDC developed these recommendations by synthesizing evidence-based protocols and recommendations already in place; discussing the scientific evidence supporting the proposed recommendations at a consultation session of institutional stakeholders and experts held February 5 in Atlanta, Georgia; reviewing established practices for maintaining Black corporeal integrity in the United States; soliciting Delphi ratings by subject-matter experts on the Black Question (formerly known as the "Negro Question") in specialty-care settings; conducting peer reviews of preliminary recommendations and supporting evidence; and discussing draft recommendations and supporting evidence during meetings of the Advisory Committee on Black Health Outcomes. These recommendations are intended to help health care providers and possessors of Black corporeality in specialty-care settings, clinical settings, workplaces, residences, streets, cars, public transit, airports, restaurants, parks, correctional facilities, classrooms, bookstores, coffee shops, love, hate, lust, situationships, heat, transition, danger, and thrall.

---

† *African American*, as used here, refers to North and South American descendants of slaves, Caribbean descendants of slaves, African descendants of Africans, willing Puerto Ricans and Dominicans, willing North Africans, all sub-Saharan Africans, eligible South Africans, and New Blacks.

*

Baltimore planted the report her father had given her on the edge of his desk. "I'm confused. This says all those protests and blackouts last year were just a health crisis. And most of it is redacted. I thought you said it explained everything?"

Vincent grabbed the report and flipped through some pages.

"Did you read all the way through it?" he asked.

"I couldn't. Everything except basically the summary and the references are redacted."

He looked through the papers again, shrugged. "I haven't had time to read it, actually. I'll see if I can get the full version, but, Bali, let's talk about this later. I've got a call with the governor in a few minutes."

Baltimore grabbed her backpack and left the office. City Hall was quiet, security guards and custodians the sole occupants. Baltimore stopped for customary conversations and life updates. These people cared about her despite her dad not caring about them, an imbalance she tried to correct though she suspected she couldn't. They asked her about her studies; she asked them about their children and weekend plans. The former tended to supersede the latter. One woman joked about the strange weather, an eighty-degree day in November, though it was the third consecutive hottest November on record. Baltimore complimented the woman's neat arches instead of quoting the almanac. The weather had cooled considerably by the time Baltimore stepped out onto Trinity Avenue. She zipped up her windbreaker then unlocked her bike and began the haul to Buckhead.

Traffic was aggressive. She was honked at, catcalled, and thrice nearly doored. The mercilessness was thorough. When GPS directed her onto an unfamiliar street and she struggled up a hill, another cyclist booed her. An actual boo, like Baltimore was bombing at an open-mic comedy show. She summoned all her strength to catch up with the smug bitch, but a second hill secured the woman's lead.

By the time she got home, Baltimore was spent. She greeted Nigel with a kiss to his forehead then headed upstairs to her room, where a small package sat on her bed. It was a plain, unremarkable thing, shipped flat rate from Last Baptist Church in Money, Mississippi, an entity and a place she had never heard of. She looked up both and was shocked to see they were real.

Had her time come? She turned the package in her hands, studying its seams, its shipping label, its integrity. The United States Postal Service had cracked down on the shipment of liquids after the bedlam of the prior year, so she didn't expect actual prune juice, as the substance had come to be known. USPS's surveillance was so thorough (inept) that Meredith had to stop copping her CBD oils from weirdos online and resort to hitting up the hawkers who hovered around New Square. They were also weirdos, but Meredith liked it. She'd sprouted a booty during her first semester at Emory and took every opportunity to put it to use. Baltimore was still waiting on hers.

She pinched the package between her fingers but didn't pull it apart. Did she even want to know what was inside? After the first batches of prune juice had arrived and turned families and households and inmates into *agents démolition*, the mysterious sender had changed tack and began sending out oblique communiqués. Baltimore had seen images of the tracts online. They ranged from annotations of transcripts of *Forensic Files* to medical bills with everything obscured but the costs to chemical formulae for compounds that no one could synthesize—or at least that no one admitted they could make. Or was alive to admit they made. It was all so loaded. Bio-weapons for black people gushing out of a black hole. What was on the other side of that event horizon?

Baltimore set the package down, closed her bedroom door, then picked up her phone. Meredith and Seth might know what to do with her winning ticket. She opened her email app and went to their thread of "pruned" memes ("pruned" was way less cool than "breaking black," as it was called in the early days, before white people started printing T-shirts, but at least it wasn't for sale). Though Seth had stopped replying to it after a black girl at Clemson had gotten beaten to death for joking she knew someone with prune juice, it seemed like the right place to go. She scrolled through months of images and mimetic responses to them. For a week, as a black mutual-aid group held a Big Tobacco executive hostage in a Hoboken apartment building demanding the imme-diate dissolution of the tobacco industry, Baltimore and the gang had been obsessed with iterations of a meme depicting Chief Keef looming over the New Jersey skyline. Sometimes he wore shades. Sometimes it was New York City he threatened. (Or maybe some bama Okie thought Hoboken and Manhattan were interchange-able.) At some point Chloe and Halle were introduced, standing on a Twinkie-yellow cab and gazing up at the sky where Chief's floating head blasted through a scrum of cloud. Do it, they com-manded the floating visage.

Baltimore burrowed down to the first message in the chain, before it became an archive of black infinitude. She had sent her friends a picture of her father in a local newspaper the day after he was inaugurated as Atlanta's first gay black mayor. "this isn't enough," she had written, words that felt no less true even after a year of "by any means" shifting from a thing niggas said through their teeth to the punctuation to the mayhem. Niggas had really turned death into an art, burning down police precincts, throwing pop-up kangaroo courts up and down Rodeo Drive and Wall Street, taking Super Soakers to Oath Keepers cookouts. The violence had alarmed Baltimore at first, who'd been raised on a strict diet of voter-registration drives and Earth Day park cleanups, but bruh, it Got Shit Done. White people were so spooked by the sight of dark liquids in black people's possession that Starbucks had pivoted to juice.

Baltimore chucked her phone onto her bed and retrieved the envelope. Her hands shook as she nudged open its seal with her thumb. What if it really was from a church and all this worrying was moot? What if she was being pranked? Some black people had stopped opening unexpected mail, fearing a nefarious government plot. Did her opening random mail mean she was a coon? Niggers'll open anything that arrives on the first or the fifteenth, as one nasty meme put it. (Seth tended to swim in the murkier online waters.) What if The Sender, like Thurgood Houser, was using their envoys for some noxious experiment?

The envelope wasn't sturdy enough to withstand a whole-ass fusillade of anxiety, so Baltimore got her answer before she even conjured a question. The envelope contained a frayed funeral program that was a single page folded over. No one was pictured on the front, and throughout words were scored with thick, furious strike-throughs that slashed and hacked through letters.

The strokes altered the formatting, too, splitting the margins into scalene cracks. The document was illegible, but Baltimore could see spots where the ink had run, had sprinted out of place, words bleeding and bending and warping until the whole text had folded in on itself as if sucked dry by a hankering flame.

One name was almost readable. Something with six letters, most of them whole except for the first, which had been reduced to what looked like an underscore. She filled the blank with possible solutions. Zaskia? Baskia? Laskia? Baltimore examined the smudge of order, unsure whether it was a hint or a mistake. She thought of Maurice White as her eyes homed in on the spot, remembering the dead end at the bottom of her deep dive and the bliss at the realization that she didn't have to look into the abyss to see her way through it, out of it.

She examined the document a final time then crumpled it and plunged it into her mouth, swallowing it in a single, pythonic gulp.

ACKNOWLEDGMENTS

Shout out my lifelines for information, imagination, and joy: rap, the AP, *ProPublica*, the DC Public Library, the New York Public Library, *coffea arabica*.

Harold, C.J., and Dustin, thanks for your critical feedback on early drafts and words of encouragement.

Ian, thanks for answering my unending and annoying questions about roasting coffee. Teri, I appreciate you answering my peculiar public health questions. Troy, that daily writing challenge was clutch, dog.

Ben, I appreciate that epic Zoom call and your granular notes on word choice and sentence structure. Kelly, your generosity and insights are immeasurable. Sheldon, you drop gems about storytelling, politics, music, and life like you have holes in your pockets. Salute.

Jackson, thank you for putting me in touch with Danielle, agent extraordinaire. Danielle, you are a peerless demystifier and resource.

Your editorial ideas and many nuts-and-bolts factoids about publishing were pivotal. I appreciated the laughs too.

Mensah, your edits sharpened every facet of the text and rewired my brain. It was a thrill to work together again. I'm really honored you saw potential in this weird novel and appreciate all the thought and effort that you and the Soft Skull team put into the book.

I also thank Anna, Kevin, Clover, Philip, Danielle J., Lucie, Nicola, Jeremy, and Geoff. None of you read drafts of *Liquid Snakes*, but your insightful notes on my other writing festered in my mind and helped me break bad habits and elevate my pen. Bless.

Rashele, Mom, Dad, Nadine, Mike, Jr, Luna—you already know. Love you.

© Stephen Kearse

STEPHEN KEARSE is an editor at *Spotlight PA* and a contributing writer at *The Nation*, where he covers music, movies, and books. His criticism and reporting have been published in *The New York Times*, *The Atlantic*, *GQ*, and *Pitchfork*, among other outlets. His debut novel, *In the Heat of the Light*, was published in 2019 by Brain Mill Press. Originally from Atlanta, he now lives in the Washington, D.C., metropolitan area with his family.